I0572580

SCARLET MASQUERADE

SCARLET MASQUERADE

JETT ABBOTT

SAPPHIRE BOOKS

SALINAS, CALIFORNIA

Scarlet Masquerade

Copyright © 2011 by Jett Abbott, All rights reserved.

ISBN 978-0-9828608-1-6

All rights reserved. No part of this publication may be reproduced, distributed, or transmitted in any form or by any means, without written permission of the publisher.

Editor: Ilene Siegel
Cover Design: Sapphire Books Publishing
Interior Design: Sapphire Books Publishing

Sapphire Books
P.O. Box 8142
Salinas, CA 93912
www.sapphirebooks.com

Printed in the United States of America
First Edition – April 2011

Acknowledgements

Thank you to the beta readers; Probingreality, Lee Fitzsimmons and Terry Baker. Your feedback was invaluable. I can't thank you enough for your suggestions, your time, and your patience.

To Ilene, the best editor I've ever worked with. Thank you from the bottom of my heart.

To Schileen. Who inspires me, makes me laugh, and loves me. You're my everything.

To Thomas, Eric, and Alex. I love you more than words could ever convey.

Chapter One

She sat on top of her chrome horse looking down at the city lights below. She had done this very thing time and time again in cities around the world, longing for that one true love that never seemed to materialize. Her "once upon a time" was over centuries ago. Now it rarely ended with "happily ever after". A.J. took a deep breath and stretched her tall, slender frame before descending the long winding road back to her reality. She could smell rain in the air and wanted to make it home before it started. She wasn't looking forward to a night spent wiping watermarks off chrome. This wasn't like the old days when she could just take the tack off her ride and let nature do the rest.

A.J. wrapped herself around her motorcycle and took another deep breath. Hoping to clear her mind of the day's events, she felt the chrome monster between her legs rumble to life. The guttural roar of the engine could rattle even the most stubborn heart to life. Realizing the vibrating iron between her legs was probably going to be the hottest thing she would have between them for a while, she settled into the leather to enjoy the ride down. It wasn't that she ever lacked the opportunity for company of any kind. It was just that she didn't want the entrapments that came with it. She knew what the end-results would be. She wasn't that naïve anymore, and she did not want to watch it end as it always did.

Rolling onto the pavement, A.J. could feel the heat bounce up to meet her. The summer nights were only a tad cooler than the days, which was why she mostly rode at night. The daily operations of her businesses made it almost impossible to find time to ride. So, she took what she could until things settled down. The motorcycle glided into the turns as she guided it effortlessly down the mountain. A.J. loved this feeling of freedom. It reminded her of flying. Well not quite like the kind of flying she was used to, but close enough. She was almost down the mountain when she felt them. The first few raindrops hit her arms. A.J. was sure now. She wasn't going to make it home in time. She needed to do the next best thing and find a place to wait out the rain. If she didn't hurry, the rain was going to make nasty work of her leather pants and vest. They already looked like a second skin on her. Adding water would only make them tighter when they dried.

Hitting the bottom of the mountain, she pulled the throttle all the way hoping to outrun the rain. The further she got, the more it rained. Clearly, she wasn't going to make it home. Down the road, she spotted a rainbow neon beer sign in the window of a building and pulled onto the walkway just under the overhang. She couldn't remember the last time she'd been in a gay bar, and she wasn't too thrilled to have to be in one now. However, she had to pass the time somehow. It was either this, or sit on her bike and wait for the storm to run its course. She dropped her kickstand and leaned the bike over settling it onto the concrete. A few women walked past her, eyeing her and the motorcycle as they entered the bar. As she pulled off her helmet long, brown hair tumbled from its confines, cascading halfway down her back.

A.J. looked around and made a mental note of where she was, not exactly the seedy part of a town but darn close to it. Why did they always put lesbian bars in the worst places and why did lesbians let them, she wondered? She shook her head as she took off her gloves and tossed them into her helmet on the seat. Walking into the bar she could feel the energy assault her senses. The predatory energy was palpable, the energy of those that wanted to be preyed upon. And then she felt something different. There was someone in the place just like her, someone who lived like she did. She scanned the dimly lit room to see if she could recognize them, trying to feel their energy as she passed them, but had no luck. Walking back to the bar she ordered a club soda. A.J. wanted to keep her wits about herself if someone like her was here. She looked around and spotted an open table off in the corner of the bar. A.J. couldn't help but notice the small dark alcove that it sat by and wondered if the table was empty for a reason.

Watching the people out on the dance floor, something caught her attention out of the corner of her eye. Something had moved in the alcove and then she heard a rustling of clothes. Her eyes focused quickly on the movement in the darkened space and realized that she was watching two people engaged in sex. No, what they were doing was hardcore, unadulterated fucking. The kind that happens when someone didn't know the other person, and they just wanted to get off. It was usually one sided and rarely happened with the same person again, especially in places like this. Trying to ignore the action taking place to her right, she focused once again on the dancing in front of her. A.J. heard a moan. Closing her eyes, she focused her hearing and heard a voice whisper from the alcove.

"You like that, baby? Huh? Yea, chicks like you usually like it rough from behind don't you?"

Her eyes adjusted to the darkness, one of her overly developed senses, and she peered into the dark alcove again. This time A.J. could see a man straddling a woman from behind. The woman's hands were on the wall as he worked himself into her. The muscles in his arms tensed as he grabbed her hips and rammed himself into the willing participant. A man in a lesbian bar? Well, it wasn't the first time she heard of a hetero couple looking for a third, so A.J. didn't give it a second thought as she heard more coming from the darkened alcove.

Grabbing the woman's hair, the guy whispered in her ear, "I knew you were going to be hot the minute I laid eyes on you. Fuck, you're the nicest piece of ass I've had in a long while. Now be a good girl and turn so I can see your face when I fuck you."

The alcove was too dark for her to see the faces, but she felt the energy falling off them in waves. It was intoxicating and she could feel herself getting stimulated. A.J. knew what she had to do, and if she didn't she would barely be able to contain her own emotions. Reaching into her tight leather pants she pulled out a small tin, opened it and pulled out two red caplets. She snapped each one and put them under her tongue, knowing that this would be the quickest way to administer her drug.

Closing her eyes, A.J. tried to shut out the rest of the world long enough for the drug to work itself into her system. Owning a pharmaceutical company definitely had its benefits when it came to controlling her condition, and tonight was just one of those times she was glad she paid so much for research and development. Without it, she would have had to handle her situation very differently, like she had in the past. That was something she just wouldn't do anymore. She had paid a deep price for how she lived her life, a life without love. She wasn't willing to throw it all away to go back to her old ways. Therefore, she would take the drugs when she needed to, period.

She felt herself being pulled back into the alcove when she heard the voice again. This time it was the woman's voice instructing her lover on the finer points of how to make a woman climax.

"Look, you had your chance. Now we do it my way."

A.J. could see the woman forcing the man to his knees as she inched her skirt higher. A long, shapely leg slung over his shoulder as she forced his face closer to her skirt. *It must be performance issues on his part.* A.J. chuckled to herself. *Now, we get to see how a sister controls her man.* Leaning back in her chair, A.J. could feel her own body responding to the commands the woman was giving to her now submissive lover.

Shit, this isn't good. I gotta get out of here before I lose it. She sat for a moment trying to control herself, and then she felt it before she heard it happen...Climax! The energy of the woman's climax ripped through her body, sending wave upon wave of pleasure coursing through her blood. A.J.'s skin flushed, her head pounded and her body tensed as she rode out the woman's orgasm. A.J. suddenly realized that this woman was the person she felt when she walked into the bar, the other one like herself. That would explain why she was feeling everything the other woman was feeling.

A.J. sat trying to calm herself, and didn't notice

the woman who had walked up to her table. Looking up, she hoped she didn't look as out-of-sorts as she felt.

"I'm sorry, but I'm not here to dance." Realizing how it sounded A.J. wanted to kick herself, but it was too late, the words were out.

"Oh, I see. Betty-Bad-Ass wants a woman to fuck. Well sorry, stud, I'm not that kind of girl. Good luck on that. I am sure with your looks and that body, you'll find someone like that here without a problem."

Before the woman could turn to leave, A.J. grabbed the dismissive woman's arm, stopping her progress. She did not owe this woman anything. It would have been easier to let her leave and just walk out of the bar.

"Look, it's not that. I'm just here until the weather clears. I'm not looking to hook-up with anyone," A.J. said, as she looked at the woman who was visibly pissed. She took her seat again and finished her drink. "Okay?"

"Fine," was all the woman could say as she walked away.

Resettling back into her seat, A.J. looked back into the alcove just in time to see two people walking out of the darkness. A smirk rose to her lips as she realized she had made a mistake. The identity of one of the individuals, he, was in fact, a she. A very butch she. Then, she gasped as she looked past her to the woman walking next to her.

"Clarissa," she whispered.

She felt as if her heart had stopped beating at the sight of the one woman who was her true "death till we part" lover. There was only one problem. The woman who was now walking out with the clandestine lover from the alcove was dead. At least she was a century ago, the last time A.J. saw her. Her mind reeled at the impossibility of the situation in front of her. Clarissa couldn't be the person she felt when she walked in, she just couldn't.

A.J. wanted to walk up to the beautiful woman and demand an explanation. Hell, she wanted to kiss her, to feel her body against hers again. A.J.'s emotions swirled around in her head as she stood to follow the two women out of the bar. She thought about the last time she had seen Clarissa. It was a couple of days before Clarissa died. Clarissa's parents had told A.J. to leave their house, so they could spend the last few moments they had with their daughter. They forbid her from being with Clarissa up until the end, thinking A.J. was the reason their daughter was dying. Now, here she was walking out of a bar. On the same continent, in the same century, and the same city she was living in. How could that be?

A.J. could hardly stop herself from walking up to the woman and demanding answers. She wouldn't confront her, not here and not like this. That wasn't her style. She watched as they strode out of the bar arm-in-arm. Maybe this wasn't Clarissa. Her hair was different, the color was brunette and Clarissa had been a blonde. Even so, hair color could be changed easily. She was also a bit slimmer than A.J. remembered. Maybe it was someone who looked like Clarissa. It was just too coincidental, a woman that looked like Clarissa and A.J. feeling another person in the bar like herself. Maybe A.J. was mistaken. No, she knew what she felt, and she felt Clarissa. It was Clarissa. A.J. was sure of it, and now she wanted to know when and who had turned her. She needed more time, more information, but more importantly, she needed Clarissa.

Chapter Two

Clarissa walked out of the bar on the arm of the butch, feeling a little less than satisfied with her experience in the alcove. It was always the same, she wanted release, she needed release, and she left feeling pathetic. Only something was different this time. It wasn't the sex, it wasn't the butch, it was a feeling. There was an energy she hadn't felt in a very, very long time. Thinking about it more, she realized that it wasn't there when she had entered the bar. No, she knew that predatory energy. It was different, warm, inviting, almost consuming in the way it made her feel. She tried to put her finger on it but couldn't until she was outside in the damp, warm air. Then it hit her, someone was in the bar just like her. But who?

Clarissa had tried to look around when she left the bar, but the butch wanted more and practically dragged Clarissa to her car. Clarissa finally pulled up short and spun around facing the over-excited stud.

"Look um—"

"Sheila," the butch replied.

"Sheila. Look, it was nice back there, but I am not really up for a long night, if you know what I mean. Besides, I explained the rules when you walked up. Right?" Clarissa asked, extracting her arm from the woman's grasp.

"Well yeah, but I figured once you got a little of Sheila you'd change your mind," Sheila said, smiling a cocky "you know you want it" grin.

"Yeah, well you figured wrong. Look, it was nice. Let's just leave it at that, okay?" Clarissa hoped that Sheila wouldn't make a scene; especially since she had made it very clear she wasn't going home with her, no matter what.

"Come on, Baby, it was good, admit it. I haven't come like that in a long time. Shit, I don't think I've ever had an orgasm like that ever." Clarissa knew Shelia was flattering her, hoping it would change her mind.

"Look, I'm flattered, but we're done. Thank you for a memorable evening. Now, if you will excuse me, good night," Clarissa said, walking to her car, not looking back. She hoped that the hormonal woman would take the hint as she walked faster to her car. Clarissa hit the remote to her car and practically jumped in and hit the lock switch.

Phew, why do women say they understand the agreement and then act as if they never heard it? Geez, I think celibacy might be a lot easier and more rewarding.

The more Clarissa thought about Sheila, the madder she got. Clarissa had wanted to wait a minute at the bar to figure out to whom the energy belonged. Now, she was left to wonder if she had really felt it. She didn't waste any time getting out of the parking lot. She didn't want to give Sheila a chance to catch up and try to stop her. Driving home all she could think about was what happened at the bar. Who could have been there? How could she have not known until it was too late? She was usually pretty in-tune with the energy around her. It was how she had survived as long as she had. It wasn't by accident. She had also taken great pains to stay out of the path of others like her.

Driving back to her house, Clarissa tried to think

about the last time she had been around someone like her. Other than Marge, she didn't know anyone else. Marge was a long time friend. In fact, she was the only person who Clarissa kept in contact with from the old days. However, Marge was in Chicago, living as a realtor last time they talked. Besides, if Marge was in town she would call. She didn't just show up without letting her know. So if it wasn't Marge, then who was it? Clarissa worked hard to stay away from that lifestyle. It was difficult, but she did what she had to do to stay alive. She didn't mingle with her kind, it was dangerous.

She found that when she had socialized in those circles it turned into a pack mentality. They acted like animals, and she wasn't an animal. She was a respectable literature professor at the university and liked her job. Therefore, she wasn't going to do anything to compromise that, period. Clarissa pulled up to the driveway that led to her house, pushed the button and watched as the gate opened. Waiting, she looked around to make sure there wasn't anyone lurking. Just in case Sheila had followed her home. She pulled forward and waited until the gate closed before she followed the short drive up to her house.

Clarissa liked her privacy and loved her house. She had searched for a long time before deciding to take the little gem in the foothills. It was quaint, had plenty of room for her treasures and her collection of rare books. And the view was spectacular. Parking her car in the garage, she laid her head back on the headrest and took a deep breath trying to settle herself. A nice long soak in the tub, a glass of wine, and she would be set for the evening. It was a bust for a Friday night, and she just wanted to put it behind her. Clarissa had nights like these, but luckily they were few and far between.

A night like tonight was one of the reasons she rarely went out. After living for over a century, she was hard to satisfy sexually anymore. Maybe it was because she liked it raw, edgy, and deep. To get that kind of sex she needed to visit places she wouldn't be caught dead in. She had her reputation to think about. Some day she would take that journey but right now, she would make do with the occasional fling and self-gratification. Besides, her encounters couldn't match her memories and fantasies. She prided herself in having a very active imagination.

###

A.J. left the bar and watched as the woman who looked like Clarissa argued with her lover. It was clear that the butch wanted more, but Clarissa wasn't having it. A.J. had decided to wait to see the outcome before inserting herself into the argument. After watching for a minute, it was clear that Clarissa didn't need her help. A.J. took out her cell phone, put Clarissa's license plate number in a text message and sent it to a friend. She was going to find out who this person was one way or the other. A.J. slipped her helmet and gloves on and waited until both women left the parking lot. She waited first for the butch to leave to make sure she didn't follow Clarissa and when she didn't, A.J. started her bike and followed Clarissa.

A.J. hadn't really thought about Clarissa in years, relegating her memory to a few quick reflections of her past. Obviously, it had happened before Clarissa's actual death, but who had brought her over? Why hadn't Clarissa tried to contact her? So many questions rolled around in A.J.'s mind, and she wasn't going to get the answers she needed tonight.

She followed as the BMW drove to a non-descript driveway and watched as it entered the gate. Pulling over she typed the address on the mailbox into another text message and sent it to her associate. She watched as Clarissa pulled in and waited for the gate to close completely before she drove up to the barely exposed house. She was cautious, A.J. noted. She had probably learned what A.J. had known for years. Location, location, location should never be given to anyone, no matter what. Not if you wanted to survive.

A.J. waited another minute and watched as a light went on somewhere above her. Taking a deep breath, she tried to center herself and not give in to the temptation to follow the one true love she thought was dead. Her skin vibrated as she remembered the sensations she felt in the bar. It had been a long time since she felt that way, and it was invigorating.

A.J. felt the hair on her neck stand up and her nipples harden as she relived the sensations coursing through her blood. Actually, her blood felt like there was a fire rippling through her body. Reaching in her pocket, she extracted the tin of pills. She wasn't sure if taking another one would help. The last time she felt like this, she had shared a night with another vampire. Putting the tin back in her pocket she guided the motorcycle onto the pavement and went back the way she had come. She needed to put as much distance between her and Clarissa as possible. What she didn't want was a confrontation with the woman who haunted her dreams, only to find out Clarissa didn't remember her. Worse, what if she didn't love her? Was she crazy to wish for that love still? Hadn't time shown her that nothing stayed the same? The past was just that, the past, and no one could live there, especially not her.

Chapter Three

Clarissa looked down at the street before she walked into the mud porch. She was feeling the tingling sensation again and knew something, or someone was close by. Her charged-up body smoldered with the raw energy. Stepping on to the bench, she sat down to take her shoes off. She looked down the drive hoping *not* to catch a glimpse of someone. It wasn't that she couldn't take care of herself, she just didn't want to have to expose herself in order to defend herself.

Squinting hard to see if someone was down there, she scanned the vast property. She couldn't see anyone. Darkness was her friend and she knew she would be able to spot anything that moved. Waiting a moment longer and still not seeing anything, she flipped the light switch to the outside on and moved into the house. Instead of feeling welcome inside the warm expanse, she felt off-kilter and disoriented. It was as if she was transported back. Back to another time, another place, another country. She reached for an open bottle of merlot on the counter as she thought about Paris, and the last time she saw Alexandra. Why that memory would come to her now confused her. She tried never to think about Alexandra, ever. She knew she was out there somewhere, stalking her next victim. Grabbing a glass, she headed for her favorite chair and flung herself into it. She rested her head against the high back and closed her eyes.

Before she could open them again, a set of piercing

blue eyes invaded her memories, Alexandra's eyes. She tingled as she thought about how Alexandra would look at her when they first met. So they had resorted to clandestine meetings. Her parents would never have approved of Alexandra hanging around their home. Alexandra had money, influence and time, things that her father disapproved of in spades. No, Alexandra was someone that she could only have met with in private. That hadn't seemed to bother Alexandra when Clarissa had suggested it. Then one night, she knew why. Alexandra was different, very different.

They had met at a social function at a Paris estate. Clarissa had attended on the arm of a rather pompous ass of a man. Monsieur De Marcus was a rising star in the medical field, and he loved beautiful women just as much as he loved himself, almost to distraction. He had asked Clarissa's father if she could accompany him to the evening's festivities. Seeing an opportunity, Clarissa's father agreed, hoping for a match of course. That night Clarissa was introduced to the men and women of high society. Then she spied a beautiful, raven-haired woman sitting in an alcove watching her. There was something about the way she watched Clarissa that made her anxious. Unsettled, she worked her way out of the woman's sight and back on to the arm of Monsieur De Marcus. After the long line of introductions were made, excluding the woman's, Clarissa and Monsieur De Marcus made their way to dinner only to find that the seating arrangements put Clarissa right next to the dark, sultry beauty.

A long determined hand reached out as Clarissa sat down. "Pardon me. I don't believe we have met yet? My name is Alexandra Locke, and you are?" The last word hung on a perfect French accent.

Clarissa stood quickly as though she were meeting the King of France. "My apologies, Mademoiselle Locke, my name is Clarissa Dumonte. It's my pleasure of course to meet you."

"I don't know why it would be your pleasure, my dear, but it is kind of you to say." Chuckling, Alexandra guided Clarissa back into her seat. "Please sit down. People might think that I am someone special and wonder why you stood so quickly. Please," Alexandra said, as Clarissa watched her glance around the room, obviously uncomfortable with Clarissa's response.

"So, Mademoiselle Dumonte, please tell me you are not Monsieur De Marcus's new engagement."

"Engagement?" Clarissa looked over at the arrogant man Alexandra was referring to.

"Yes, engagement. Monsieur De Marcus has quite the reputation as a ladies' man and you seem rather, well, let us just say you don't seem to be his usual type." Alexandra looked directly at Clarissa, making her blush.

"I am sure I don't know what you mean, Madame Locke but —"

"Please, call me Alexandra. The other is so formal. Besides, be honest. Monsieur De Marcus is so…well, he is a cad and you don't seem to be in need of a cad. Am I right?"

Blushing, Clarissa turned to her napkin and placed it on her lap, picking at a thread that had come loose. Before she could say another word, Monsieur De Marcus patted her on the forearm sitting next to her.

"Ah, Clarissa, I see you have met Madame Locke," he said, nodding in Alexandra's direction.

"Madame Locke." Curtly acknowledging Alexandra, he placed a possessive hand on Clarissa's, which had come to rest on her lap. Clarissa jerked her

hands from his grasp and scooted towards Alexandra without realizing it. "Alexandra has quite the racy past, Clarissa. Careful, it's said she loathes men since her husband died."

"Things are not always as they seem, Monsieur De Marcus. You of all people should know how people talk. If we were to listen to them, then one would think you are a dastardly cad that uses women whom are never to be seen again," Alexandra bantered back.

Clarissa watched as Alexandra became more animated in the conversation with her date. Alexandra's stunning features captivated Clarissa. She had never seen such blue eyes before and she felt drawn to them, almost mesmerized. She felt a hand draw her back into the conversation before she realized she had been staring at Alexandra the whole time.

"Don't worry, my dear. Monsieur De Marcus and I have a long, long history together. He is only jealous that I did not fall for his charms years ago."

Alexandra's touch sent a chill through Clarissa. To quell the tingling in her fingertips, Clarissa clasped her hands tighter together. Turning toward her date, she watched him flash a feral grin. A definite chill had settled in the room and she felt as if she was the prey between two fighting dogs.

"Please accept my apologies, Mademoiselle Dumonte. I will seek other seating arrangements for dinner. I don't want to ruin your evening."

With that, Alexandra was at the head table discussing new seating arrangements with the host. Quickly, she was replaced with a rather portly gentleman who had been enjoying too much wine and reeked of his overindulgence. Clarissa watched as Alexandra sat next to a younger man who was obviously happy with the new *seating arrangements, as he rose to seat Alexandra in her spot. Alexandra nodded and rendered a smile to Clarissa, who was shaken by a sudden jealousy, while she watched Alexandra engage the young man with a sweet laugh at something that was said between them.*

After dinner, the only thing Clarissa wanted was fresh air and a quiet spot. Sitting between the two men had been an exercise in feigned enjoyment. On one side, one man sat and talked incessantly of himself. On the other side, one had belched non-stop throughout dinner, without the decency of apologizing. It made her want to retch, since he often did it right in her face while talking to her. As they rose to retreat to the parlor for dancing, Clarissa begged her date's apologies, informing him that she needed to freshen up before dancing. When he rose to escort her, she explained that she knew the way and that he should take the opportunity to mix with the other gentlemen. Clarissa knew full well Monsieur De Marcus would corner another young woman as soon as she was gone. Turning, she quickly made her way out through a set of doors, not caring where they led, as long as it was outside. As her eyes adjusted to the darkness, she made her way to a balustrade that edged the porch. She was far enough out of sight to be missed. Yet, close enough that if someone came looking, she would see them first.

Clarissa leaned back against the bulk of the ornate balustrade and reached behind with her hands, balancing herself. She let her head slowly roll back and took a deep breath. The warm night air hung with perfumed wisteria that was in full bloom. It felt good to relax and enjoy the quiet of the evening, even if it was for a short time. Soon, she would be home and in bed wishing she had never accepted her father's suggestion of a date with Monsieur De Marcus.

Clarissa practically jumped off the porch when she heard the low rumble in her ear.

"You know, you should be careful out here unprotected, Mademoiselle."

Clarissa could barely make out the silhouette of a person standing in the shadows.

"I'm sorry. I didn't know anyone was out here. I didn't mean to intrude on your privacy."

"Please, don't apologize. I was only enjoying the evening, as you were." Alexandra came out from the shadows slowly and stood next to Clarissa. She was close enough to recognize the perfume, hints of honeysuckle.

"Besides, I am sure you are ready to slit your wrists after having to sit between two remarkable specimens of the male species. So, you need the quiet more than I do," she said, as she turned to go back inside.

"Please, wait. Don't go…I mean, you don't have to go in just because I am here. The porch is big enough for two, or more."

It was a good thing it was dark out. The blush that seemed to accompany a conversation with Alexandra was creeping its way back up Clarissa's neck again. Without looking, she could feel Alexandra's eyes on her. The thought made her shiver. Clarissa told herself it was the thought of talking to an unaccompanied woman that made her curious. It was rare in Parisian society that women went to parties unescorted. It was thought to be in bad taste. The idea that a woman couldn't get a man to escort her meant something was wrong. She should stay home and be thought of as respectable. The fact that Madame Locke did not stay home intrigued Clarissa. At least that's what she told herself. No, there was something more about Madame Locke, but Clarissa couldn't quite put her finger on it.

The silence between the two was almost deafening as Clarissa was startled back to reality by an owl flying by.

"Ah, we seem to have company."

Clarissa looked around and didn't see anyone.

"Excuse me, but I don't see anyone."

"The owl. Don't you hear him?" Leaning in, she whispered into Clarissa's ear, "There, don't you hear him?"

Alexandra's nearness was overwhelming Clarissa and she took a step back, only to be stopped by the balustrade behind her.

"Relax, you aren't for dinner tonight...." Hearing a squeak, Alexandra continued, "...the mouse, he is dinner."

Clarissa felt a wave wash over her as she inhaled Alexandra's perfume. Relaxing against the bulk of the balcony, she turned to see Alexandra staring at her again. She returned the gaze, determined not to weaken under the intense scrutiny. Her gaze roamed over Alexandra's face. She noticed a smile meander across Alexandra's lips and teeth, oddly reflecting the moon's light. A tingle ran down her spine as she watched Alexandra run her tongue along her top lip.

"Well, I have kept you too long. Your date will wonder where you have gone off to. Perhaps we can have lunch sometime, Mademoiselle Dumonte? Next week, before I leave for my summer home in Italy." Alexandra reached down and clasped Clarissa's hand, caressing it before lowering it. "But, then again, I will understand if your date has influenced you against me?"

"No, I barely know Monsieur De Marcus. Besides, I can make my own decisions. I would love to have lunch. What could it hurt?"

"Indeed, what could it hurt?" Alexandra asked, walking back into the shadows. "Then I will send a carriage for you. Is Tuesday okay?"

With that, Alexandra was gone off the porch and back into the house, leaving Clarissa to wonder why she had accepted the invitation to dine with someone she barely knew. Someone who, according to her date, had a very racy past and hated men.

Clarissa twisted the glass of wine between her fingers as she was pulled back into the present. Remembering the first time she had met Alexandra seemed like yesterday and yet it was over a century ago.

Chapter Four

A.J. sat back on her bike and watched the moon as it moved on its protective path across the midnight sky. How different she was back then. She had been a vampire for almost seventy-five years when she met Clarissa. Suddenly, memories of her own turning flooded her mind. She had innocently taken her horse out for a simple ride through the forest when she lost track of time. One minute it was a beautiful, sunny, warm day and, before she knew it, night had fallen throwing her into the darkness of the forest and waiting arms of a vampire. He had been stalking her since dusk, moving stealthily through the forest waiting for his opportunity to strike. Her horse spooked and she was thrown, or so she thought. Landing on her back, she was straddled by a man with shining, almost glowing black eyes.

"You really shouldn't be riding alone, my dear. Things happen in the forest. Haven't you read the children's stories of things that go bump in the night?"

Alexandra raised her hips against the dead weight that sat firmly on her, but with no success. She tried to squirm loose but he only laughed at her attempts to dislodge him.

"Please, you're only delaying the inevitable, my love."

"How dare you?" Alexandra questioned the audacity of the man straddling her. "If you are set about to rape me, I assure you my family will hunt you down like

*the animal you are and kill you. Release me." Alexandra
felt the cold hand of fear squeeze her heart as her body
tensed.*

*"Oh, I assure you I'm not here to rape you my love,
oh and you will be my love when I am finished with you.
You'll have no choice. You see," continuing as he bared
his fangs, "I intend to own you. A bite will do more than
a kiss any day and you will be mine."*

A simple ride in the country had cost her
everything she valued at that time. Her parents, her life
and her freedom. To say her master was benevolent was
like saying a snake could be kept as a pet. Of course the
snake is always a snake and they eventually do what
nature intended, kill, as does a vampire. He taught her
to control her urges, how to be discreet and how to blend
in with society. With time she was free to lead her own
life without his tutelage or guidance. She had heard that
his life was forfeited when he tried to turn the wrong
person. A blacksmith had struck him through the heart
with a hot poker when her master had tried to attack his
daughter. A fitting end to a man who had lusted for too
many and taken much from his victims. But that was
another time, a lifetime for everyone else, but young in
her lifetime.

Remembering Clarissa though was another gentle
reminder of her past life. It was Paris in the eighteen
hundreds and A.J. was rich, beautiful, and independent.
It was a time when women were like children, never
meant to be seen or heard from, unless their husbands
gave them permission to do so. Clarissa, on the other
hand, was young, beautiful, and single. She had a fire in
her that A.J. loved, and it was what drew her to Clarissa
immediately when they had met. The role A.J. played at
that time was the one of a rich, widowed woman who

loved to travel and had estates in several countries.

For as long as A.J. could remember, she always knew she was a lesbian. She never fell in love with men. It just wasn't who she was. She liked to play with women, and she played a lot. She just didn't play in her own backyard. That could be dangerous. She also had a rule and that rule was simple, she didn't feed where she played. She could feed on a lover and she could turn them. She just didn't end their lives, she loved them too much.

A.J. worked hard at constructing what would be seen as a normal life for a woman back then. She was seen with men so often that no one would have guessed she disliked them. She had never slept with them and she hadn't dated them longer than a few months. She had traveled and enjoyed what life had to offer. She had more than her share of closeted lovers, too. It wasn't hard to find women who liked other women, actually. Parisian men had their own lives and vices and that often left lonely, horny women at home, a situation she found ways to take advantage of. Befriending a wife was easy. She often met them at social engagements where they would become friends. They would go to lunch or meet for tea, talking about what beasts men were, how they violated their wives or had affairs and there she was to comfort the poor things.

She tended to her own affairs, took care of estate business and lived much like a man did. She even opted for wearing men's clothes when she was home. She liked working her estates and primarily loved working the grounds, a fete most of her staff admired, especially when she shared small talk about their families or ate a meal with them. She had hated those who treated their staff like slaves, ordering them around, paying them meager wages and rarely giving them time off to raise their families, let alone see them. She had learned at a young age that if you wanted respect you needed to give it. If you wanted loyalty you needed to earn it. She still missed her father's guidance and wished he had lived long enough to see how she had succeeded.

Back in the present, the ride through the city was quiet and calming, the night finally cooling. The streets were barren and lifeless as she made her way to the parking garage of her apartment complex. She hated the city, actually. It made her feel dirty and hopeless. The high-rise cement skeletons that made up the living spaces for the inhabitants reminded her of crypts. Only these crypts were filled with people who paid five bucks for coffee and yet walked past a homeless man and offered only scorn for his condition. She had chosen to live close to work so she didn't have the long commute every day, but it was beginning to wear on her. A.J. thought she had seen it all, but lately, humanity was showing how low it could really sink into the abyss. The senseless gang shootings, the drugs, and now the Middle East war that seemed to go on forever. It was beginning to make her wonder why she had chosen to stop feeding on humanity. And she was the evil everyone in the world worried about? *Please, one less scumbag in the world, who would notice?*

Her life had become a series of patterns. Lonely, lifeless patterns that repeated themselves every fifty or so years. However, tonight that pattern had shifted, skewed because of one woman. She thought about Clarissa again as she dropped the kickstand down for the third time that night. Walking to the elevator she stopped, inserted her key and punched the button for the penthouse. She stood listening to the hum of the elevator waiting to be lifted to her sanctuary. She wondered what had happened to Clarissa since she'd last seen her. How had she survived? Did she have someone in her life now? Where did she work? What was her name? More questions than she could give attention to swirled in her head as she watched the doors, waiting for them to open up and swallow her inside. She felt herself become dizzy and reached for the cold wall, one knee buckling slightly as she swayed towards the support. What was wrong with her? She had seen unspeakable tragedy. Created unspeakable tragedy in her life and now, the mere thought of Clarissa was making her light headed.

Entering her apartment and tossing her keys in the tray by the door, she looked around and wondered what Clarissa would think of her place. It was functional, yet sterile. It had the dark wood tones of mahogany and soft accent lights that displayed a few token art pieces she kept for entertainment sake. She didn't entertain often, but when she did, she wanted her apartment to be serviceable. Walking to the bar, she poured a triple malted scotch. She had acquired the taste decades ago. Its soft oak undertones and smooth taste warmed her, if you could call it that. It was amazing what time and evolving had done for her. She had learned to enjoy the sun again, slowly. It had taken decades, and sunlight-reproducing lamps, to get her accustomed to small doses of the warming rays. She often thought of herself as a snake, coveting the short-lived warmth of the sun on her skin, but instantly becoming cold when it was gone. Now, she could live outside with little damage to herself. She wouldn't be living in the Bahamas anytime soon, but she could survive in the areas where coastal fog was more of a companion than the sun.

Walking to the length of windows along the

southern wall, she looked out over the dimly lit city and scanned it. She watched for seekers, vampires that preyed on unfortunate individuals who were careless as they strayed out at night. There was little she could do for those unfortunate individuals once they were caught, but she prayed for them none-the-less. Seekers had no honor. They lived, no survived, on the pain of others and made no apologies for it. If she hadn't had the breaks she had, would she have ended up a seeker? She didn't dwell on it, but she did wonder. She had heard that seekers' numbers were dwindling. They were becoming a part of the shifting tide of the underworld. Like any other group, seekers hung out in gangs, and what happens when gangs collide? Violence. They dealt drugs, they hustled, they survived on the pain of others, and then they killed them. However, they hadn't counted on human gangs being so virulent, so violent. Times had changed from the days when people didn't venture out at night. Today's gangs lived in the cover of darkness and so did seekers. Too many people battling for the same turf meant one thing - only one would survive. And right now the odds were even. However, that wasn't A.J.'s world. It would never be her world.

Chapter Five

Purrrrrrr."

Clarissa slowly released a long sigh arching her back and stretching out from beneath the blankets. The warmth of the blankets made her purr like a kitten being stroked by its owner. She loved her heated blanket. It almost made her feel like she was alive again, the warmth seeping into her bones.

"Come here, Nefertiti." Reaching out, she felt the soft fur glide across her palm. "Come here sweetie, mommy wants to pet you."

Squeezing the black cat, she purred back, "Where were you last night when I got home? I missed you, silly girl."

Clarissa closed her eyes and rubbed the side of her face along the soft fur.

"I was worried."

Picking up the purring engine, she looked into the slanted green eyes. When she first saw Nefertiti, there was an instant connection between the two. Looking into her eyes now, she wondered if the cat could sense something was off last night and had decided to beat it.

"You're not a dummy, are you Nef?" Pulling the cat into her, she began the morning ritual of cat cuddling, as she liked to call it. Nefertiti tolerated her owner's need to cuddle and Clarissa tolerated Nefertiti's need to bring dead animals to the door. Gifts, she told herself. They were always warm, and that was a bit offsetting to

Clarissa. Did Nefertiti know what she was?

"No, of course you don't. You're just a cat. Right?"

Continuing the ritual, Clarissa laid back and smiled. If only she could find someone to wake her up like this, she would be in heaven.

She lay there stroking the now sleeping feline as she thought about her life. Looking back, her life had changed so quickly when she left England and came to the U.S. But even more dramatic was the change her life took when she left France, De Marcus had made it clear that she was to do exactly as she was told. He informed her that as her only source of protection, she needed him for everything. Her very survival depended on him and only him. She was bound to him, forever. Clarissa had no choice but to follow him. The rules of the Coven were clear back then. The vampire who turned you owned you, period. Only death changed the order. And since a slave never laid a hand on their master, it was rare that one died without help.

She had been smart and created a life around education. It was easy to get lost in the stacks of books that it took to do research. She loved learning. It challenged her when everything else seemed to fail her. So, she reverted back to those experiences she found comfort in. European literature was an easy choice as well. It didn't change, it was familiar and it was home, so to speak.

The sun began to peek through a crack in the drawn curtains. She shielded her eyes with an arm. It always took her some time to get accustomed to the brightness, but she had slowly conditioned her body to the transition through the decades. Her eyes still stung occasionally from the exposure, but she found if she wore the darkest shades she could find it was tolerable. Resting her head in her palm, she scanned her room, looking at the remnants of a very long life. Was it time to rid herself of a few mementos from her past? Was that why she had thought of Alexandra the night before? Looking around, her eyes paused on her jewelry box. It had been a gift from Alexandra. It still played the soft melody that often took her back to that past. A past she hadn't thought of in years, no decades. Except, on those rare once-in-a-blue-moon times when she would wind the jewelry box on a whim and would listen to the minuet it played.

Clarissa had thought about looking Alexandra up after De Marcus died, but De Marcus had told her Alexandra had killed her family. Clarissa knew if she sought her out it would be for revenge. Besides, the rules were clear and her fate had been sealed with one kiss. He ruled her with an iron fist. He had brought her over and she was his to do with as he pleased. Those were the rules of vampires and of the Coven. You owed your very existence to the one who turned you. Until they released you, you were theirs.

She had resigned herself to her life and waited. Lucky for her, De Marcus was always into a new woman every few months. This time it had been his undoing. He had decided to have a tryst with a barmaid from the local pub that night. Sneaking her into a nearby barn, they had climbed up into the hayloft to have sex. While in the throes of passion, De Marcus slipped out of the loft and onto a combine blade. The blade piercing his heart, he died instantly, leaving the poor girl in a panic. She ran screaming from the barn and straight into the path of a local patron of the bar, who was stumbling home that night. Together they had gone back into the barn, only to find De Marcus truly dead. Fate had been on her side when he died.

Clarissa had found out the next day, when the constable had knocked on her door to inform her of her husband's death.

"Mrs. De Marcus," he started. "I am afraid I have some rather bad news for you this morning."

"Please come in, Constable Johns." Clarissa ushered the police officer in, quickly shutting the door behind him to keep the sun out. "May I get you some tea?"

"No, thank you." Looking rather nervous, Constable Johns continued, "I am sorry I have to tell you this, but we found Mr. De Marcus dead early this morning."

Casting his eyes down, he continued, "It seems the Mister was a..." Now visibly distressed at what he had to say to Clarissa, he cleared his throat and continued. "Um, well it seems, he had a dalliance in the hayloft at old man Rogers' place. Fell out of the loft and landed on the combine," he said, tugging on his collar. "He a...he was killed instantly."

"I'm sorry, did you just say my husband is dead?" Clarissa stumbled back against the kitchen table.

"Oh, I'm so sorry Mrs. De Marcus. I..." Constable Johns reached forward and steadied Clarissa.

"And the woman he was with, is she dead too?" Clarissa wasn't sure how she should act. She didn't want to see an innocent woman hurt because of her husband.

"No, no, she's fine. Seems he slipped out backwards and just took himself down. Lucky for her."

It was clear the conversation was taxing on the poor constable and Clarissa didn't want to prolong his agony any longer.

"Well, I don't know what to say, Constable. I never suspected he would do something like that." Lying, she

turned to cover her face just in case the constable was watching.

"Can you tell me what the next steps are? I mean, where is my husband's body? I need to make arrangements for his burial."

"Well, that's the strangest thing. Seems Mr. De Marcus's body has gone missing. I mean, well, we went back with the mortician to pick him up and there was nothing there but his jacket and some ash. I called my captain and he's searching the barn again. For right now, we can't seem to find him."

"I see."

"I am sorry, Mrs. De Marcus. A respectable woman like yourself deserved better." Turning and reaching for the door he continued, "If there's anything we can do, please let me and the wife know."

"Thank you, Constable Johns. I appreciate the offer."

Feigning a show of her sudden loss, she dabbed at her eyes and sniffled. "If you'll excuse me, Sir, I think I need to lie down. I am starting to feel as though I might faint. Could you show yourself out please, Constable?"

"Oh, of course, Mrs. De Marcus. I'll have my wife stop by later and check in on you. Again, my deepest condolences on your loss. When we find Mr. De Marcus, I will send an officer over and let you know."

Tipping his hat in her direction, he quickly closed the door behind him. Clarissa was sure he was happy to be done with the messy business De Marcus had created.

As quickly as it had started, it had ended. Her service to De Marcus was over. Clarissa was a free woman, so to speak. She no longer had to submit to anyone. She was free to roam and live as she wanted. She was lucky he had made such a show of marrying her, or she would have been left penniless. No, fate had been on her side when De Marcus died. As her life changed so did Clarissa. Changing her name to a more common English name like Graham helped her fit into her new life better. Shedding the De Marcus name had been like a cleansing, both physically and mentally. Clarissa stroked Nefertiti and slid back into the present. Glancing over at the clock, she realized she was going to be late for her lecture if she didn't hurry.

A.J. tossed aside the covers, swinging her long legs off the bed. Taking a deep breath, she twisted her head to release the kinks that always seemed to develop when she had trouble sleeping. It was a rare night when A.J. tossed and turned. It was usually the condition of a young woman sleeping in her bed. This time she knew the reason, Clarissa.

Trying to rub the creases out of her forehead, she sat and waited for the headache to ease. She had thought about Clarissa all night. She briefly contemplated a drive out to Clarissa's house, but then what? A knock on the door? A peek into a window? She had enough control over herself to abandon any ideas of stalking the poor woman. However, she couldn't get Clarissa out of her mind.

Slowly standing, A.J. walked to the velvet curtains and paused as she stroked them. The softness reminded her of her home in France. She hadn't thought about France in years and now, all she could think about was that time, decades ago, when she first met Clarissa. Sliding one side open, she squinted her eyes as she adjusted to the brightness. She arched her neck back as she felt the warmth envelop her. The sunlight gently warmed her breasts as she moved closer to the shear panels that covered the long expanse of glass. Pressing her naked body against the warmth, she shuddered and felt her nipples tighten. Something about the sun energized her. It was almost as if she was flirting with death when she was out in it. It hadn't been that long ago that a mere sliver of sunlight would have been her undoing. Now, she basked in its warmth like a snake lying in the middle of the road at night, soaking up the last bit of warmth. It was a guilty pleasure she relished. She knew of only a few like her with this ability. The research she paid for made it possible for her to enjoy the sun, and she did as often as her job allowed. A.J. was shaken out of her daydream when the phone rang.

"Hello." A.J. turned and made her way to the bathroom.

"A.J., I wanted to let you know I have a line on that license plate you texted me last night."

Kevin was one of her most trusted friends and employees at her company. They had transitioned at relatively the same time, meeting by accident one night over 'dinner'. They had spotted the same man in a back alley in France and pounced on him at the same time. If it had been a fight, A.J. was sure she could have taken the lanky man, but he had been a gentleman and retreated to the shadows. She had not killed the poor man in the alley, but had offered Kevin a fair share of him. Since then, they had been quick and deadly friends. At some point though, she had outreached Kevin in drive and motivation. Kevin was happy to play second mate to her captain, going along for the ride. They had parted ways three decades back, when A.J. had decided that killing was no longer her forte. Kevin, on the other hand, wasn't ready to give up the vampire lifestyle. He had wandered back into her life eighteen years ago by accident. He had answered an ad her company had placed in the trade papers for a hemoglobin researcher. Seems Kevin had worked for a foreign company as a researcher of some type. He had landed back stateside when the company expanded its operation and then left it when they couldn't compete in the U.S. market.

"Hey Kev, what do you have for me?" A.J. held her breath as she waited for Kevin to divulge what he had learned.

"Well, it seems that the plate belongs to a woman named Clarissa Graham. I did some digging and she is a professor at the university. I have someone checking her out as we speak. So, I should have more for you when you get in to work."

A.J. felt as if someone had just punched her in the stomach as she replayed the information over in her head.

"Hey, you still there?"

"Yeah, yeah I'm still here. Could you tell me her name one more time? I don't think I heard you." A.J. braced herself on the sink and closed her eyes.

"Sure, her name is Clarissa Graham. She teaches comparative literature studies at the university, specializing in European literature."

"I see." A.J. paused and briefly considered the implications of what she had just been told.

"Kev, I'll see you at the office in about an hour and you can fill me in on the rest."

Hanging up before Kevin finished, she felt herself begin to lose control. She slammed her phone against the wall. She clutched her stomach and felt her body begin to morph into something she hadn't been in a long, long time. Her eyes unfocused, she stared into the mirror. She felt her body become ravaged by the beast she tried to control for over a century. Her nerves felt like they were on fire as she trembled with the power overload. She threw her head back and let her mouth drop open wide to make room for the quick growth of incisors. She pricked her tongue as she ran it over the tip of one. A trickle of blood slowly made its way out of the corner of her mouth as it contorted into a grimace. The intense pounding of blood in her head forced her to her knees as she struggled to control herself. Clenching her hands into tight fists, she pounded the tiled floor. The delicate tiles gave way under the force of her blows. An eerily haunting moan escaped A.J.'s lips as she began to retch from the torment. Finally, falling to her side, she contorted on the bathroom floor in pain.

Chapter Six

"Professor Graham, wait," a short blond student called after Clarissa.

Clarissa slowed down briefly. "Shirley, hurry. I'm late for class. What can I do for you?"

"Well, I was hoping we could talk about the masquerade ball, when you get a minute."

"Sure, but not now. How 'bout we meet after classes? Around three?"

"Okay. See you then," Shirley said, running in the opposite direction.

Clarissa had started the masquerade ball as a way to get the students interested in European literature eight years ago. Now, it was a full-fledged fundraiser at the university. It had garnered its share of wealthy supporters, who loved the idea of playing dress-up once a year. It never ceased to amaze her how the opportunity for anonymity gave people the courage to dress up in tights and broadcloth. Given the chance, a few would probably even dress up as courtesans, if they were guaranteed not to be found out.

"Good morning, class. We're going to be discussing the literature of the crusades this week," Clarissa announced, setting her bag on the desk.

"So I hope you take good notes, because there'll be an essay due at the end of the week."

Three hours and just as many classes later, students began to file out of the standard issue classroom at the university. Clarissa rarely gave it a second look, but this time she looked around the room. Was it time to make a move? Had she overstayed her time at the university? The events from the night before played over again in her mind. She hadn't been caught off guard like she had last night in a long time, and it unsettled her. Students milled about as she made her way to her office, which was tucked in an unusually small corner. She was grateful she didn't have to share an office, as most of the newer faculty did, so she was content with its quaint size.

Shirley stood waiting at her office door. "Hi, Professor G. Ready to get started?"

Clarissa keyed the lock and swung her office door wide so they could both enter. Pulling the shades, Clarissa flopped down in her chair.

"Sure." Clarissa dropped her pumps on the floor, under her desk, and stretched her toes. She hated "office drag" and wished she worked at a less formal institution. It had been made clear when she was hired, the university had "standards" when it came to faculty attire. She was accommodating if she was anything. Besides, it came with the territory, she told herself. *If you want to be taken seriously, you need to dress accordingly.* That was her mantra, especially when she found herself griping about the amount of stockings she went through in a year.

"Okay, so where is everyone else?" Clarissa said, clearing a spot on her desk.

"Oh they're on their way. Mark had a test and the rest of the crew is late as usual. You know, 'college time'," Shirley said, as she made air quotes.

"Well, 'university time'," Clarissa said, making the same air quotations, "means being on time or else."

"We're here. We're here," said a tall, cute student,

as she entered the office.

"Good. Now we can get started, finally," Clarissa said, grabbing the folder for the masquerade ball.

A few hours later, Clarissa closed the folder and placed it on the desk. "Well, it seems we are on track with everything, but donations. Donations are down, everyone, so we need to make those follow up calls to those on the past donors list. They probably just need reminding, but we are short on time and long on things that need to be done." Standing and turning, she stretched and rolled her shoulders. "Okay, let's meet next week, same time. If something comes up, email me, and we'll deal with it."

Everyone said their good-byes, and Clarissa closed her eyes and took a long deep breath.

"Hey."

Startled, Clarissa jerked around. "What the fu—"

"Whoa, hey, sorry. I didn't mean to scare you. I thought you heard me walk in."

Carol Hayes was a long time faculty member and was assigned as Clarissa's mentor teacher when she was hired. They had become fast friends, one of only a few Clarissa had on campus. It was a dog eat dog world in academia. The publish or perish mentality created enemies before you even got on campus, so Clarissa was glad to have someone from another discipline assigned as her mentor teacher.

"Oh, sorry. I guess I'm just a little jumpy lately." Clarissa waved Carol to the sofa in her office and joined her.

"Are you okay?" Carol asked, as she patted Clarissa's leg.

"Yeah, I just had a weird experience last night. That's all."

Carol had no idea who Clarissa really was, but she was the closest thing to a confidant Clarissa had.

"What happened?" Carol leaned in closer so that Clarissa wouldn't be overheard.

Clarissa knew she would never truly tell Carol everything.

"Have you ever felt like something wasn't quite right? Like someone was watching you, but when you looked around, you didn't see anyone?"

"I don't know. I guess," Carol said, watching Clarissa as she talked.

"Well last night I went out, and I had this feeling like I was being watched." Clarissa rolled her head back on to the couch and sighed. "I'm probably just overly tired, with all the planning for the ball and no time to myself." Lifting her head up, she looked back at Carol. "Crazy, huh?"

"Well, you have been working a lot. Maybe you need to take some time off? Winter break is coming up. Maybe you should go somewhere and relax. Hey, how about Barbados? Sun, surf, and men." Carol rocked her eyebrows up and down, "Doesn't that sound like fun?"

"I think I'm more of a cabin, snow, and hot toddy kinda gal," Clarissa said, as she thought about last night again.

"Well, why don't we go get some dinner, and we can discuss your plans when the masquerade ball is finally over." Carol wrapped an arm through Clarissa's and dragged her to her feet. "Besides, you can treat. I believe it's your turn this time."

"Okay, okay. Let me grab my stuff. I'll pay, if you pick," Clarissa said, as she shut the door behind her.

Chapter Seven

A.J. jerked on the floor of her bathroom, as she still fought with the internal beast trying to work its way out. It had been hours and the best she could do was lay there convulsing. A knock, then a banging on the penthouse door, couldn't bring her out of her self-induced comatose state. As she lay there, she could hear someone calling her name in the back of her mind. The beast is playing tricks on me, she reasoned.

"Geezus, A.J. What the fuck?" A warm blanket was thrown over her and she felt someone's breath on her face. "What the fuck happened?"

Kevin turned A.J. over and picked her up. "What the hell happened here, A.J.?"

A.J. felt her eyelids being pried open and a dim light pierced her mental fog.

"Kevin," she whispered, "I'm gonna kill that bastard."

A.J. turned and grimaced as she felt a shooting pain throughout her body. Her body ached, like she had been someone's punching bag. She knew immediately what had happened. Looking up, she saw Kevin sitting in an armchair by her bed.

"How long have I been out?" she whispered.

"Define out?" Kevin asked, as he got up and moved to the edge of the bed. "If you mean sleeping, a couple of hours. If you mean creepy, crawly out, I don't know."

"I didn't leave this penthouse, if that is what you

mean by creepy, crawly out." A.J. closed her eyes and took a slow, deep breath. "Ouch."

"Yeah, well if you hurt as bad as that bathroom floor looks, ouch is an understatement." Kevin held two red capsules and nodded, "I think you need these. I don't want you going all creepy, crawly on me. If you know what I mean."

Taking the capsules, A.J. cracked each one and put them under her tongue. She felt like someone had just given her food to level out her blood sugar. The effects were immediate.

"Thanks."

"Okay, I just have one question. Who is it you want to kill?" Kevin moved back to the armchair, just in case he was on her short list.

"Don't worry, it isn't you." Sitting up, A.J. adjusted the blanket to cover her naked body. Not that it mattered now, but she didn't need Kevin focused on anything but the orders she was about to give him.

"I need you to find someone for me." A.J. felt herself become angry again and took a minute to compose herself. "His name is Jean Pierre De Marcus. He could be going by the title Dr. De Marcus, or he may have changed his name altogether. However, I doubt it. He's an arrogant asshole."

"I'm confused. Does this have anything to do with the name I gave you this morning?"

"I am afraid it might. He was one of us, back in the day, and the woman you told me about..." A.J. bit her lower lip and then gave a piercing stare at Kevin. "She was my lover, but she wasn't a vampire. I am afraid the bastard turned her."

"Okay, I'm still confused. Why didn't you turn her?"

"Because she didn't want to be turned." A.J. stood-up, wrapping the blanket around her. "She was dying, the last time I saw her. Her parents forbid me to see her, and I thought she died."

Wrapping the blanket around her, A.J. got up and walked to the window, looking out over the night skyline. Below, cars crawled to stoplights and a few people milled around. She watched as the first drops of rain began to slide down her high-rise window. The popping of umbrellas started to line the street below as people began to scurry faster.

"Look, I don't know anything about her life now, so I want you to find out as much as you can. Okay?" Walking to her closet, she tossed the blanket and pulled a sweater on. Reaching for some jeans, she yelled over her shoulder, "and find that bastard, De Marcus. Because I am gonna kill him for what he did to her."

"All right, I'll see what I can do. I'll call you when I find something out," Kevin said, as he closed the door to the penthouse.

A.J. walked back to the window and put her hands on the cool glass. Wishing she could feel the connection with Clarissa again, she closed her eyes and opened herself up to the emotional energy surrounding her. She had felt her last night. Maybe she could reconnect with her. She jerked immediately as she felt a twisting in her gut. It felt like a knife piercing her. Taking a deep breath and tightening her stomach, she lowered her head. Looking down to the street, she tried to see who, or what she was feeling. This was a dangerous game she was playing, and she knew it. She hadn't been connected to Clarissa in over a century. There was no way of knowing if she could still feel her, even now. She had shut herself down to those connections for a good reason and this wasn't a time to act on emotion. Pulling herself back in, she looked down and scanned the street and park below, knowing she probably didn't want to know what had just happened.

Walking to the desk, she picked up the phone and dialed Kevin. Waiting, she wondered what she was going to do now. Confront Clarissa or wait and kill De Marcus.

"This is Kevin."

"Hey, Kev, I need a cell phone and any more information you might have on Clarissa Graham." A.J. steeled herself for the blow she knew was coming.

"Yeah, I kinda figured you needed a new ball and chain when I saw it in pieces on the bathroom floor. Over on the bar is a box with a new one." A.J. heard Kevin cover the mouthpiece of the phone before he responded to the second part of her statement. "Sorry, that was the P.I. I hired. Okay are you ready for this? Maybe I should come over, just in case something happens?"

A.J. could sense Kevin's nervousness through the phone.

"No, I'll be fine. Just spill it." A.J. poured a glass of scotch and plopped down in the leather armchair by the desk.

"Okay, I haven't had a chance to go through everything, but let me see if I can give it to you in a nutshell.

"Well, Clarissa Graham, according to university records, is single. She has been with the university for about—hhmm, eight years. She lives at the address you gave me and hasn't had a speeding ticket, accident, or come up on anyone's radar during that time."

"Actually, she doesn't come up on anyone's radar before 2001, when it says she graduated from college with a degree in comparative literature. She's good, if she can keep this low a profile."

"Hmm," was all A.J. could say. "What about Mr. De Marcus? Anything on his whereabouts?" A.J. shifted, throwing her long legs over the arm of the chair.

"Well, that's the report that was just delivered to me, so let me look real quick."

As A.J. waited, she wondered why Clarissa was single. When someone transitioned, they were usually bound to the person who brought them over. Something wasn't adding up and it only made A.J. angrier, to think about all of those years she had wasted, when Clarissa was alive and this close.

"Okay. You still there?"

"Yeah"

"I've looked over the report and there is nothing about a Jean-Pierre De Marcus in the United States. You want me to do a detailed investigation on him and see if we can come up with more info?"

Rubbing her fingers across her lips, she thought about whether she really wanted to find De Marcus. If she found him, she knew she would kill him. That wasn't the question. However, did she need more information or time to find out about Clarissa? That was the real question.

"Tell you what; I'm going to give you a starting point to look for this bastard. Then I want a detailed report on Clarissa. Where she goes? What she eats? Who she sees? The works."

"You got it. Are you coming in tomorrow?"

"Yeah, I think I need to rest tonight. Then, I'll be ready to start fresh in the morning." A.J. slowly and methodically detailed everything she knew about Jean-Pierre De Marcus. His dealings with women, his former address in Paris and even where De Marcus's parents were buried.

"Alright, I'll see you tomorrow then." A.J. was sure Kevin's head was reeling, but she needed to be sure he found the bastard and quick.

"See ya tomorrow."

Hanging up the phone, she laid her head back. She drummed her fingers on the leather, thinking about De Marcus. *Where was he and why was Clarissa by herself?* She wondered.

Nothing was making any sense. She had lived long enough to know some vampires treated their underlings like trophies. The bigger the herd, or harem in De Marcus's case, the more prestigious you were. A follower would often be set free, as the responsibility of always watching their underlings soon became too much of a burden to the vampire.

Then there was the question of whether Clarissa was even still a lesbian. Hadn't they been intimate during their time together? They had been more than casual lovers. They had talked of a future together, moving to somewhere different and starting a new life. Had it all been just a game to Clarissa? A.J. had met many a woman who liked to, "try it out", but usually they were pretty up front in the beginning. The whole thing was starting to make her angry again. De Marcus, Clarissa, the lies. Her hands began to shake as she thought about putting them around De Marcus's neck and choking the life out of him. No, the thought of driving a stake through his withered-up heart would give A.J. the satisfaction she needed to avenge Clarissa.

She knew she needed to stop before it started all over again. She got up, went to her room and put on her running clothes. She needed to get out and try to release this energy quickly, before it took a turn for the worse. As she stepped out into the cold night air, she took a deep, long breath and clipped her cell phone to her waistband. Twisting her neck from side to side, she felt the pop and stretch as she tried to loosen herself up. Running wasn't her favorite exercise, but it helped keep her in shape. With her lifestyle, sometimes it didn't hurt to be able to outrun someone just like her. *Better to run away than have to fight to the death,* she told herself.

Running towards the park, she felt herself begin to relax into her pace. She liked mindless labor sometimes. It gave her the chance to clear her mind and not think about things, only focusing on the thump, thump, thump her running shoes made when they connected with the pavement. Her long strides ate up the distance to the first marker on her run, a century old oak that had seen some of the same things she had seen in her lifetime. The only difference, the oaks didn't repeat their stories.

She could feel her body rebelling against the strain of the run, especially after what she had just put it through earlier, in the bathroom. Looking down at her hands, she saw the remnants of the pounding she had delivered to the tiles. Their stiffness reminded her that had the tiles been a person, they would have probably been dead. *I guess I need to call a contractor and get that fixed,* she thought running past a group of ducks. Their heads were tucked under their wings, in for the night. Running faster, her body started to relax even more. Her mind began to clear from the fog she had been clouded in. Her ears picked up drifting conversations as she passed by people walking home. Work was often the topic, but occasionally, she heard the whispers of an intimate conversation, making her smile. If people only knew they could be heard by others like her, maybe they would be more careful.

Thump, thump, thump was all she focused on as she clicked off the markers that made up her journey. The century oak, the cluster of picnic benches on her right, the white light posts that lit the edges of the path she ran on. Her skin prickled as she ran closer to the lighted phone booth on her left. Someone stood under the light in the booth with his back to A.J. as she passed. A.J. felt her body tighten when she cleared the phone booth. Something was wrong, very wrong, and there was little she could do as she was tackled from behind and thrown to the pavement. Rolling with the attacker, she tucked her head and dropped her shoulder, so that she could position herself on top of her unsuspecting attacker.

A guttural, throaty growl assaulted her ears, as she straddled the now victim under her. A punch landed squarely on her jaw, throwing her head sideways and threatening to unseat her off him. His stench was overwhelming and made her want to throw up. Jerking her head back, she worked her arms between his iron grips on her jacket and grabbed his throat. Pulling him closer, she could see the dried blood in the corners of his mouth, alerting her to whom she was fighting. Her gaze caught a brief glimpse of sharp incisors meant for her.

"Wrong idea, asshole." A.J. felt her body begin its second attempt to morph on the same day. Her grasp tightened on the slender neck, and she let her body continue its transformation. *Timing is everything,* she thought, feeling her skin tighten with anticipation. Her eyes became piercing and she began to stand up pulling her attacker with her. She could hear his windpipe crunch, as she continued tightening her grip. A.J. felt his grip on her jacket release when he moved to grab her wrists, trying to pull them from his neck.

"You just made the biggest mistake of your life," A.J. said, through grinding teeth.

Chapter Eight

"Okay, so what are your plans for the break?" Carol asked, wiping dressing from her lips.

"Hmm, I don't know. I guess stick close to home." Clarissa pushed her plate away and looked at Carol.

"So, tell me about last night," Carol said, looking down and picking through her salad. "What happened that made you jumpy?"

Taking a long, deep breath, Clarissa dropped her head on the back of the high booth seat, closed her eyes and remembered. Exhaling, she started to tell Carol about the night before, at the bar.

"So tall, dark and dyke didn't like the rules huh? Gee, I wish I had your problems, but only in the male department." Pushing her plate away, Carol smiled at Clarissa. "So what happened then? You said you felt like someone was watching."

Clarissa rubbed her fingertips across her eyebrows, trying to work out the stress that had deposited there. "I don't know. Maybe it was just the run-in with Sheila. It probably left me off-kilter."

"Naw, I've seen you take on some of the most aggressive men on campus and make hamburger out of 'em. You're sure it isn't something else, kid?"

"When are you gonna stop calling me kid? You're only a few years older than me." Chuckling, Clarissa knew she was easily a hundred years older than Carol.

"Aw, you look like a kid to me. You know how it

is. When you've been here as long as I have, everyone just starting is a kid, regardless of their age. Just my way of thinking."

"Hmm."

"Okay. Well, I need to get home and grade papers. The end of the semester waits for no one, as they say in academia." Carol stood and grabbed her coat and purse. "Besides, it's your treat right?" Flashing Clarissa a smile, she winked and reached for her hand, helping her out of the tight booth.

"Yep. You got last time."

Clarissa followed Carol out of the restaurant and into the street. Just as she stepped to the curb, her neck and shoulders began to tingle, and goose bumps covered her body. Tensing, she froze and pulled her jacket tightly around her neck.

"Hey, are you alright?" Carol asked, reaching for Clarissa's shoulder.

"Huh?"

"What's wrong? Are you alright?" Carol leaned in and looked into Clarissa's face. "You look like you've seen a ghost? What's the matter?"

Clarissa knew what was wrong immediately. A vampire was close. Twice in two days. What were the odds? She had spent years without ever feeling one close by and now two days in a row. She was on alert.

"I just remembered, I need to go back to the university. I left my office unlocked." Clarissa turned and started walking towards the university. She needed to get as far away from Carol as possible. If she was with a human, they were in danger, and she didn't want anything to happen to the only friend she was close to here.

"Hey wait, I can give you a ride," Carol said, trying

to catch up.

"No, I'm good. I need to walk dinner off anyway. I'll call you later," she said, waiving Carol off. "Good night." Clarissa's body was starting to charge up as she walked further away from Carol.

Good, as long as they follow me and not her, she thought.

She walked faster towards anywhere but where Carol was. She felt her heart start to race and blood to surge faster through her veins. Her fingers tingled and she felt her nails start to lengthen as the small hairs on her body started to vibrate out of control. If she didn't know better, she would have thought she was having a sexual reaction to someone. Looking around, she tried to pick out anything that might give her a clue as to who was following her or where that person was. Slowing down, she walked casually to a corner window and peered into it. Scanning the reflection in the glass, she tried to see the few people walking towards her. It had been a long time since she had been on alert. Now she wished she had stayed focused.

Looking at her reflection in the glass, she watched as her eyes became the color of blood, and the pupils dilated fully. She was transforming and needed to get out of sight, fast. Spotting a parking garage, she ran for the entrance and ducked behind a pillar. Her body was in full control, and her mind was lagging behind. Her nostrils flared as a familiar scent assaulted her. Lust. She was close to another vampire in transformation and could feel its sexual energy vibrating through her body. Her nipples hardened as she tried to control the urge to come. Every muscle in her body reacted, tightening, and then spasming almost to orgasm. Inside her mouth, she tasted blood, her blood, as her incisors lengthened.

Whoever was close was feeling the same thing she was, or she wouldn't be reacting this way. It had been a long time since she had this kind of reaction. It wasn't unpleasant, just the wrong place at the wrong time. Not to mention, she could be in danger if she lost control and transformed in front of the wrong person.

On her hands and knees now, she panted as she tried to regain control of her body. She slowly moved further back into the garage, watching every movement around her. Her ears tuned in to a conversation a few cars over.

"Aw, come on baby, for me?" said a husky male voice.

"No, it's dirty in here. Besides, we have a perfectly good bed at home. You can wait," a softer female voice whispered.

"Please."

"Mike, I said no. No means no. Don't bug me until you get your way."

"Fine."

A car door slammed and then another, followed by screeching tires. Clearly, those were not the people responsible for the energy Clarissa was feeling. Moving further into the dark garage, she wanted to put distance between her and the other vampire. She stood leaning against the cold cement wall, bracing both hands on it. Her body started to shake again. Her clit lengthened and she felt a cold caress move up her body. As long as she faced the wall, she was vulnerable. Taking her jacket off, she leaned against the cold wall and looked around again. Nothing. She could see in the darkness, and yet she could see nothing. But she was definitely feeling someone.

Her body started reacting again, clenching and

spasming. She felt a breath on her neck and an erotic caress against her breast. Only a seasoned vampire could be so aggressive, so controlling. De Marcus was the last one she had been with that could command her to come without touching her, and he was dead. Before she could do anything, she shuddered as an orgasm took control of her body. Grunting, she fell to her knees and moaned as she felt her body convulse repeatedly. She thought she felt a hand touch her clit, causing her to come again as she begged for another touch.

"Please, stop. Please," she pleaded into the darkness, as she arched her back and clenched her jaw trying to control the pleasure. She panted as she struggled to regain control of her body.

She cleared her mind and remembered what De Marcus had told her about letting other people try to control her. The lessons had been brutal at his hand, but she had learned them quickly. He didn't want her influenced by anyone other than him, so he beat it into her. Remembering the lesson instantly brought her back into control of her body. She expected De Marcus to be standing over her as she remembered the lesson.

"Control it, Clarissa. I said control it, damn it." He swung the leather strap over her back.

The sting of the leather bit into her back as she lay naked on the floor of the cottage. Her body was betraying her mind. Another bite of the leather across her back and she felt her incisors lengthen.

"I said control it, you bitch," he said, as he swung again.

Clarissa cursed him under her breath. He watched as another vampire brought her to orgasm again, only to beat it out of her. She panted as she tried to focus on something other than the betrayal of her body. Another tingle shot through her body and then the strap hit her again.

"If you don't learn to respond only to me, you will be at anyone's beck and call," he said, hitting her again.

"Fuck you," she said, spitting blood at him.

"Oh I will, but not before you learn your lesson, my love. Trust me, this hurts me more than it will hurt you if this happens again," he said, swinging the leather strap across her back.

"De Marcus, must we—"

"Shut the fuck up. She needs to learn that I am her master and only me."

"Fine, but I am done with this folly. She has learned her lesson, I'm sure. Don't call me again if this is what you want next time." Reaching down, the man caressed Clarissa's shoulder and said, "I'm sorry, Clarissa. Please forgive me."

With that, the lesson was over. Clarissa lay on the floor for quite some time as De Marcus smoked a cigar and preached to her the virtues of self-control.

Clarissa found herself lying on the garage floor. Her body recovered from the almost pleasurable experience. Getting to her knees quickly, she reached for her jacket and scanned the garage. Still, she didn't see anyone or hear anything as she pulled her coat on. Running her tongue across her lips, she tasted the remnants of blood left behind from her bite. Panicking, she focused on the entrance of the garage as she ran towards it. Clarissa barely missed being run over by a car speeding towards the exit.

"Hey, watch where you're going lady. Geez."

Chapter Nine

A.J. stopped dead in her tracks when she saw Clarissa exit the garage. She had been chasing the seeker who attacked her in the park. She had lost her focus earlier when she heard someone walking by, afraid she might be caught. She had turned her head to see where they were and lost her grip on the bottom-feeder, and he took advantage of the opportunity to run, with A.J. giving chase. They ended up fighting again by the garage Clarissa was now leaving. It explained why A.J. felt her body reacting sexually to someone else. The energy she was giving off was sure to be felt by Clarissa, so she waited.

Making certain the seeker was gone, A.J. felt herself start to tingle as she followed Clarissa down the street. Clarissa's long hair flowed in the soft breeze that was blowing and A.J. could smell her. She could smell her perfume, her shampoo and her — orgasm? A.J.'s body was starting to react again to the tension that was rolling off Clarissa. Stopping, she waited until Clarissa had crossed the street and walked further before she followed. A.J. watched, puzzled by the thought of Clarissa meeting someone in the garage for sex. Maybe Clarissa had changed since the last time they saw each other. The thought of Clarissa being straight played on A.J.'s mind again. Maybe she had been wrong about Clarissa all this time. She remembered the bar and Clarissa with the big, strong butch, with her demanding ways and Clarissa's climax.

A.J. had changed, so it was reasonable to think Clarissa would change too. Gay to straight though was a big stretch for A.J. to accept, but stranger things had happened. The swing of Clarissa's hip brought A.J. back to the moment. She watched Clarissa look around as if she was waiting for something to happen. Maybe she had felt A.J. when she was in the garage? Vampires were in tune to everything around them. It was survival or death if they didn't pay attention. Darkness protected A.J. as she followed Clarissa, sitting on a bus bench every once in a while when Clarissa paused and looked back. If she wasn't careful, Clarissa would see her and then what would she do? Picking up a stranded newspaper, she pulled it open and shielded herself from another gaze from Clarissa. A.J. had to make a choice, follow or go home. Either way, she would eventually have to stop when Clarissa got to her car. A few more blocks, A.J. told herself. What could it hurt?

Before she could get up to follow Clarissa further, her phone vibrated on her waist.

"Yeah," A.J. said, looking down the block at Clarissa.

"Hey, where are you? I've been knocking on your door for ten minutes. I think I'm pissing the neighbors off," Kevin said.

"I don't have any neighbors, Kevin. What's up?" A.J. stood and started walking down the street towards Clarissa.

"Well, I've got some more information on that De Marcus guy. But, you better be sitting for this one."

A.J. watched Clarissa key the alarm on her car and get in.

"I'll be home in about ten minutes. Wait for me,"

A.J. said, closing the phone as she watched Clarissa drive away.

A.J. made the run back in exactly ten minutes. Walking past Kevin, she turned the handle on the door.

"Why didn't you just go in?" she asked, walking to the refrigerator and grabbing a water bottle. "Want one?"

"No, I'm good. Thanks."

"So, what have you got for me?" A.J. tossed her jacket over the back of the chair and flopped down in it.

"Well, it took a lot of digging and—"

"I knew you could handle it," A.J. said, smiling at the frustrated man. He hated it when she interrupted him, but she did it anyway. "Go on."

"Thanks. As I was saying, this person, De Marcus, doesn't come up on anyone's radar anywhere. So, I had a friend do some digging in France's records and nothing, except a marriage license for a De Marcus and a Clarissa Dumonte. After that, nothing in France. So I had him check out the surrounding countries and bang, up pops De Marcus in England. He bought property in England and then promptly died about a year later."

A.J. stroked her neck and thought about how she wouldn't have the pleasure of killing De Marcus. Things were starting to make a little sense, but very little.

"How did he die and are you certain he died?"

"Well, the report is that he was screwing around in a loft and fell on a combine. It killed him instantly. The records are from the coven in England, not local police records. Those burned in a fire."

"Something doesn't sound right about this. I want you to keep looking for De Marcus, Kev." A.J. squeezed her eyes shut as she tried to think about De Marcus alive.

Was it possible? Could he have faked his own death to get away from everything? She wouldn't be surprised if he did, but this put Clarissa in danger. If he was still alive, he would eventually come back for her. It was inevitable.

"Okay. Any particular place you want me to start looking?"

"Well, he was a doctor back then. It was all he knew, so let's start there."

"I'll call London tomorrow and see what I can dig up."

Looking over at Kevin, A.J. raised an eyebrow at his unintentional pun.

"Sorry, I meant find." Kevin blushed realizing his mistake.

"Okay," A.J. said, now stroking her forehead. "Something happened tonight to Clarissa. I want you to put someone on her, a protector. Make sure he's trustworthy. I don't want anything to happen to her." A.J. was now worried someone or something had spooked Clarissa. Her behavior tonight was too out of the ordinary, not that she knew what that was anymore for Clarissa. It just didn't seem normal.

"Why? Did something happen?"

"I don't know, but she was acting weird when I saw her, like someone was after her." A.J. wished she had paid more attention to what was going on around her, but she was so focused on the seeker that seeing Clarissa took her by surprise.

"I don't know, Kev. I tangled with a seeker in the park this afternoon while I was on my run." A.J. threw up her hands. "I'll tell you later. Just put someone you trust on Clarissa and make sure I get a report twice a day. Sooner, if something happens. He has 'shoot to kill' orders if anyone tries anything. Got it?" A.J. stared at Kevin and gave him her business face.

"Hmm, A.J. That might be a problem."

"A problem? For you, Kevin?" The menace in A.J.'s voice wasn't disguised as she quizzed Kevin. "What kind of problem, Kev?"

"Yeah, well, there are only two people available right now. Brax and Selene."

The silence was deafening as Kevin waited for A.J.'s response. A.J. and Selene had history together, and it was a history that couldn't be rewritten, even if she wanted to. And she didn't want to. Beautiful, sexy, and dangerous were all words used to describe Selene, but so where deadly, vicious and vindictive. A.J. had seen both sides of the beautiful assassin in her former life. In fact, she had loved the danger Selene had brought with her. But Selene had changed after losing her lover decades before and now she walked through the night like a thief, stealing what wasn't given freely and killing what pissed her off. She had to keep Selene away from someone as innocent as Clarissa. Clarissa would be no match for the gorgeous assassin and A.J. didn't want to resurrect that part of her life, either, no matter how enticing it was before.

"A.J.?"

"I'm here. Shit. How reliable is Brax?"

"On a scale of one to ten, I'd say he's a seven or eight. But Selene is the best, A.J. and if you want the best you go with her. She's trained in this kind of stuff and she doesn't mind getting her hands dirty."

"Yeah, I remember. I can't believe I've kept her on the payroll."

"Look, she doesn't know who hires her. She just works."

"Go with Brax."

"You sure?"

"Kev...."

"Okay, whatever you say, boss. Anything else?" Kevin asked, taking out his phone.

"Yeah, I want you to find out what Clarissa likes, what she's involved with, and if she's seeing anyone." A.J. stood and stretched. "Get it to me by tomorrow."

"Geez."

"Is that a problem?" A.J. asked, her tone suddenly menacing.

"Nope, it's all good."

"Good. Shut the door on your way out." A.J. started for her bedroom. "And Kevin—"

"Yeah."

"No screw-ups like last time." A.J. had trusted Kevin to protect a client. Instead, the client mysteriously died in her limo waiting for her, while the protector was nowhere to be found, leaving A.J. with a lot of explaining to do when the police arrived. "Has he been found, by the way?"

"No, not yet. Look, how was I supposed to know that—?"

Before Kevin could finish, A.J. had her hand around his neck choking him. Her eyes blood red and her fangs exposed.

"You always know, period," she said, dropping him to his feet. "That's what I pay you for. There are no more second chances, Kevin. Not this time, got it?"

A.J. left Kevin standing in the front room rubbing his throat as she slammed her bedroom door behind her. If Kevin screwed this up, he would regret the day they met, A.J. vowed to herself.

She grabbed a towel and made her way to the

bathroom. A hot bath sounded good right about now, and she needed to think about everything that had happened. She felt like she was losing focus and that was the one thing she couldn't afford to lose. Not now. Just like she had told Kevin, A.J. knew there were no second chances for her, either. Maybe it was time to start setting up a new life. Things were getting complicated.

Chapter Ten

Clarissa watched as the gate closed behind her. She took a deep breath and parked her BMW in the garage, putting the garage door down. She rested her head against the head rest and thought about what had happened in the parking garage. Something wasn't right. She had been here for years and never once did she run into another vampire. Now, she had felt them two nights in a row and it left her unsettled. Tonight though, she hadn't just felt one, she had responded to one. She had a sexual encounter without her consent, and it left her uneasy and scared.

Winter break is just around the corner, she told herself. The free time would do her some good. She could stay home cooped up in her house, or she could go somewhere cozy and get away from it all. Pulling her briefcase and her books out, she went inside and dumped them on the bench in the mud porch. Nefertiti slid against her legs and purred.

"Well if it isn't my favorite mouser," she said, reaching down and picking up the cat. Looking around the house for any "gifts" Nefertiti might have left her, she asked, "So what did you do all day? Huh?" She stroked the cat as she went to the bathroom and started a bath.

"I think I need a glass of wine and a nice long bath, Nef. What do you think?" she asked, placing the cat on her bed. The ringing of the phone made Clarissa jump. "I think I need that glass of wine more than I realized," she said, reaching for the phone.

"Hello?"

"Hey kid, are you all right? I was worried about you."

"Carol," Clarissa said, with a sigh. "Yeah, I'm fine."

"You don't sound fine. Why'd you take off? I could have given you a ride back to campus, silly."

Clarissa wished she could confide in Carol. She needed someone to talk to, but she just couldn't risk it. She would have to call Marge later and tell her everything. Marge had been her only friend when she left Paris with De Marcus and landed in England. She had befriended Clarissa and for that she would always be grateful. Marge had also helped Clarissa navigate between the human world and the vampire world after De Marcus's death. Hopefully, she would have some advice for Clarissa.

"No, you needed to get home and do your grading, remember?" she said, trying to sound upbeat. "Besides, I needed to walk off that dinner. I'm not getting any younger, you know."

"Right, you're practically rail thin, and you're worried about your weight. Why don't you let me give you a few pounds? Besides, you look like you need a cookie or two, Honey." Clarissa was always surprised when Carol referred to herself as fat. Gone were the good old days when women were nice and voluptuous. Actually, Clarissa reminded herself, those days were a century ago; when being fat was considered a sign of wealth.

"Hey, are you still there? Are you sure you're all right? I can come over and talk if you want."

Clarissa was tempted by Carol's offer, but she just would be lying to her if she came over and they talked.

"Yeah, I'm good. Really. I'm pouring a bath and getting ready to have a glass of wine to relax. How about I call you tomorrow when I get up, assuming you're not otherwise engaged."

"Alright, but are you sure you don't want me to come over for some girl talk?"

"Nope, I'm good. I need to check the bath, so I'll call you tomorrow. 'Night." With that, she hung the phone up and sighed. Why did it have to be so difficult being different?

Putting her merlot on the side of the tub, she stripped off her clothes and flung them at Nefertiti, only her tail swishing about. Clarissa slid into the lavender scented bath and sunk up to her neck.

"Hey, Nef, wanna join me?" she asked of the inquisitive cat who now sat on the toilet seat. "Water's fine, jump in." Tossing a splash of water toward the cat made her instantly disappear.

She rubbed a kink out of her neck and then laid back against the tub, closing her eyes.

"Pardon, Mademoiselle," said a sultry voice. "I think you are waiting for someone, no?"

She looked up at the woman whose voice was responsible for the goose bumps popping up all over her body. Shielding her eyes, she could barely make out the woman.

"Madam Locke?" she said standing.

"Oh, you are cold. Should I ask the waiter for a table inside?"

"No, no, I'm fine. A slight breeze must have caused them." Clarissa looked down at her arms and wondered what else Madam Locke could see. *Perhaps her hardened nipples pressing against her bodice?*

"Please, why must you stand? I am no one special.

Didn't we have this conversation the other night at dinner?" Alexandra asked, sitting across from the beautiful woman.

"Of course. My apologies," Clarissa said, dropping her head submissively.

"Oh my dear, you really need to get a backbone," Alexandra chuckled. "Or you will be the object of affection of every eligible man, and some not so eligible men, in the city.

"Excuse me?" Clarissa sat pondering Alexandra's statement.

"My dear Mademoiselle, men love submissive women. It allows them to train you to their liking." Alexandra motioned for the waiter. "Besides, you are not ready for marriage are you?"

"Excuse me?" Once again, Clarissa was on the receiving end of yet another question by this seductively, sexy woman.

"Perhaps it is you that I should be concerned with, Madam Locke. I hear many interesting things about you." Clarissa blushed when Alexandra steadied her gaze on Clarissa's breasts.

"Touché. See, you can volley across the court." Alexandra smiled, pouring the tea that had been deposited on their table. "So your boyfriend, De Marcus. Will he be joining us?" Looking up from tossing a sugar cube in her tea, she smiled demurely.

"He is not my boyfriend. We had this conversation the other night, remember?" Clarissa said, stirring her tea fervently. "Perhaps this was a mistake, Madam. If you will excuse me—"

"Please, forgive me, Clarissa." A hand stopped Clarissa from getting up. "I don't know when to stop baiting such beautiful women. I promise to behave if you *will stay. Otherwise, we will just have to make a date for another time."*

"What makes you think I would do that?"

"Again, I am being presumptuous. See, I don't know when to stop." Alexandra sat back in her chair staring at Clarissa. "You are not a prisoner here, Clarissa. You may leave if you would like. I hope you don't, but I understand if I am too forward for someone so beautiful and so young."

Clarissa stared into Alexandra's blue eyes and felt drawn to them. She wondered what power this woman had over her to make her want to stay, to continue the repartee they were exchanging. Clarissa's goose bumps returned as she watched Alexandra slide her tongue over her top lip, then close her mouth in a pout.

"Oh mon ami, you are cold. Let me call the waiter. No, wait, here. You can wear my shawl. It should keep you warmer." The soft cashmere shawl slid down Clarissa's arms and enveloped her with a scent she remembered from the other evening, honeysuckle. "There. Are you warmer?"

"Yes, thank you, Madam."

"Please, call me Alexandra. We are friends, no?" Alexandra's eyes twinkled when she smiled at Clarissa. Clarissa felt like she was cheese in the clutches of a very smooth mouse.

"Yes, I would like to be friends."

"Good. Let's order something. All of this friendship is making me hungry. Waiter."

An hour later, Clarissa and Alexandra had finished a light dinner and ended it with interesting conversation of Alexandra's travels. Clarissa was enthralled with the tails of travel and adventure. Clarissa learned that Alexandra had been married only once. "Once was enough," according to Alexandra, to know she wasn't suited for it.

"Well, perhaps next time you can come with me to my summer home. It is beautiful. The vineyards are heavy with grapes and we can relax and swim in the pool at the estate." Clarissa felt Alexandra's hands grasp hers and stroke her palms. "I usually have business during the day, but in the evening we can venture into the vineyards, eat grapes and swim in the pool. It will be fun."

"I would love to come. However, my father would not approve, I'm afraid."

"Perhaps I can speak with him on your behalf?"

"I don't think that will change his mind."

"I can be very persuasive. Trust me."

Clarissa smiled at Alexandra's determination. It was clear she rarely took no for an answer.

"All right, but don't say I didn't warn you."

"Hmm, don't be surprised if you're at my summer home soon."

Smiling to herself, she realized she liked this dark, secretive woman. Something about her was dangerous, yet protective of Clarissa. Looking down at her arms, the goose bumps were back, and a tingling had vibrated through her body when she took Alexandra's arm. Clarissa looked up at Alexandra and studied her as they walked arm in arm down the street. Yes, Alexandra was definitely an interesting woman she wanted to learn more about.

Clarissa relaxed in the bath as she thought about the masquerade ball. She loved the opportunity to dress up in period clothing, especially a period familiar to her. There was still so much left to be done that she needed to make sure the students stayed on task. There was only one problem. This year a major donor had pulled their funding because of the rough economy. She was surprised more donors hadn't done the same thing, but was thankful for the few who had assured her of their long-term support. This event wouldn't be a success if the club couldn't replace that donor. The economy had hit everyone hard, including the university. Dean Marsh had made it clear no money would be coming from the university. Carol had recommended a few of the bigger companies that did research for the university, so tomorrow she would send a letter to each and find out what their level of interest might be. One company looked promising. A research and development company had recently set up a lab on campus and had made it clear that they were interested in helping the university in any way they could. No one on campus knew much about the company so the details were light. She had asked the grants and finance department to send over what they could about the new company.

She thought about Marge and the call that she needed to make. After the experience in the garage, she needed some grounding and Marge was just the person to help her. Marge had lived twice as long as Clarissa had and would be able to give her some much needed advice.

Clarissa had led a protected life for the past eight years, but now she was worried she had been too careful. With the exception of Marge, she didn't have any friends like herself. She stayed out of the culture for a reason, but now it looked liked her past might be looking for her. She had heard of a sub-culture of vampires called seekers, but she hadn't seen any evidence of them. Maybe last night had changed all of that. Clarissa tingled as she remembered how easily her body had worked into the orgasm. The only person who could do that to her would be an older, established vampire like De Marcus.

De Marcus wouldn't hide though, he would take what was his. And she was still his, if he was alive.

Dunking her head under the warm water, she tried to rinse the prior evening's memories from her head. Things were getting complicated and maybe it was time to start thinking of moving. But, first things first. The masquerade ball and then deal with the insanity that was starting to swirl around her.

Chapter Eleven

A.J. grabbed the first available elevator and made her way to the back. Her shoulders pressed firmly against the wall. She always stood in the back, watching who got on and who got off. This time though, she noticed there were a lot of new faces. She didn't like new faces, even if she didn't get a vibe off them. She liked knowing who worked for her. It was what kept her safe. Getting off at her floor, she half smiled at the receptionist in the lobby and went straight to her office. It was still early and Kevin wouldn't be in for another half hour. That would give her plenty of time to walk the floors and check things out. She didn't like it when she lost focus on what was important, and this company was important to her.

The new high-grade blood replacement could change the way she lived, and she was enjoying the stuff R & D had sent for her to try. A.J. was the guinea pig when it came to stuff like that. If something went wrong, she could handle it, so she tried all of it out. This new drug showed a lot of promise, and she was happy with the results. She hadn't fed on real blood in ages, and she felt better than she ever had. It had taken years to develop the formula that they experimented with now. The highly concentrated blood in the pills acted fast enough that A.J. could resist the urges that took over her body when she needed to feed. Her motivated staff was well compensated for their discretion and it was amazing what money could buy. Loyalty, privacy, dedication and an iron clad contract that made it impossible for her employees to work in the industry if they quit. Few left, and on the rare occasion one did quit, she had ways to protect herself. She told them that the project was top secret for the military, a blood replacement for war that was both convenient and portable. Rehydration was the reason for the high concentration, she told them.

"Hey boss lady."

A hand slapped her back causing her reflexes to spike, her body to go rigid and her nails to grow before she could control it. Taking a long deep breath, she stuffed her hands in the pockets of her tailored black slacks before she sliced the idiot.

"Mike, how many times have I told you not to surprise me like that, or call me 'boss lady'?" A.J. felt the bones in her neck pop when Mike slapped her on the shoulder.

"Hey, lighten up. Life's too short to be so uptight. Right?" Mike sat down at his desk and turned his computer on. "Besides, we haven't seen you in a while. You okay?"

Mike was an underling that hadn't learned his place in the world yet. Perhaps it was time she gave him a lesson in decorum.

"A.J." A.J. heard Kevin call her down the hallway by her office.

"Mike, you and I are going to have a conversation on employee and employer boundaries this afternoon," A.J. said, finally able to pull her hands out of the shredded, interior pockets of her pants. "See you at 1 p.m., and I wouldn't be late if I were you."

A.J. walked past Kevin and into her office, sitting down on the leather couch.

Seeing the exchange, Kevin said, "I'll talk to him."

"No, I'll talk to him. What the fuck is wrong with everyone? Shit."

"A.J., relax. You're just off kilter right now. It stands to reason. You just found out a woman you thought was dead, is alive. She lives a couple of miles from here, and she doesn't even know you're alive, yet." Kevin looked at A.J., hoping logic would take over from emotion.

"Don't patronize me, Kev. We've known each other way too long." A.J. made her way to the window and pulled down the sunshade. "What did you find out about Clarissa's daily habits?"

"Well, like I said before, she's an assistant professor over at the university. Teaches literature, English, stuff like that. Oh, I did find out something interesting. Every year she puts on the Renaissance Masquerade ball. They have donors that contribute large sums of money and that money goes to scholarships and grants at the university for the students."

Shaking her head, A.J. said, "That sounds like something Clarissa would do. She was always putting others first. Okay, get me more information about donating, tickets, that sorta stuff. I want to see her up close and in action."

"You think that's a good idea, A.J.? I mean she doesn't know you're here. Don't you want to keep it that way?"

"Kevin, why must you always second guess my actions?" Sitting down at her desk, she called for her assistant. "Kevin, if you can't handle working with me then maybe we need to reassess your position with the company." A.J. motioned her assistant to come in.

"A.J., it isn't that and you know it." Leaning over her desk, he whispered, "I just want you to be careful, that's all. I don't want to see you get hurt."

"Thanks buddy." Shooing him away, she finished, "I think I can take care of myself. Now, find out what you can and give me a status report this afternoon."

"Okay."

A.J. turned her attention to her assistant.

"Gail, can you pull Mike Tyler's file. We're having a meeting this afternoon."

Chapter Twelve

Good Morning, little Miss Sunshine," Carol said, closing the door behind her.

"Hmm, well aren't we chipper. I see you met someone new." Clarissa poured herself some coffee and passed a cup towards Carol. Clarissa noticed a bruise on Carol's neck and instantly the hairs on her arm stood, and a chill worked through Clarissa.

"Well, if you must know, I just met him the other night."

Raising an eyebrow, Clarissa looked at the darkening mark on Carol's neck. "So I see."

"Oh, that." Carol reached up to pull her collar closer to the mark, "It's my sweet spot, he says."

"Is it a bite? I can't quite tell," Clarissa said nonchalantly, ruffling through paperwork on her desk.

"It's a hickey, silly. Kinda embarrassing, but it happened so quickly." Still trying to pull the collar closer, she asked, "Can you really see it? I mean really see it?"

"Naw, it's barely noticeable. Besides you can always tell the students it's a curling iron accident." Clarissa started chuckling at the bad joke.

"So what does this guy do?"

"Well...he's a teacher."

"Really. Hmm, I would've thought he was—"

Carol cleared her throat cutting Clarissa off as a few students walked towards them. "Well, I gotta get to class. Hey, are we on for lunch today?"

"Sorry, I have an appointment with that new research company, Knight-Pharmaceutical, on campus. I need to try to fill that donor's slot we lost. How about I call you later and maybe we can do drinks or something," Clarissa said, as they started walking down the hallway.

"Okay, sounds good. Let me know what they're like over there. I hear they do animal experiments."

"No, they don't. The university has a policy on that. Geez."

"Hey, I'm just telling you what a student told me. Besides, maybe you'll meet some gorgeous researcher over there."

"Is that all you ever think about? Sex?"

"Hey, Ms. Woods, nice hickey," said a student as she passed by the two women.

Clapping her hand to her neck, Carol glared at Clarissa. "I thought you said you couldn't see it?"

"No, I said it was barely noticeable." Grinning, Clarissa watched as Carol took out her compact and started dabbing make-up on it.

"Oh right, well…." Carol fidgeted with her collar again, trying to cover her neck, looking embarrassed.

"Well, at least you have the decency to look embarrassed. Don't you two get enough?"

"Well…I'm advising him on changes he might want to make to his lesson plans."

"I didn't know he was teaching sex ed.," Clarissa smirked. She knew Carol fell fast and hard, but a hickey on the first date? That was fast, even for Carol.

"Well, I gotta run, Ms. Smarty Pants. Call me after your meeting and let me know what happened." Carol kissed Clarissa on the cheek, and made a beeline for the door. "See ya later." Tossing a wave over her shoulder, she was gone.

Something about Carol's boyfriend was making Clarissa nervous. She couldn't put her finger on it, but it was clear he was already having a huge affect on Carol. The hickey, if it was only just a hickey, was strange behavior for a male his age and profession. Clarissa suddenly had an urge to meet Carol's boyfriend. The sooner, the better.

Pulling out her notebook, Clarissa found the number for Knight-Pharmaceutical. A minute later, she had confirmed her appointment with someone Clarissa figured was the person who ran interference for the head of the donations department.

A.J.'s office door opened a crack as Kevin peeked around the corner looking for A.J.

"A.J.?"

"What, Kevin?" The darkened room clearly reflected A.J.'s mood. She had been pissed with herself for her rash decision to dispense with Mike Tyler earlier. She had wanted to keep a level head when she met with the young man, but he had done everything he could to push her buttons, and she felt he had left her with few options.

"Um, I heard you had a meeting with Mike Tyler earlier. How did it go?" Afraid he knew the answer, he stood by the door just in case he needed a quick retreat.

"Let's just say Mr. Tyler's working remote for a while. What do you want, Kevin?"

Fidgeting with the door handle, Kevin felt the door yanked from his grip. A set of steely eyes glared through him.

"A.J., I just got a call from our grant department. Professor Graham's coming over this afternoon to discuss a possible donation from Knight-Pharmaceutical. What do you want me to do?"

"Write her a check." A.J. slammed the door shut, then flung herself against her leather couch so hard, she practically knocked the breath out of herself. She hated when she lost her temper with people she worked with, but lately, she had been on edge and it was showing. *It's all Clarissa's fault*, she thought, rubbing her temples. Everything was fine until she saw Clarissa, not once but twice. Now, Clarissa would be at the company, A.J.'s company. On the same floor as A.J.'s office, and close enough that A.J. would be able to feel her energy, and reacquaint herself with Clarissa's scent. A.J. wasn't sure she would be able to maintain a safe distance if Clarissa were that close, close enough to touch.

"A.J.," Kevin whispered through the closed door. "How much?"

"How much what, Kevin?"

"How much do you want me to write the check for when she gets here?"

Jumping up, A.J. pulled the door open so hard it slammed against the wall, burying the handle. A.J. could see perspiration dot Kevin's upper lip as he avoided making eye contact with her. He was playing the subordinate role well. He knew his place in the pecking order and A.J. knew he would never step beyond it, not any more.

"Sit down." A.J. pulled the door out of the wall and quietly closed it behind them. She crossed her arms as she watched Kevin still avoid eye contact with her. Something was wrong. She knew it because she knew Kevin. "What's going on, Kevin?"

"What do you mean?" Kevin quipped, running his hands down his slacks.

"Why are you so nervous? This doesn't have anything to do with Clarissa, does it?" A.J. leaned closer to the nervous man and he flinched with the motion. Her voice lowered to a menacing level as she asked him again, "What the fuck is wrong with you, and you better tell me now. Understand?"

"Look, we might have a problem." Kevin twisted his neck and an audible pop echoed in the room.

"I told you, Mr. Tyler's working remote, not six feet under, if that's what you're worried about." A cold stare met frightened eyes.

The tension in the room was palpable now, and A.J. was past losing her patience. Within a second, A.J. had leapt over the coffee table and was straddling Kevin, his neck in her crushing grip.

"Listen, I'm past twenty questions. What the fuck is going on?" Spittle dropped from grimacing lips moving closer to Kevin's neck. "Now, or I snap your neck."

A gurgling sound pushed passed Kevin's windpipe as the veins in his neck started bulging. A.J. licked her lips and moved closer. An audible pop as A.J.'s fangs broke from their hiding place made Kevin's eye bulge, as he tried to twist out of the relentless death grip. Clawing at her hands, Kevin gurgled again and tried to sit-up.

A.J. relaxed her grip waiting for Kevin to answer her question. "Well? What's the problem?"

"The guy I sent over to watch Professor Graham—" A.J. started tightening her grip again as Kevin talked. "A.J., please."

"Kevin, this doesn't sound good, and I told you what would happen if he screwed up." Slowly, she applied more pressure.

"Someone else is watching her, too," Kevin blurted out, trying to avoid passing out from the tightening on his neck.

A.J. stood, pulling Kevin up by his collar, snarling with her fangs still fully exposed. "Who? Who's watching her?"

"I don't know, but I wanted you to know as soon as possible, especially since she is coming to the office. Her being here might blow our cover, especially if the someone following her is a vampire."

A.J. dropped Kevin on the sofa and stepped over his limp body. Leaning against her desk, she scrubbed her face with her hands, trying to make sense of the past few days. She had been on edge, but she figured it was because of Clarissa. Now, she had to consider other possibilities. First seeing Clarissa, then the attack in the park, and now someone following the same person she was. It wasn't a coincidence. She didn't have those. Instead, she found life had patterns and reasons for why things happened. Now she needed to find out what those reasons were.

"You're gonna meet with Clarissa today," A.J. said, turning to her desk and taking out her checkbook. "I want you to chat her up, find out what she's been up to. That is if she'll tell you anything. She hasn't lived this long being stupid, so you're gonna have to be patient and careful." She handed Kevin a check, then took out a bottle from her desk and tossed it to him. "Here, take two of these. They'll relax you enough so you won't give off any extra energy she could pick up on."

"A.J., she's gonna know. Like you said, she's been around a long time." Kevin was still rubbing his neck when he felt a trickle of blood cover his palm. "Geez,

A.J., what's gotten into you?"

"I'll be in the other room watching the interview on close circuit T.V. Just tell her you need some background information for the application process. Tell her it's something we do for all grants and donations." A.J.'s body reeled at the thought of being so close to Clarissa. She knew it was a bad idea, but she stopped being logical a week ago when she saw Clarissa in that bar.

"A.J.—"

"Just do it, and if you can't do it, I'll find someone else who can." A.J. moved close enough to Kevin that she could feel his fear. It was rolling off him in waves. "Have I made myself clear?"

"Crystal."

"Good." She sat down in her chair and steepled her hands as she thought about what to do next. "What do we know about the person following her?"

"Nothing yet. Our guy just picked him up this morning when she left for work. I told him to stay as close as he could."

"I want you to put another person on her. This one watches both of them, our guy and the other one. If this guy makes the tail we have on Clarissa, chances are he won't figure we have two."

"But A.J...." Kevin said, wringing his hands, "I only have Selene available."

"I know, I know."

"She's the best and you know that. You wanna tell me what the deal is between you two?"

A.J. knew Clarissa would be in good hands. She just didn't want her in that set of hands. A.J. didn't want Kevin to know that she and Selene had a history and the last thing she wanted was to relive that history anytime soon. "Nope, and I don't want her to know I'm involved in her hiring in any way. Understand?"

"What do you want me to tell her?"

What did A.J. want Kevin to tell her? It would be sticky and Selene would sniff out a lie quickly. A trained assassin over one hundred and fifty years old was not someone to be played. Whatever Kevin told her would have to be believable, or Selene would ask questions.

"Tell her it's a private contract, she needs to keep her distance, and that someone wants Clarissa dead. That should keep her on her toes and deadly."

"Anything else?"

"Yeah, tell her she'll get a big bonus if she keeps Clarissa alive without her knowing it. Remind her there is another person working the case, too. I would hate for her to accidentally kill him, thinking he was the enemy."

"Okay, you're the boss. I'll let you know what she says."

"Kevin," A.J. said, waiting for Kevin to turn around and face her. "She doesn't know I'm involved. Do I make myself clear?"

"Crystal."

As Kevin reached for the door, A.J. whispered, "Sorry about your neck."

"I know."

Chapter Thirteen

The Knight-Pharmaceutical Research Center was a monstrosity of glass and steel, and standing under its huge cantilever entrance sent a chill through Clarissa. Its sterile look reflected the sunlight onto the other smaller building it dwarfed. A huge glass door was opened for her as she moved towards the entrance.

"Good morning, Miss. May I be of service?" a stout gentleman asked, ushering her in to a direct contrast to the exterior. Dwarf Aspens and other deciduous plants were strategically planted to create a picturesque environment. It gave the appearance of a primeval forest indoors. The only thing Clarissa noticed missing from the picture were birds chirping or hopping from the treetops. It was clear the intent was to give one a sense of what was missing outside in the concrete jungle. *But why?* Clarissa wondered.

"Miss?"

Clarissa was drawn back to reality as she scanned the last of the interior landscaping.

"Impressive isn't it?"

"Very."

"So, how can I direct you?"

"Oh, I have an appointment with the director of grants and funding." Extending her hand, "My name is Clarissa Graham. I believe they're expecting me."

Looking down at his clipboard, he noted the

time and highlighted her name. "Do you have any identification?"

Pulling her faculty ID from her jacket, she flashed it at the guard. After closely inspecting it, he handed her a detailed map of the building with a highlighted path directing her exactly where to go. As she stood in the elevator, Clarissa's palms started to sweat thinking about what she would say to the grant manager to convince her to donate to the university. She could only imagine what Knight-Pharmaceutical already donated to have the huge research center at the university and it wasn't like a masquerade ball was as prestigious.

Clarissa stood dumb-struck when she exited the elevator on the third floor. If she thought the atrium was breathtaking, the décor on this floor was staggeringly expensive. The first thing that caught her eye was the enormous stained glass ceiling. A renaissance scene that reminded her of her own childhood graced the entire expanse of the ceiling. If she didn't know better, she would have thought someone had delved into her past and recreated it. And there it was, right before her eyes. A chill went through her as she stood transfixed, staring at it. The craftsmanship was brilliant and no detail was too small, including the bees that hovered over a budding rose. In fact, that particular rose was from France, strange that she would remember.

A moment later, a tall man exited one of the doors and walked toward Clarissa, holding out his hand. "Good afternoon, you must be Mrs. Graham. My name is Kevin Armstrong."

Confused, Clarissa shook his hand. A surge shot through her when he grabbed hold of her hand. "I'm sorry. I thought I had an appointment with Ms. Reinhold?"

"Well you did, but she was called into a meeting and asked if I would take her place. I assure you I've been briefed, but if you would like to reschedule I can call her assistant and do that for you?"

Time wasn't Clarissa's friend at this point. She needed to replace that donor and if Knight Pharmaceutical couldn't help her, then she needed to find another soon.

"No, no please. I was just expecting Ms. Reinhold."

"Please, this way then," he said pointing to another door. "I have us set up in the conference room."

Clarissa had a strange feeling as she followed him, almost as if she knew him. "Have we met before, Mr. Armstrong?"

"I don't believe so, Mrs. Graham. Why?"

"Ms. Graham."

"I'm sorry, I just assumed that you were married. Please accept my apologies." Kevin dipped his head in apology and opened another door, allowing her to pass.

"Please have a seat. Can I get you something to drink? Coffee, tea, water perhaps?"

"No thank you, I'm fine." Another surge shot through Clarissa's body, catching her off guard. Feeling light headed, she turned quickly grabbing for the chair. "Perhaps I'll take some water, if you don't mind."

"Of course, I'll be right back."

Clarissa eased herself into the chair and looked around the room. Perhaps the fact that she missed lunch was the reason for her being lightheaded, she reasoned. Clarissa closed her eyes and took a deep breath, and then another. Rubbing her temples, she tried to relax. She needed to keep her wits about her and now wasn't the time for her to get overly stimulated. That could have disastrous results.

"Here we go," Kevin said, passing Clarissa a bottle of water and a napkin.

"Thank you." Clarissa took a deep breath and tried to relax again.

"Okay, I have the paperwork here for our donation process. I'll need to ask you a few questions, if you don't mind, and then we can see where this leads."

Clarissa watched as Kevin shuffled through the paperwork, rearranging it in some order. As they went through the questions, Clarissa could start to feel herself becoming more agitated. The sporadic surges were now one continuous tingle, and she knew what that meant. She was about to change, and soon. Something was wrong, and she knew it. She had been having these feelings for the past week and now they were starting to take control over her ability to stay grounded.

A.J. sat in the darkened room watching Clarissa on the monitor. Clarissa was still as beautiful as ever, and A.J. ached to touch her. A soft wisp of hair fell into Clarissa's face. A.J. watched as a delicate hand reached up and flicked it behind her ear. It was a gesture she had witnessed often in the past. A.J.'s eyes then focused on Clarissa's full lips. The seductive movement hypnotized her as Clarissa answered Kevin's questions. At least it looked seductive to A.J.

The questions were just a rouse to keep Clarissa in the conference room so A.J. could see her up close, study her, make sure it was Clarissa. A mole on Clarissa's neck caught A.J.'s attention. She remembered kissing that mole many times. The memory sent a shiver through her body. The curve of Clarissa's face, the tiny gestures she made today, reminded A.J. of the nights she had spent watching Clarissa sleep. They had spent few intimate evenings together in the past and she had committed each one to memory, knowing she wouldn't have forever with her lover.

It was Clarissa. A.J. had no doubts now. But the question now would be how to reconnect to someone she thought was dead. Someone who probably thought she was either dead or a blood-sucking seeker. The last thing Clarissa would remember about A.J. was clearly not the person she was today. Clarissa had seen a side of A.J. that no longer existed, a heartless nightwalker who lived off others.

It was all A.J. could do to stay in her seat and watch. She wanted to walk in the conference room and demand answers to all her questions. No, what she really wanted to do was to sweep Clarissa into her arms and kiss her. To tell her how she never stopped loving her, and she haunted her dreams still after all of these decades. Time didn't have a way of making a person forget someone, it only added to the pain that already had taken up residence in A.J.'s heart. She just didn't know how hard her heart had become, until she saw Clarissa again.

A.J. continued to watch Clarissa and noticed that Clarissa was starting to fidget more. In fact, she could feel Clarissa's energy escalating. She was sure Clarissa was starting to feel her presence so close. A.J. recognized the signs of someone starting to turn and she knew Clarissa didn't have long before she was in the throes of it. A.J. needed to act fast, for Clarissa's sake. Pulling her phone, she dialed Kevin's number.

"Kevin, get her out of here. She's starting to turn, I can feel it," A.J. whispered into the phone.

"What?"

"I said get her in a car and get her out of here. I'll call a car around front. You can escort her down to the lobby. Make sure she gets into that car." A.J.'s agitation was evident in her voice now.

"Yes Ma'am," Kevin said, closing his phone.

A.J. watched as Kevin concluded the meeting with Clarissa. She wished it could have lasted a little longer, but she knew Clarissa was fighting hard to stay human. She watched as Kevin did exactly as he was ordered, escorting Clarissa to a waiting car. A.J. continued watching and listening as Kevin informed her that since it was late, he wouldn't feel right if she took a cab back. Relieved that Kevin could think fast, A.J. relaxed a bit as she watched the car pull away from the building. Now that she was away from A.J. and Kevin, Clarissa would be able to control her demons. But the longer she stayed in the building, the greater the chance she would turn and then her secret would be out. She would lose Clarissa forever if that happened.

Movement on the camera caught A.J.'s eye, and she watched as Selene followed Clarissa's car. *Damn, she's already on the job,* thought A.J. when Selene disappeared. Well it was what she wanted, wasn't it? Clarissa protected. A.J. wasn't one to second guess herself, but she knew if Selene found out she was behind the protection order, no good would come from it. But where was Brax? He should have been right behind Clarissa.

Kevin walked into A.J.'s office, dropping onto the sofa he had been pinned to earlier. "God, I don't know how much longer I could take that. She was throwing energy all over the place. I thought I was about to lose control. Thanks for picking up on her like that." Kevin brushed his hands through his hair.

"Selene is already on her?" A.J.'s gaze raked Kevin. "Where's Brax? I didn't see him following Clarissa."

"Brax is at the house. I figure if Clarissa's here and Selene is here it's all good. So I told Brax to stake out the house." Kevin sat up when he realized he could feel A.J.'s anger peek.

"I don't pay you to change the plans. I pay you to follow them. Understand?" Her was anger seething now.

"I'm sorry, but I didn't have time to consult you. I thought we needed him there, besides I got Selene on the case ASAP. Like you said." Kevin pulled at his collar. "Look, A.J. I don't know what's going on with you, but you're really starting to lose control. This morning I thought you were—"

"Gonna kill you?" A.J. finished his sentence for him. She knew she needed to apologize for earlier, but she just hadn't been able to. Her pride had gotten in the way. Now she needed to or she would lose Kevin as a confidant, a friend and her hider of secrets. "Look, I'm sorry about earlier. I guess the stress is getting to me." Leaning her head back, she rubbed her temples.

Up until recently, she had led a boring life. However, in one week, she had learned that an old lover was still alive, she had changed into a vampire for the first time in years and she had a run-in with a seeker, which never happened to her. The fact that someone, possibly another vampire, was following Clarissa only added to the stress she was feeling.

Chapter Fourteen

Clarissa pushed herself into the seat of the car as she tried to control herself. She had fought hard not to change in front of Kevin Alexander. She couldn't remember the last remnants of their conversation because of her fight, but she was sure she thought he had said Knight-Pharmaceutical could help her with a donation. If only she could remember how much he had promised.

She looked through the tinted back windows and watched as the street lights flickered past her. She was struggling to keep her sanity lately. The bar, the incident in the garage and now her meeting at Knight-Pharmaceutical made her wonder if she was changing somehow. She hadn't had human blood in years so was her body telling her it needed to refresh? She had heard of vampires who had gone too long without it suddenly losing control and gorging on it for days, even weeks. Was that happening to her? Clarissa was starting to feel as if her life was spiraling out of control. She didn't like thinking about what she might have to do to bring her life back to the center. It either involved a dark trip on the sexual side or a blood lust, neither of which she was ready for. Clarissa remembered the last time she had taken that dark trip for her lustful cravings.

"How can I help you, my petite flower?" a leather clad gentleman said, stroking his goatee. As he looked her up and down, she knew he was trying to assess her.

"Perhaps a little spanking and then some tickling. Yes?"

Clarissa did her own assessment of the slender, fragile looking man. "Hmm, no, but I am interested in something a bit more physical." Pulling an envelope out of her purse, "but..." waving a negative finger at him, "not with you." Smiling, she set the envelope on the counter. "Please bring me...a female, taller than me and striking to look at. Do you have someone?" Clarissa looked around the darkened room and noticed there were several people lounging. Doors on either end of the room opened to barely lit corridors with more doors.

"Well, that depends." Picking up the envelope and thumbing through the bills in it, he motioned at the bartender, and a drink was quickly deposited in front of Clarissa. "I think I have someone who can help, but she isn't for the faint of heart, if you know what I mean."

"Perfect," was all Clarissa could say, her body tingling at the possibility of being released from her torture. Clarissa grabbed the man's arm as he raised a hand to summon someone. "I make the rules. Understand?"

"For this amount of money, you can beat the shit out of Franco over there," he said, motioning to a huge beast of a man.

"That won't be necessary." Downing the drink, she motioned for another. "Just make sure that this woman is beautiful and skilled, if you know what I mean."

"Yes, I know exact what you need. Follow me." Clarissa was led into a plush room, ornate by dungeon standards. "This is for our exclusive guests. Please make yourself at home. I'll send in Selene and if she doesn't meet your standards, then you can pick someone else. Okay?"

"Thank you." Clarissa laid her coat on the back of the over-sized sofa and tried to relax, but it was no use. She was primed and ready for release. If she didn't find it

this way, she would have to find it in a blood lust and she wasn't ready to concede to that, not yet.

A soft knock on the door and a small woman came in with a bottle and two glasses. Quickly depositing them on a table in the corner, she bowed and whispered, "Compliments of the house." Her quick exit was followed by another knock and then silence.

"Come in." Clarissa was pouring the bubbly liquid into two glasses when she watched a delicate hand cover hers.

"Allow me." Following the delicate fingers up her arm, she felt her skin tingle along the path the fingers had just traveled. "My name is Selene."

Clarissa ran her tongue over her lip as she looked into slate grey eyes. Selene was beyond beautiful. In fact, she was breathtaking. For a moment, Clarissa was lost in the gaze of her soon to be torturer.

"I'm sorry?" quickly realizing she had been asked a question.

"I asked, what did you have in mind for tonight?" Selene's low seductive voice mesmerized Clarissa immediately. She was exactly what Clarissa was looking for tonight. She could feel her body tighten with excitement, and she thought about the promise the night held for her. A quick appraisal of Selene, and Clarissa let a slow, seductive smile flash briefly.

"You're perfect," Clarissa said, then took a sip of champagne. The soft curves of Selene's body caught Clarissa's attention as she assessed her companion again. The robe she wore opened slightly and Clarissa caught a quick glimpse of a generous breast. She was sure the robe opening was no accident, but averted her eyes anyway. A quick glance back at Selene and she was sure the woman was flirting with her.

"So, Michael has told you that I am not for...." *Moving a finger to her lips, Selene looked as though she were searching for something.*

"You're not for the faint of heart, I believe he said." *Clarissa let her gaze linger on Selene's lips and then licked her own.* "I'm sure I can handle you, but I have a few rules of my own. If we can't agree, then I will be happy to have someone else see to my needs." *Clarissa knew she wanted Selene and she knew Selene wanted her. Clarissa explained what she wanted for the evening. The seductive banter between the two women was short lived as Selene rose and walked out of the room.*

Another knock on the door and the same woman who delivered the champagne had a small bundle in her hands. Handing it to Clarissa, she informed her, "Selene said that you should undress and wear what you like out of these items." *Casting her eyes down, she retreated and closed the door again.*

Clarissa felt herself starting to lose control. She needed to be released and soon or she was going to do something she didn't want to do. She picked up each item, each one smaller than the last. Finally deciding on a small robe, a halter and a pair of panties, she heard the knock on the door again. This time, Selene didn't wait to enter. Clarissa watched as she carried the items for the night and meticulously laid each one out on the sofa."

"Are you ready?"

"I...I think I need to explain something before we start." *Clarissa looked at each item on the sofa and felt a chill run through her body. She could get this started soon enough but she had to warn Selene before they stared.*

Putting a hand up, Selene stopped her, "Please, I know why you're here and I know what you need."

"But—"

"Trust me." Clarissa noticed Selene had changed and wore the accoutrements of her job. Tall leather boots and a small, barely there outfit, left little to the imagination and yet it would be what Clarissa would fantasize about for years. Selene grabbed Clarissa's hand and softly stroked it. "Trust me, I can handle you."

Clarissa felt herself relax into Selene's touch and nodded her agreement. Selene slowly disrobed Clarissa and made a show of picking up the blindfold she had brought in. Clarissa felt herself being assessed by Selene as she walked around her. The blindfold draped over Clarissa's eyes and she felt it tugged tight against her head as Selene knotted it. Her mind and her body were on fire as her senses took over. She felt a hand glide up and down her arms and she tingled at the touch. Cuffs were closed around her wrists in the front and she was lead to her right, her arms then stretched over her head. Clarissa could smell Selene as she nuzzled her nose in Clarissa's hair, then pulled it to the side and in front of her body.

A snap of leather echoed behind her as she felt the vibration of it in the air. Clarissa's body tensed knowing she was about to find relief for her tortured mind. A firm whack against her backside surprised her.

"Relax. I want to get your body ready to accept my stroke." A cool hand smoothed over the hot welt on her ass. "Besides, now is the time to relent if you want to change your mind." Another whack against Clarissa's ass, and she shook her head no. She hadn't come this far to not find release, so she just stood there waiting for another. Sweat covered her body and she knew it would enhance her experience even further. This time leather slicing the air caught Clarissa's attention followed by a stinging strike. She could feel her body responding to the torture and knew she would be able to ease her pain tonight. Each

strike brought her closer and closer to release, and her soul started its journey to unraveling.

A cool hand caressed the red marks that criss-crossed her back and ass. A glass was pressed against her lips with a command to drink slowly. Then she felt a tongue smooth its way down her. Her body tightened at the contact as Selene's tongue traveled back to her ear.

"You taste delicious. Do you mind?" Clarissa's mind was in a fog at the contact and she felt something else taking over as she pushed into Selene. "I thought so. Relax, the night is young still." A hand reached around and caressed Clarissa's breast. Her body vibrated from the beating as she requested more from Selene.

Snap, snap, snap. Each strike was driving her closer to release. She remembered her lessons from her husband as she faded into the memory. Each stroke was harder than the last until, finally, she was consumed in the pain. Her demon released itself as she orgasmed. Sliding further into the memory, she felt her body finally relax, but a sharp pain brought her back to reality as she felt Selene bite her breast.

"What the —"

Blood assaulted her senses, she felt lips press against hers. "I know what you are."

The kiss lingered and then Clarissa tasted blood, her blood, on the tongue that thrust into her mouth. Her head was pulled back and she felt flesh pressed into her mouth and another command, "Bite."

As she bit, she felt Selene's hand caress her, squeezing one nipple then the other, and then Selene roughly palmed Clarissa's clit. She jerked at the hard contact but moved into it, slowly feeling herself starting to come again. The taste of blood and her body still throbbing from the torture all made Clarissa's senses climax. She was no longer in control, her body's needs were and she let them take over.

"That's it my love, enjoy what I have to offer. Oh, shit. You're gonna make me come, too. Fuck." Clarissa felt another bite as Selene pulled her body into her, grinding herself into Clarissa's ass. "Release, lover." Her head pulled back made her relinquish her hold on Selene's arm, but she felt another climax roll through her body as Selene grabbed her neck and sucked. It had been decades since she had been with another vampire and this time it was an unexpected pleasure to find one without realizing it. Her body convulsed as Selene tortured another orgasm from it.

"Enough," she whispered, relaxing against Selene. "Please, I can't take any more."

Clarissa felt her hands drop in front of her and was carried to the couch. When the cuffs were removed, she felt Selene gently massage her wrists then slide onto the couch.

"How long has it been since you've fed?" Selene whispered into Clarissa's ear. Clarissa felt herself pulled into Selene's body and gently caressed.

"Decades." Clarissa relaxed into the firm body behind her and reached up to remove the blindfold, but was stopped.

"Not yet. I may want more. The night is still young."

Clarissa shuddered remembering the beautiful brunette. Selene, as with Alexandra, had been what her fantasies had consisted of the last few decades. That was a different time, a different Clarissa, but a memory worth saving and treasuring, as twisted as it might seem to someone else. The car slowed to a stop in front of her house, with a promise that her car would be delivered that evening if she left her keys with the driver.

Chapter Fifteen

Selene watched as the limo disappeared behind the iron gate. She had been hired to watch and protect the young woman, but there was something niggling at Selene as she watched the woman get into the car at Knight-Pharmaceutical. She looked familiar, but then again, everyone had a look she'd seen in almost two centuries. From her vantage point along a utility easement, she watched a car slowly pass by in the other lane. The tinted windows were a dead giveaway to whom or what might be inside the vehicle. Slowly sitting back up, Selene watched it pass by her and turn into a driveway down the road. Another vehicle, this time a truck, made a slow pass on her side of the street. It was clear someone was watching the woman. In fact, a whole lot of someones.

Selene wrote the license plates down for future reference and then made herself comfortable. She had a feeling it was going to be a long night watching three people, two of whom were definitely on her list of possible playthings tonight. Picking up her cell phone, she dialed her employer.

"Kev." She waited until recognition hit the person on the other end.

"Selene? What's up?" She heard suspicion in his voice and wondered why. She and Kevin had a working relationship that went back decades, but she didn't trust him. She didn't trust anyone. Life did that to a vampire, and if it didn't it would soon enough.

"I have two plates I need info on. One's planted themselves outside the little bird you want me to watch, and the other I figure better be your guy." Dictating the numbers, she watched as someone got out of the car parked down the street. Darkness barely hung in the sky, almost guaranteeing they weren't human. "You better hurry on that one because he's on the move to the bird cage." Selene slammed the phone closed, pulling on her gloves and watching the dark figure moving up the hill. The truck from earlier passed in front of her again, this time slowing to a crawl as the driver looked up the hill trying to see something or someone.

"Shit," was all Selene said. She gently closed the door on her car and bolted across to the roadside culvert. She watched as the truck continued down the road, slowing when it saw the parked vehicle. Brake lights made it obvious the driver was probably taking down the license plate. *It must be Kevin's guy,* Selene thought watching the truck speed off. *So, that makes this scumbag the bad guy, so to speak.*

Selene slowly started up the hill, parallel to the stalker. She loved the hunt. The smell of the wet decomposing leaves the stranger kicked up took her back to a different time, a time when she only ventured out in search of food, a warm bed, or a distraction. She was like a cat with a mouse who played dead to save its life. They both knew what the outcome would be and it was just a matter of time. She felt her body start to spasm a bit, the chase energizing her blood. The rustling of leaves and a twig breaking assured her she was almost on top of him. She slowed down, not wanting the thrill of the chase to cloud her mission.

She could hear his breathing as he struggled to

make it up the hillside. *Poor fellow, he needs to take better care of himself. Why did vampires always let themselves go?* Selene wondered. It was taking all she had not to pounce on the obviously out of shape stalker. Clearly, he wasn't as in tune as he thought he was, or he would have picked up on her energy. Selene relished a good fight, especially since she hadn't had one in a while, but she was patient. It was why she was so good.

Selene stealthily climbed up a tree, opting for a better view and to wait until the idiot did something worth getting worked up over. From her vantage point, she could now see the house that sat nestled on the hill. She watched a naked woman busy herself around the quaint home. Naked! The buxom woman walked around the kitchen, her breasts gently moving back and forth as she grabbed a robe and slid it on. *Maybe she knows she's being watched,* Selene wondered. A shiver ran through Selene as she continued to stare at the beautiful woman, recognition shaking her. A flash of memory put her back in her club, decades ago. A beautiful woman, her arms above her head moaning. The memory almost sent Selene tumbling from her perch. Clarissa! Selene knew she was oblivious to the eminent danger she was in, but that wouldn't last, not for long. Tearing her eyes away from Clarissa, Selene looked around the landscape. She noted her exit points, the hill behind the house and the only other way out, the way she came in. There wasn't much in the way of plant life this time of the year, and she was thankful poison oak didn't affect her when she saw the abundance of it throughout the hillside.

Another twig breaking brought her back to the man slowly making his way to the top of the hill. It was time for Selene to do something before he reached the driveway and had a clear shot to the house. She knew once she hit the ground the stalker would be alerted, so she had to make sure she landed as close to him as possible. Pushing off the massive oak, she aimed herself to land a few yards from his feet. Surprise would be on her side if she kept her feet under her and ran like hell at him. Landing, she did better than she hoped, but she had a knee down on one side causing her to roll towards him rather than take a run at the fat man. Righting herself, she caught a punch to the jaw that staggered her back.

"I thought I heard something back there, stupid bitch. You should really be more careful." Another punch caught her in the chest, buckling her to her knees. Selene put her hands up in time to block a knee aimed at her face and catch the heel of her attacker. Pivoting her body around, she knocked his other leg out from under him and watched his face plant into the composting. As she twisted his leg, she positioned it between hers and wrapped her one arm under his neck throwing and positioning her other arm behind his head locking it in place.

"You wish, asshole. You're breathing so heavy you couldn't hear a cheeseburger drop right in front of you." Tightening her grip, she felt her incisors drop and a surge pulsed through her body. He was a dead man, but she needed to know who he worked for before she snuffed his candle. "So who sent you, and be smart or this is going to be a very long night for you. You decide."

Pulling tighter, she felt him squirm more, the pressure in his neck causing his veins to bulge. The temptation was too great for Selene and she quickly nipped the bulging artery. His blood tasted old, and muted, not fresh and vibrant like she was used to. She spat it out. She would have to be happy killing him and leaving his blood for someone else.

"Look, you're in no shape to fight me, so why don't you just tell me who sent you, and I'll make it painless."

"Fuck you. I'm not saying shit."

"Oh yes you will. You'll just wish, when it's all said and done, you would've told me sooner. Cause trust me, this is gonna hurt."

"I told you, I'm not saying shit. So fuck off!" His hands were pulling on Selene's arm as he tried to roll her off. He only succeeded in rolling them both onto Selene's back. Selene knew she was eventually going to have to release him so she could get to her dagger, but she was in control and would let him tire himself out. He continued to push with his one free leg, using their bodies to clear a circle in the leaf debris. After ten minutes of rolling around, Selene realized the man had more stamina than she expected so she had to come up with a plan B or choke him out.

"Listen to me, fat man. You're not getting out of here alive, and you definitely aren't getting to that woman, so give me a name, and I'll be quick about your death. Otherwise, we're gonna be here all night, and I have better things to do than screw with you." Arching her back, she pulled tighter on his neck, hearing buttons pop off his shirt as she stretched him backwards.

If he were a thinner man, he would have been able to reach Selene's face as he tried to reach back for her, but his bulk prevented him from even making it to her upper arms. Laughing, she whispered in his ear, "Whoever hired you is a stupid S.O.B."

Selene heard a pop as he transformed, his body morphing into his original form. "You might think I'm stupid, but even a mouse gets a break once in a while." His now sharp nails dug into her upper arms shredding her jacket and drawing blood. Selene recoiled enough that the attacker took the advantage and rolled forward and curled, throwing Selene from him. Landing on her back, she scrambled upright, her own transformation complete. His black eyes transfixed on her every movement as she circled him. She watched as he licked the blood off his fingers.

"Hmm, you're young. So, who sent you?" he asked, licking his last finger clean.

Pulling her shredded jacket off, she tossed it at him as she tucked her head and slammed into him. An audible exhale escaped him as he tried to toss her off. Pushing, Selene backed him into a tree and slammed her knee between his legs. She reached up and pulled his head down and made contact with a knee to his face. A double strike with her hands to his back and he was bent over groaning. Stepping behind him, she pulled his head back and pressed her dagger into his spine.

"Now, I'm gonna ask again. Who sent you?"

"Who sent you?"

Selene pushed the dagger into the fat that encased his back. "I asked you a question. Who sent you?"

"For what?"

Pulling the dagger towards his head, she felt it hit each rib as it moved upward, slicing fat and muscle along its path. Stopping just under his shoulder blade, she twisted the dagger sideways and pressed it between two ribs. The razor sharp dagger slowly entered his body barely touching his heart. The smell of his blood wafted up towards her nostrils making her skin tingle. It wouldn't be long now, and Selene knew it. The smell of death hung around him.

"Even if you kill me, he'll send another and another, until he gets what he wants."

"Who will send another?" Staring down into his dark eyes, she twisted the dagger a quarter turn. "Who?" The question hung in the air, as the smell of blood assaulted her senses again. Licking her lips, she watched as he squinted at the pain, his eyes starting to glaze over into a death mask.

"You're wasting your time, I'm not telling. He owns me and I owe him. That alone means I would rather die at your hand than his. So finish the job, bitch."

"So you'd rather die on your knees than fighting? Pathetic." Plunging the knife into his heart, she felt her body start to spasm as his blood coated her hand. Grunting, Selene let his body drop forward watching the life ooze out of him. This wasn't what she had hoped for, but it was clear he wasn't going to tell her anything. He was too afraid of whoever sent him and that meant death by her hand was more welcome than to go back and face the wrath of his master. Selene was shaking as she fought the urge to drink his blood. The animal that controlled her body commanded her head, doubling her over as she fought back. The smell of him was starting to make her sick, so she backed away from him, dry heaving into the pile of leaves that had formed from their fight.

Selene reached for her shredded jacket as her phone vibrated in the pocket.

"Yeah."

"Selene, I got that information you wanted. The car is registered to a—"

"It doesn't matter. He's dead and—"

"What? What do you mean he's dead?"

Selene heard Kevin choke out the response as she continued, "He's dead. I just killed his sorry ass. He said he would rather die than go back and face his master."

"Shit."

"Look, he said that whoever sent him will send someone else. So you better come up with a plan for the little bird I'm watching, or I'm gonna be killing these guys 'til you do. You got it? So you go back to whoever hired me and tell him that."

"Are you sure he said 'him'?"

"Positive." The silence on the other end of the line made Selene uneasy. Surely, Kevin had known this was a possibility. She was an assassin for god sakes. Her reputation wasn't exactly stellar when it came to this sort of work. Besides, she had been hired to protect the woman in the house, and that is exactly what she did, protect.

"Can you make it look like an accident, Selene?"

"It's gonna cost you more. This guy's a fat son of a bitch."

"Do whatever you have to. Just make it look like an accident."

"Okay."

Snapping the phone shut, Selene wiped her hands on the shredded jacket and cleaned off her dagger before putting it back in her boot. Wrapping the jacket around her waist she bent over and heaved the obese man onto her back. "Thank God it's downhill."

Chapter Sixteen

Kevin looked down at the closed phone, and then across the desk to A.J.

"That didn't sound good." A.J. turned the light off on her desk. It was starting to give her that rare headache she got from too much light exposure. She pushed her chair back staring at Kevin in the darkness. "Well, what happened?"

"Shit, A.J., this is getting messy. Selene killed the guy stalking Clarissa. He wouldn't tell her who sent him, only saying that he would rather die at her hand than go back to his master."

"Interesting." A.J. stroked her chin as she leaned on the desk. A long sigh escaped her lips alerting Kevin she was pissed. "What the hell happened to Brax? I thought he was supposed to be watching Clarissa and Selene was watching both of them? Where was he when this whole thing went down? I don't like this. I don't like this one bit."

"Brax called me after Selene did asking for information on the same car Selene saw. So obviously he was there, too." Kevin palmed his phone in a nervous gesture as he watched A.J.

"Nothing is obvious here, Kev, nothing. I want you to call Selene back and tell her to watch Brax real close. Something doesn't add up. He should have been the one on top of this guy, not her. Her role was secondary, not primary, and that makes me wonder." Again, A.J.

sat back in her cool leather chair, her eyes closed as she thought about what she knew about tonight. She wasn't surprised that Selene had killed the guy stalking Clarissa. What did surprise her was that Brax wasn't around when it all happened. If that was the case, the stalker could have easily gotten to Clarissa, and Brax wouldn't have been there to stop him. It was looking worse and worse by the minute, and she knew what she needed to do.

Jumping up, A.J. grabbed her keys and jacket heading for the door. "Didn't you just tell Selene to make this guy's death look like an accident?"

"Yeah, I figured that would buy us some time before whoever hired him realizes he's dead. Why?"

"Cause that means Clarissa is unprotected, that's why."

"Brax is there."

"If Brax was there, why didn't he help Selene? If Brax was there, why didn't he try to kill either one of them, especially since they were within yards of Clarissa's house? Something isn't right here."

"What're you going to do?"

Running down the hallway to the elevator she yelled back, "I'm gonna protect Clarissa and hope I don't get caught in the process." Punching the panel, she felt like ripping the doors back and vaulting down the shaft to get there quicker. It took everything she had not to, as she yelled back at Kevin running behind her, "Call Brax and find out where he is. Tell him security was breached and that Clarissa is down at the mall or something. I don't want him anywhere near her until Selene gets back and we can check his story."

"Are you sure you want to do this? I mean he's been with us for decades. Come on, A.J. It's Brax." Chuckling nervously he continued, "I mean, shit, he's our go to guy. He knows where the bodies are buried."

"Exactly." A.J. jumped into the elevator and inserted her over-ride key in the panel, punching the garage floor. "Call me when you know more."

A.J. watched the floors clicking off the overhead panel thinking through the events of the evening again. Things had twisted out of control since seeing Clarissa in the bar last week, and this wasn't the first time she had thought about how the events were spiraling out of control. But now things were getting messy. Someone, a seeker, was suddenly watching Clarissa, A.J.'s tangling with a seeker just the other night, and now an AWOL Brax. Thank God Selene had been there to prevent anyone from getting to Clarissa. But now Clarissa was alone, and unprotected. A.J. stopped as the elevator doors opened to the garage and realized Clarissa wasn't just anyone. She was a vampire who had survived a century obviously without her protection. *That was before the events of last week though*, thought A.J.

Peering around the doors of the elevator, A.J. looked around the garage and then sniffed the air. Nothing. Closing her eyes she listened, trying to hear anything that might be out of place in her personal space. Slowly, she eased into the garage and pulled her keys from her charcoal slacks. She was determined she wasn't going to be surprised again like she had in the park. She smiled when she thought about the ass-whipping she delivered to the unsuspecting seeker. Drugs were getting to be a problem for seekers and they couldn't function like normal vampires, feeling each other's energy and avoiding their fellow vamps. Sad really, thought A.J. keying the lock to her Land Rover. Seekers and gang bangers were going to be the death of each other and that was fine with A.J. The problem was, seekers could make more seekers before they died, while gang bangers just killed each other.

"Not my problem," A.J. said, sliding into the black Rover. Keying her ear piece, she rang Kevin. "Hey, what have you got for me?"

"Well…."

"Kevin…."

"Look A.J., I'm doing the best I can. Brax isn't answering his phone."

"Keep trying. Let me know when you get him. I want to talk to him."

"Okay."

"And Kevin, call Selene and tell her to get back to Clarissa's and let her know what we suspect about Brax so she's prepared. Just in case."

"A.J., I think you're way off base here on Brax."

"Wanna stake your life on it? Pun intended." A.J. waited for Kevin's reply. When she didn't get one she keyed her ear piece again and tossed it on the seat next to her. "Kevin, you're just way too trusting. You're lucky you've made it this far."

Clarissa tossed the rest of her students' papers into her briefcase. It was an exercise in futility trying to grade them. She had been on edge ever since coming home from Knight Pharmaceutical and couldn't concentrate. She had struggled to control herself as she sat talking to Kevin Alexander about the funding he was offering. The whole experience had put her into a frenzy and she was grateful Mr. Alexander had rushed their meeting. Something was off, and she felt it. Her soul felt it. Clarissa had thought that when she got home she would be able to work through her demons, but she was wrong. She was restless, hungry and wired. Nefertiti caught Clarissa's attention pacing on the window ledge. Stopping, Nefertiti focused on something outside, alerted like she was when she was watching a mouse in the yard. Clarissa stood, walked to the window, and peered into the darkness. Suddenly, Nefertiti hissed and ran past her, hiding under the couch. Looking back outside again, Clarissa felt her skin prickle and a tingle shoot throughout her body, alerting her something was out there.

"Come here silly girl. What's wrong?" Reaching down, she grabbed at Nefertiti just as the cat swiped her paw at Clarissa. "Hey, what's gotten into you?" Pulling back, Clarissa felt her skin jump again. Now, she definitely knew something was wrong. Even the cat felt it. She wished she didn't live so far out from town. At least being around people gave her cover. Living remotely provided the solitude she craved, but it didn't afford her the luxury of having living energy around her to keep her safe. Bolting the doors wouldn't keep anyone out that wanted in, but she checked her locks anyway. Turning the lights off throughout the house, she positioned herself by a window that gave her a decent view of the driveway and the front half of the house. If something was coming, she at least wanted to be prepared.

Things were changing around her and now she knew it was time for a move. Thinking about how many times she had moved, she knew that nothing lasted forever. Not friends, not lovers and not living arrangements. She considered giving her notice at the university and moving on. At least she had a while before she needed to make any permanent changes, hopefully.

For the fourth time in as many days, she felt like someone was watching her, stalking her. Looking out the window, she scanned the side yard. Nothing. Not a movement, not a sound, nothing. Maybe she was just being paranoid? Taking a deep breath and holding it, she heard it. A groan. Stepping back further into the shadows, she surveyed the yard again, squinting to try and block out the glowing light from the moon. The ominous shadows from the tree line did little to help assuage her fear. Another sound, a grunt, pulled her attention further back into the forest that bordered her driveway.

"Shit."

Skirting the island in her kitchen, she made her way to the bedroom, tossed her robe and pulled on a pair of sweat pants and a sweat shirt. She knew if anything was going to happen, she was going down fighting. The recent events had left her too unsettled not to take whatever was happening outside seriously. *It could be an animal*, she reasoned. Living in the country, she had definitely seen her share of snakes, deer, and raccoons. Then she felt it again. Her skin was like an internal alarm lately and she knew enough to trust her instincts. Clarissa pulled a gun from the dresser drawer. The weight of it felt calming in her hand. Pulling the clip, she checked to make sure it was loaded. Nine rounds caught her eye as she slipped the clip back into the automatic, clicking it into place. As she pulled the slide, she heard another sound. This time it was different, like branches breaking.

"Fuck."

The way her body was reacting she knew it wasn't a mere human close by. It was a vampire. Clarissa gently slid the sliding glass door back and eased onto the porch.

A gentle step and then another put her on the outskirts of her deck. Looking into the darkness, she still couldn't see anything, but she definitely heard something now. The protection of the house had muffled the noises before, but now she could make out what sounded like a one-sided conversation. Someone was on her property, but not just anyone. Squatting down in the shadows, she listened as another groan reached her, then a thud. The smell of blood filled her senses and she felt a hunger start to control her. The thud, the smell of blood and a conversation told her that two people were close by. Standing still she tried to control her breathing, but the smell of blood was pulling her.

"Yeah."

Clarissa stopped dead in her tracks. A woman's voice drifted up the hillside. "He's dead…"

Clarissa felt a panic race through her. Did the woman just say someone was dead? Now what was she going to do? Frozen, she waited. She couldn't make out the rest of the conversation and she didn't want to move. Whoever was down the hill was, hopefully, too busy to have heard her movements above them. She sat waiting in the shadows as she listened again.

"Thank God it's downhill," said the anonymous woman, followed by another grunt. Clarissa could hear footsteps walking and sliding down the hillside. When there were no more sounds, Clarissa slowly made her way to the side of the slope. Crouching down, she could barely make out the form of someone carrying something down to the street below. Letting the smell of blood guide her, she made her way to a partial clearing. It was clear there had been a fight. The leaves and broken branches gave away the evidence of the struggle. A dark patch caught her eye. Fingering it, she brought the stain to her nose and could smell the freshness of the blood. Snaking her tongue out, she sampled it and then spit it out. Clarissa's stomach started to clench as the blood lingered on her tongue. She hated the taste of human blood. In fact the reaction was so visceral that she started to heave and puke. She had survived without human blood, but that hadn't always been the case. When De Marcus changed her, he had forced her to consume, rather gorge, on the red gore. He told her it was her destiny and she should embrace what those whom he brought home gave so she could live. He invited his "lady friends" over for a party and would then force Clarissa to watch as he languished in the blood orgy. When he was finished, he would force her face into the lifeless body and make her finish his victim. Clarissa shuddered as she thought about the pain that had etched itself on each of his victims. The mask of beauty and suffering were never far from her memory when she thought about feeding. Focusing back on the dirty stain, Clarissa knew it was old blood.

Peering back into the darkness, she chastised herself for being so afraid. She had grown soft and weak in her advancing years, and now she had paid the price for not paying attention to what was happening around her. After tonight, she would be on her guard.

Chapter Seventeen

A.J. drummed her fingers on the steering wheel speeding through town towards Clarissa's place. Her soul felt like it was drowning in her need for Clarissa. All she could think about since Clarissa had come to the office that day was how badly she wanted her. Her body ached. She was in a constant state of arousal since seeing Clarissa in the bar. A.J. would have to take care of business when she got home that evening. She had learned that the solitary life had certain requirements, and lately she had been meeting those requirements, a lot. A.J. shuddered through another phantom touch across her body, her nipples hardening at the memory of Clarissa.

She needed to explain things to Clarissa. That was if Clarissa would even talk to her. Why wouldn't she? A.J. hadn't been the one to leave Clarissa in her hour of need. Clarissa's parents had seen to it, but did Clarissa know that? A.J. could only imagine the lies they had probably told Clarissa about her. Another hurdle she would surely have to overcome with Clarissa considering everything else her parents had told her.

A.J. thought about De Marcus and what he had probably done to Clarissa. She knew him as a ruthless vulture that preyed on young women. Usually though, he didn't let them live after he had his fun with them. He had been a known sadist in the coven and rarely apologized for it. If the truth be told, it was an excepted idea in those circles. If a vampire could suck the life out of someone, why shouldn't they have their fun with them before they died? It was thought that the adrenaline in the body enhanced the blood somehow, but A.J. doubted it. It was only an excuse for those that loved violence.

A.J. slowed down somewhat trying to think about what she would do once she actually got to Clarissa's house. A.J. couldn't risk exposing herself yet to Clarissa. But she could no longer just sit by and let everyone else take care of her business. Selene had killed the vampire that was stalking Clarissa, but according to Kevin, whoever hired him wouldn't stop even if he was killed. The very idea that a vampire would rather die by Selene's hand than go back and face his boss let A.J. know the assassin's master was ruthless and not someone to be underestimated. Death at Selene's hand wasn't pretty.

The interstate had changed to two lanes as she entered the foothills. A.J. would be easy to see now driving into the narrowing canyon. She hadn't had her window blacked out like most vampires did, opting to let in the daylight instead. She had lived in the shadows so long she didn't like who she became when she hid in them. The light gave her a different perspective on life and how she wanted to live it. But the darkness was always lingering just off her shoulder, never letting her forget who she was.

Turning her lights off, she slowly cruised down the street edging closer to Clarissa's driveway. She could see two people at a tow truck hitching up a car. Watching from her vantage point, she couldn't make out if they were men or if one of them was Selene. Except for today at the office, she hadn't seen Selene in decades, which was fine with her. As she watched the tow truck drive off, the other person walked towards their car, but not before they were tackled to the ground. A.J. gasped as she saw the glint of a knife arc in the air and then descend on the lone figure. Gunning her SUV, she sped at the two wresting on the ground, her high beams aimed right for them. As they rolled towards the hill, A.J. saw Brax flashing his fangs in her direction as he tried to straddle his victim, Selene. Slamming on her brakes, she slid into the combatants. The light blinded Brax, causing him to shield his face, giving Selene the time she needed to send Brax head over heels. A.J. watched as Selene jumped to her feet, fangs bare, and ran after Brax up the hill.

A.J. waivered. Should she chase after them, exposing herself to Selene? Or did she wait and see who came back and deal with them then? If Brax came down the hill, A.J. knew she would have to kill him. He had double-crossed her for whoever hired the other assassin. Brax had been hired to watch Clarissa and being AWOL proved he was dirty in A.J.'s mind. A.J. was sure Kevin had made it clear this was a life or death mission. If he wanted to live, he would take care of Clarissa, regardless of whoever was stalking her. If he failed, death was his only option. Now she was certain of his betrayal. If Selene came down the hill she would remain in the shadows.

She parked her SUV down the road and around the bend. She grabbed her cell phone from the passenger seat and started to dial Kevin's number, but stopped. Kevin had been positive that Brax was trustworthy. He almost staked his life on it. What was she missing? Was Kevin in on whatever was going on? Had he betrayed her too? Turning off her phone, she slipped it into her pocket. She knew Selene would call Kevin if she killed Brax. How would he explain Brax's death to A.J.? He had been so certain about Brax. No, she would wait to see what Kevin would do. She needed to think about what she would do when he told her. *Presentation is everything, Kevin my man,* she thought, quietly getting out of her car.

A.J.'s skin tingled at the smell of fresh blood. Her body surged, but she had to control the urge to change and run towards the fight she knew was happening above her. She hadn't hunted in decades, but her natural instincts fought with her present day logic. The need to feed was hard to ignore for a vampire and she had felt herself begin to unravel earlier in the week when she was attacked in the park. Seeing Clarissa walking out of the garage was the only thing that kept her from killing and feeding off the seeker. Now, though, she fought hard to maintain what little control she had. Her mouth watered as the scent of blood grew stronger. She reached deep into her pocket and pulled out two "safety pills". Popping each one, she placed them under her tongue and waited. The energy around her shifted as she darted behind trees, making her way up the hillside. Wave after wave of energy hit A.J. as she made her way closer to the fight. It was hard to maintain control fighting the change that lay just under her skin. She knew Selene would be engrossed in what she was doing and too overcome with bloodlust to feel A.J.'s own bloodlust surfacing. The autumn breeze blew again and the smell of something else caught A.J.'s nose. A familiar scent, Clarissa!

Clarissa had stood transfixed, still staring at the bloodstain in the dirt. Her senses taking over her body, a shift was taking place and she fell to her knees. The blood pounding in her head was so loud it blocked out everything around her. Her nose flared and she inhaled deeply, the blood calling her. Rational thinking was slowly ebbing from her mind, a deeper need taking its place. Opening her mouth, she let her fangs drop. Her vision sharpened as she watched the tow truck down the hill drive off. She watched as the person left behind was tackled, the flash of a knife catching her attention. Then the lights of a car skidding towards the two helped Clarissa see the fangs of a vampire as he faced the headlights. She didn't know him, she was sure. So why was he here and who was the other person he was fighting? She wasn't alone anymore, but now what? Was he the person responsible for the bloodstain before her? She watched him tossed like a rag doll onto the ground. The person beneath him was obviously stronger even with a stab wound.

Fully transformed, she quietly made her way down the hill edging closer to see the two fighting. As she watched, the man started running up the hill towards her. Shit. She realized she couldn't risk being seen. Turning to run back up the hill, she knew she would never make it before they were on top of her. Looking up, she saw her only chance for cover, the trees. Scrambling up a redwood, Clarissa concealed herself almost at the top and tried to slow her out of control heart beat. There was no telling what would happen to her if she was found out. The blood stain already revealed the depths that someone would go to, and she didn't want to be next. Peering around the massive trunk she watched as the two pummeled each other, neither having a big advantage over the other. Each punch moved them closer and closer to Clarissa and she wondered if they would eventually make it under her location. The energy buffeted her and she felt her body responding like an animal in heat. Vampires gave off energy when they fought, fed or when they were intimate, and only a very experienced vampire could tell the difference. Right now Clarissa could see the difference, but her body was responding not to what she saw, but to what she felt. A cut had opened under the eye of one of the attackers and the other's nose had started to bleed. The smell beckoned to Clarissa and she slid a tongue across her lips, savoring the scent that hung in the air. To expose herself would mean certain death, especially since both attackers were deep in bloodlust. She watched the male slide his tongue across his knuckles.

"You're gonna taste even better after I beat your ass," he taunted his rival.

"I wouldn't be so sure about that. You see, I already killed your buddy. I'm sure you can smell his blood, can't you?" A husky female voice answered.

Clarissa stood staring at the woman. She had heard that voice before, she knew that woman. It was Selene.

###

A.J. slowly inched her way up the hillside towards Selene and Brax. Her senses were on overload smelling fresh blood and Clarissa's fear. Or was that excitement rolling off Clarissa? She struggled again to maintain control. Each wave of sensation was stronger than the last washing over her. The backlighting from the house exposed the fighters as they punched, kicked and rocked each other over and over again. Selene was slowly starting to lose ground and A.J. could only think it was because of the stab wound she had suffered at the bottom of the hill. A.J. wondered if she should insert herself into the fight and help Selene, but movement caught her eye as something in the trees moved. Clarissa was watching the same fight from the top of a tree, almost directly over Selene and Brax. That was her answer. If she exposed her position and helped Selene, Clarissa was sure to figure out who she was. No, this wasn't the time or place for a reunion, or a rebuff. Selene would have to make it on her own if she was going to survive.

A.J. watched Brax raised his knife again, aiming for Selene's throat. Selene dropped to the ground and swept Brax's feet out from under him, the knife still swinging wildly towards her. A.J. observed Brax land on his back, the wind knocked out of him for a brief moment, but long enough for Selene to stand and land a kick to his jaw. A deafening crack echoed through the forest as Selene landed another kick, this time to the ribs he exposed reaching for his now shattered jaw. Then she was straddling him, pummeling his face. Selene arched her back, bared her fangs and buried them in Brax's neck. A slow gurgling sound was the last thing to seep from his lips. The air around Selene electrified with energy, heat and intensity as she pulled the life from Brax's body, savoring each intense blood pounding moment.

A.J. looked up at Clarissa and wondered how she could keep her position watching Selene feed. Vampires had a pack mentality when it came to feeding and once it started they wouldn't stop until the body was drained completely. She slowly eased her way back down the hill, moving backwards as she watched Selene and Clarissa, making sure she wasn't spotted by either. A.J. watched as Selene's body pulsed with each suck, the outline of her muscled arms holding Brax down shimmered with sweat and slowly engorging with the energized blood. Selene's body pulsed as if it was orgasming. The heat was almost too much for A.J., feeling herself start to tighten in anticipation of her own orgasm. Selene's energy pulled at A.J.'s body and she felt her clit harden and her skin tingle. An orgasm would be a welcome release as she closed her eyes and absorbed the intensity. Her demon coiled and pulsed throughout her body. Her mouth watered again and she knew she had to do something quick. Pulling her "safety pills" from her pocket, this time she popped four, rather than her normal two. She had to make sure she could control herself enough to get the hell out of there. Letting them rest under her tongue, she watched Clarissa slowly squirm as she had done in the office earlier. She wasn't sure what she was going to do to help Clarissa, but she knew she needed to do something or Selene would have a dining partner soon. Pulling her phone from her jacket, she dialed Kevin.

"A.J. What's going on?"

"Kevin, listen to me carefully—"

"A.J., why are you whispering? Is everything alright?"

"Shut up and listen. Call Selene, now!" A.J., frantic that Kevin couldn't hear her, repeated her order, "Do you hear me? Call Selene now."

"Okay."

A.J. waited what seemed like hours. Then she heard Selene's phone ring above her. "Pick it up, damn it." It rang again and again. "Pick it up," she said as if willing it would make it happen. Then, suddenly, the phone stopped ringing. Pausing, A.J. held her breath.

"What the fuck do you want? I'm a little busy. Make it quick."

A.J. could hear the one-sided conversation and breathed a sigh of relief. Luckily, Selene hadn't said Kevin's name or Clarissa might have put two and two together, or at a minimum come to the wrong conclusion about Kevin.

"Yeah, he's in the trunk, but I got a little side tracked." A.J. watched as Selene wiped the corners of her mouth, lick her lips and continued, "Let's just say that your man, Brax, is a traitor and he's dead, too."

A.J. couldn't help but wonder what lies Kevin was telling Selene, as Selene's eyebrows furrowed. A.J. recognized the distrustful look on Selene's face.

"Look, that isn't my problem. He jumped me and before I could ask him any questions he ended up dead. I wouldn't want to be in your shoes when you explain this to your boss. By the way, this is gonna cost you more. I wasn't hired to kill anyone, just protect the girl."

A.J. realized that Selene was walking right towards her as she talked to Kevin. She crouched down behind some brush and watched Selene walk past her towards the car. Looking back up at Clarissa, she was grateful Clarissa probably couldn't hear the conversation. She watched Clarissa slowly make her way down to the floor of the forest and hesitantly walk towards Brax. Bending down, Clarissa touched his neck and brought her fingers to her nose. *Don't do it,* A.J. silently pleaded. If Clarissa tasted his blood, A.J. was sure she would feed, and probably expose herself to Selene. She watched again as Clarissa wiped the blood from her fingers in the dirt. *Good Girl, now go.* Once again, A.J. pleaded for Clarissa's sanity to return, *Damn it, get the fuck out of here.* She looked down to see where Selene was. A.J. reached into her pocket again and pulled her cell phone.

"Kevin, call Selene again. This time try to keep her talking for a few minutes." Gently closing the phone, she looked back up at Clarissa, who was trying to look down at Selene. A few seconds went by. Then Clarissa quietly crept back up the hill, watching Selene as she disappeared over the top. A.J. took a deep breath and relaxed. Slowly, she scooted backwards, deeper into the forest and farther away from Selene and the now dead Brax. Her mind was spinning as she stood. Suddenly dizzy, she sat back down before she fainted. It had been a long time since she had watched a vampire feed so close, and the experience left her light headed, hungry and edgy.

Chapter Eighteen

Selene threw the phone into the trunk, watching it shatter into pieces. She grabbed the back of her car to steady herself as she felt her body react from the flood of energy from her feeding. Twisting her head around, she tried to pop the kink out of her neck. She hadn't expected the attack from Brax and, because of that, he had been able to stab her easily. She reached up and rubbed the stab wound in her shoulder. She could feel it starting to heal already, but it would take a few days to completely heal and a few weeks for her to be back to her normal fighting self. The adrenaline Brax had in his blood had given her even more energy than she'd expected. It was rare that she could feed off a vampire, very rare, and one who was in full transition was even rarer. He had fought her with everything he had but, like most men, he had underestimated her. *As usual,* she thought pulling the tarp off the other guy she had stashed in her trunk.

"Geez, what am I gonna do with two dead vampires?" she said to the dead body in the trunk. "You got any ideas buddy? No, I don't suppose you do." Slamming the trunk shut, she started to walk up the hill. "They don't pay me enough to deal with this shit. Maybe I need to find a new line of work." Snapping the tarp in front of her to open it up, she mumbled to herself again, "Naw, then I might have to get a real job or something. What would I do with all my free time?"

Continuing up the hill, something caught her eye. She acted as if she hadn't seen the movement. Laying the tarp down by the dead body, she made her way back down around to the movement in the brush and then stopped.

"Hello A.J." Selene saw A.J. visibly flinch and then stand-up. "Look, don't do anything stupid. I'm not in the mood for it." Selene raised her hands and shrugged her shoulders, "But if you want to go a round or two, I think I can manage it."

"Hello Selene. It's been a while." A.J. raised her hands in a defensive posture in response to Selene's. Selene's body still vibrated with energy and knew A.J. could feel it flowing off her in waves. Obviously, A.J. had seen the whole thing; it all made sense to Selene now. She had felt another vampire in the area, but was too busy with her fellow combatant to look around.

"So, let me guess. You're either the one that hired me, or you're the one that wanted this lady dead. Which one is it?"

"I hired you."

Selene shook her head and swung her fist at A.J. connecting with her jaw. The punch sent A.J. reeling backwards.

"I owe you that for the last time we met. Remember?" Selene rubbed her knuckles and eyed A.J. as she picked herself up from the ground.

"Yeah, I remember." A.J. rubbed her jaw and spit blood on the ground. A.J. remembered their shared past as if it were yesterday. A woman. It was always a woman with them. But this time, A.J. got the girl and Selene didn't. She had known that this one was special to Selene. In fact, Selene had told A.J. she wanted to bond with her, making their relationship permanent. Bonding occurred when two vampires, who loved each other, fed until orgasming. Biting while having sex wasn't unusual between vampires. But add love and it was considered a connection that outlived time. It was a bond that could rarely be broken unless…well, A.J. didn't want to think what it took to break that connection. The woman had seduced A.J., but she didn't have the heart at the time to tell Selene the truth. So, she let Selene think she had run the woman off, telling Selene the woman had gotten cold feet when she found out what Selene intended.

"Good, I would hate to have to remind you what an asshole you are. Now, if you don't mind, why don't you explain what the fuck is going on around here?" Selene said, pointing to the dead body just up the hill from them.

"Okay." Pointing to Brax's body, "He's mine, or was supposed to be working for me. The guy in the trunk, I have no idea. Your guess is as good as mine and her…" Pointing up to house, "She's none of your business."

Selene rubbed her chin looking over at Brax. "Did he know I was working for you?" Selene watched A.J.'s eyes. She could tell when someone was lying. It's what she did and if A.J. was lying, Selene would kill her. Because that meant she wanted Selene dead, too, and had sent Brax to do the job.

"Nope. Brax was supposed to be watching the dead guy in your trunk. He was AWOL and we couldn't find him. Brax wasn't returning Kevin's phone calls, nothing."

"And?" The question hung in the air like wet laundry.

"And you stumbled on spooky dude over there…" A.J. pointed in the direction of Selene's car, "and he…" pointing to Brax, "jumps you after you kill spooky dude."

"I saw someone drive by this guy's car earlier and they looked like they were writing down his license plate, or I assumed they were writing down his license plate. But maybe it was this guy..." Selene pointed at Brax, "making sure he..." Selene pointed to the trunk, "was doing his job and killing the girl." Selene pointed to the house on the hill.

"I don't know."

Selene watched as a puzzled look made its way across A.J.'s face, which was then replaced with frustration.

"Okay, well we need to get out of here before someone sees us and starts asking questions. I have two dead bodies that I have to dispose of so." Selene motioned with her head towards Brax. As A.J. turned to leave, Selene grabbed her arm. "By the way, where does Kevin fit into all of this?"

"I don't know. Nowhere I hope, but I can't be sure now."

Selene looked at the confused woman and wondered if she was worried for her friend or if A.J. really knew what was going on. A.J. never struck Selene as an idiot, but time had a way of changing people, even vampires, and rarely for the good.

"Well, while you try and figure that out, I need to clean up this mess." Selene tossed the tarp over Brax and rolled him in it. Dragging him down the hill, she looked back at A.J. "I'll stay on the girl. Call me if anything changes."

"We need to talk, Selene."

"I know." Selene knew that they would eventually need to clear the air, but she wasn't ready to deal with A.J. now, if ever. Some business just needed to stay unfinished.

Chapter Nineteen

Clarissa gently slid the door open and squeezed through the small opening. She didn't want to draw any attention from the vampire that was left standing. After placing the gun on the counter, she rubbed her hands on her sweats. She could still smell the blood, the scent lingering in her nostrils. She had come so close to joining the woman in her feeding frenzy. It wasn't just any woman, though. It was Selene. She hadn't seen Selene in years. Their last meeting ended in a night of passionate love making on a couch in a non-descript bondage club, in a city she didn't even remember. That was a different time in her life and she wasn't sure she wanted to go back there again. How ironic that she had just relived that very memory earlier, and here Selene was killing not one, but two men in her own backyard. But why?

Clarissa washed her hands and braced herself against the sink. Her body pulsed with tension, her skin tingled, and tendrils of pleasure washed through her body. Her sweats felt like they were rubbing her nipples and clit raw, so she stripped and tossed the blood stained clothes in the garbage. Without thinking she ran her hand down her body and touched herself, first one stroke and then another, and another and suddenly she was moaning as she orgasmed.

"Fuck, Fuck." Clarissa's body vibrated as she climaxed again. The memory of Selene's body as she arched over her victim tonight clouded Clarissa's thoughts. The moonlight reflecting off Selene's hard body, muscled arms and shoulders exuded power, and danger. Remembering how Selene's body throbbed with sexual energy as she fed had almost caused Clarissa to join her, uninvited. The blood pounding in Clarissa's body pushed her closer and closer to another orgasm and finally pushed Clarissa over the edge and she relished the long, hard orgasm. Clarissa retreated into her thoughts trying to control herself once again, but clearly the night's events had taken their toll. She relinquished her hold on reality long enough to lose herself in the moment. It had been so long since Clarissa had a strong lover and tonight reminded her of why she didn't mingle with her own kind. She could easily cross over to the dark side, her multiple orgasms and urge to feed tonight a violent reminder of that.

Clarissa's body jerked one last time releasing the breath she was holding. She laid her head against the wall and slid down sitting motionless on the floor. *How had things spiraled so out of control?* she asked herself. It was a rhetorical question and she knew the answer. She had tried to be normal, human. Her slow change over the years, from a night stalker to a day walker allowed her to fit in. She had changed her eating habits, she changed the way she lived and she had assimilated to the point where she had lost her edge.

"You are who you are, Clarissa." She remembered, De Marcus telling her one day when she tried to open a window in their home in England.

"You will never be free of me and you will never walk in the daylight anymore. So you should just accept your fate and get on with your life," he said, shutting the curtains and smiling at her.

"What life? This isn't a life. What you have given me is a walking death." Clarissa covered her face, the slight burns from the sunlight reminding her of her hopeless plight.

"Please don't be so dramatic, my dear. It just takes time to adjust. Look at me. I've been alive one hundred and fifty years and I've seen civilizations fade into the memories of time. Some gradually and some with the fervor of a spectacular bonfire."

"You aren't alive, you live off of life." Clarissa suddenly felt her neck squeezed, gasping for breath.

"You're an ungrateful bitch. Enjoy the gift, I have given you. As easily as it was given, it can be taken away just as easily."

Clarissa rubbed her throat at the harsh memory of her torturer. De Marcus still had an effect on her. She wondered when she would be able to relegate her past to exactly that, the past. Perhaps he was right. She was who she was, a vampire. Standing, the smell of blood lingered around her. She needed to shower and try to get the stench of the night off of her and she needed to think about what her next move would be. The hot water coursed over her body as she lingered under the shower, trying to clear her mind. She felt numb thinking about what could have happened tonight. She was clearly the object of whoever Selene had killed. She kept nothing of value at the house, she didn't know people in power and she held no one's secrets. So why was she being targeted for death? Turning the water off, she toweled herself dry and slipped into clean sweats. Something didn't make sense.

Suddenly, Clarissa started to panic. She wasn't safe here anymore. She needed to get out of the house and fast. Clarissa ran to her room and pulled two suitcases out and started packing them. When she had finished with them she packed up her school work into her briefcase and tossed the bags into her car. Clarissa looked around her house and wondered if she would ever be back.

Looking at the mementos, pictures and things she had collected over the years, a realization started to set in. She could run or she could stand up and fight and protect herself. She hadn't lived this long being a victim. That was what was wrong with society today. Everyone was a victim. She had lived for centuries and had faced other vampires and survived. Hell, she had survived De Marcus, and, if she could survive him, she could survive anything. Seekers were everywhere. She needed to tune in and maybe, just maybe, this was her wake-up call. At least she wanted to look at it that way.

No, she wasn't going to run. She was going to find out what the hell was going on around her and face it head on. Trying to replay the night's events, she tried to remember what Selene had said on the phone when her feeding had been interrupted. Her brain had been in such a fog because of the thirst she felt watching Selene. What had she said? *Think, think, think.*

Now she remembered, *"Look that isn't my problem. He jumped me and before I could ask him any questions he ended up dead. I wouldn't want to be in your shoes when you explain this to your boss. By the way, this is gonna cost you more. I wasn't hired to kill anyone, just protect the girl."*

Selene was there to protect her? From what? From whom? *Selene referred to me as "the girl", so does that mean Selene doesn't know it's me? Obviously, or she would have said my name.* Pulling her suitcases back out of the car, she headed back into the house and picked up the phone. She knew what she wanted to do, but she knew what she needed to do too. She punched in the number she knew by heart and waited.

"Hey, it's me. I need a favor...."

Chapter Twenty

A.J. sat motionless in her car watching Selene dump Brax's body in the trunk, joining the other assassin's lifeless corpse. A quick wave over her shoulder at A.J. and Selene was gone. A cool breeze drifted through the open window, finally clearing the odor of stale blood from her nostrils. The beast coiled in her waiting to be released. Its tendrils ached throughout her body. She had watched Clarissa as Selene fed and she knew Clarissa would need to be released, too. Would she hunt or had she learned to control it as A.J. had? Tonight the ache was like no other time in her life. She burned with both hatred and hunger. She had no way to exorcise either option so she popped two more pills. Another deep breath and A.J. knew what she had to do, confront Kevin. Someone in her organization was a traitor and she only had one person close enough that knew her secrets.

Strumming her fingers on the steering wheel, A.J.'s heart battled with her mind. Her heart wanted to go to Clarissa. To feel Clarissa's soft skin as it slid against her naked body. She wanted to immerse herself in Clarissa's essence and relish their reconnection. But A.J.'s head wanted revenge. Not the sweet savory taste of revenge, served cold and heartless, but the bitter, spicy type that made you relinquish yourself to that darkness. A.J. knew that kind of revenge would slice a piece of her soul as payment to the devil that waited for his remittance.

Trying to calm herself, she slowly realized that maybe right now wasn't the time to confront Kevin. If he knew she suspected him, he might run and then she wouldn't know who was trying to kill Clarissa. No, she needed a plan and with the masquerade ball only a week away she needed to keep Clarissa safe and Kevin close. A.J. hit Kevin's number on speed dial and tapped her ear piece.

"A.J., what's going on?" Kevin's inquisitive tone didn't fool A.J.

"Kev." A.J. closed her eyes and concentrated on her breathing. She didn't want to give anything away. "I just saw Selene toss someone into the trunk of her car and drive off."

"Shit."

"Have you heard from Brax yet?"

"Brax? Yeah, he just called me. He's been watching the university…" Kevin wasn't good at lying and now he just confirmed A.J.'s worst fear. "Yeah, he thought Clarissa went to the university to pick up her car. He's been staking out the parking lot in front of her office all this time."

"Okay, well get his ass over here and let's make sure nothing happens to Clarissa."

"I'll call him right now. Are you on your way back to the office or are you going home?"

A.J. gripped the steering wheel so tight she felt it start to bend, her anger starting to get the better of her.

"No, I need you to meet me at the office so we can go over the plans for the donation to the university."

"I thought we discussed that already? I have the check right here ready to drop off at Clarissa's office tomorrow."

"After what happened today, I think we need to change that. I don't want to give Clarissa another chance to pick up on your energy and put two and two together. I'll have a courier service drop it off tomorrow. Besides, I have other stuff I need you to handle."

"Okay. I'll meet you at the office. Say in about twenty minutes?"

"Sounds good. See you in twenty." A.J. tapped the ear piece and tossed it on the seat. "Fucker, you lying piece of shit." A.J. closed her eyes and scrubbed her face. "You're gonna pay, you traitorous bastard."

A.J. was having a hard time controlling herself. All she could think of was Kevin's betrayal. Well, she had a place for people who betrayed her and he wasn't going to like it. But first she needed to know who he worked for. Eighteen years Kevin had worked for her and she never suspected a thing. *How could she have been so stupid?* She wondered. She trusted Kevin with everything, every secret, every lie, everything in her life. She tried to think back to anything that might have tipped her off, anything that she might have overlooked, because it was Kevin. Nothing, nothing came to mind. He had played the part of confidante well and she had fallen for it hook, line and sinker. It had taken eighteen years for Kevin to weasel his way into her inner circle, but he had been a reliable second in command. Never once had he questioned any of her orders. Oh, he had made an occasional fuss, but nothing outright.

Had this been his plan all along? To wait until A.J. had found Clarissa? He didn't steal from her, at least not that she knew of. He hadn't balked at any of her orders when it came time to pick everything up and move. In fact, he had been Johnny on the spot when it came to a new move. He took on even the most difficult tasks without being ordered to. He knew everything. How she worked, where she lived, and how she survived. Every secret she had in the last ten years had been his for the taking. The more she thought about it, the more it made sense. It had been a gamble for whoever hired Kevin. On the one hand A.J. and Clarissa might never meet, but on the other hand if they did, Kevin would be right there waiting.

"Shit, shit, shit." Banging on the steering wheel she screamed as loud as she could. "I led him right to her. Shit." Looking back up the hill, A.J. wished she had never entered that bar. If anything happened to Clarissa, she would never forgive herself. Grabbing her phone she dialed Selene's number.

"I need you to get back here asap."

"What? Now?"

"Yes, now. I need you to get back here and protect the girl." A.J. rubbed her throbbing temples. Her anger was starting to get the best of her, but she needed to make sure Clarissa was safe first.

"What the hell do you want me to do with the two in my trunk? They can't stay there all night. They'll start to stink and I like this car."

"I'll take care of them. Just get your ass back here now."

"Look, I don't know who you think you're talking to, but—"

"Selene, I don't have time for this. I need you here to watch the girl, now. I'll take care of the bodies. Just get back here." A.J. had lost her patience a long time ago and if she wasn't careful she was going to take it out on Selene.

"Don't push me, Alexandra," a menacing voice echoed through the phone. "You might write the check, but I don't have to cash it. Do I make myself clear?"

A.J. knew she had pushed Selene's buttons earlier

and now Selene was pushing back.

"At this point, as bad as it sounds, you're about the only one I can trust. Money makes strange bed fellows and right now you and I are in bed together for the duration."

"That does sound bad, A.J. and I am sure it's killing you to say it, too."

"You have no idea, Selene. No idea."

Just then, Selene's car rounded the corner and she pulled up to A.J.'s SUV.

"Open the trunk," A.J. commanded.

Selene popped her trunk and tossed A.J. her keys. "I'm not taking 'em back out again. There's a can of gas in the trunk and a few flairs. Give me your keys." Selene stuck her hand out for A.J.'s keys and closed the trunk.

"What?"

"Look, we aren't playing musical bodies. Take my car, do what you need to and I'll take your car if she leaves. Besides, you look like you can lift them, or do you need my help?" A.J. watched Selene check out her body.

"You look like you can handle 'em, but if not—"

"I got it. You just make sure you stay on top of her."

A.J. watched as Selene's eyebrows shot up and a smirk crossed her face.

"Not like that, Selene. Not like that."

"You ready to tell me why she's so important?"

A.J. grabbed her cell phone and pushed a button. "Not yet. Besides…Kevin, I'm not going to make it back to the office tonight. I'm just too tired. Did you get a hold of Brax yet? Okay, if you're sure he's gonna be here in five minutes I'll go ahead and take off. If anything happens call me. Got it?" A.J. smirked as she listening to him lie to her again. "Yeah, I'll see you tomorrow in the office." A.J. slammed the phone shut and stuffed it into her pocket.

"I thought you said the dead guy in the trunk was Brax?" Selene squinted at A.J.

"It is."

"Okay, then…."

A.J. looked at Selene and wondered how much she should tell her. It wasn't like they were strangers, but it had been a long time since she had seen Selene and things had changed, a lot. She watched as Selene crossed her arms and leaned against A.J.'s SUV. Clearly Selene was settling in for an explanation, regardless of what A.J. wanted.

"Well?" Selene questioned again.

"Really, Selene. Right now?"

"I got all night, all month, heck I got a year, so spill. Now"

"I've got a traitor in my organization and I just found out."

"Kevin?"

"I think so. Look, it's a long story, but I think he's been waiting until I found the girl up there to do this. I think he's working for someone who wants her dead."

"Why?"

"I don't know why, but trust me, I'm gonna find out." A.J. tossed Selene her keys and walked over to Selene's car. "I'll be back in about an hour. Guard her as if your life depended on it, Selene. We'll talk when I get back."

A.J. spun the car around, leaving Selene in a cloud of dust as she hit the gas. She knew exactly where she would dispose of the bodies and no one would ever find them. The drive gave her time to think about Kevin and her past. She never would have suspected Kevin if Selene hadn't killed the first vampire. She was sure Kevin was trying to figure out what to do next, now that the assassin was dead and he couldn't find Brax. She would play along, it would buy her time. As long as he thought Brax was still alive, Clarissa was safe. Whoever he worked for wouldn't send a replacement if he thought Brax had taken care of Selene. So now she had to work out something with Selene to keep Kevin busy and away from Clarissa.

A.J. turned off the paved road and onto the gravel road that led to the abandoned quarry. It was deserted and forgotten. That's why she had bought it. It had come in handy when she needed a place to practice her shooting and drop off a few of her "things". No one ever went past the three locked gates and the barbwire fences she had installed. Opening the last gate she took one last look around, just in case someone was stupid enough to "accidently" trespass. A.J. weaved her way around the mounds of leftover rock from the quarry's heyday. Arriving at the empty shaft, she backed the car up and put the trunk at the opening. Pulling each body out, she doused them in gas, lit them on fire and rolled them down the shaft. Suddenly a roar of flames came back up the shaft and A.J. had to jump sideways to avoid them. Vampires exploded when they caught fire and for that, A.J. was thankful. Now there wouldn't be a trace of anything left, just in case something didn't burn.

Chapter Twenty One

Clarissa sat at her desk chewing her lip as she contemplated the future. Another masquerade ball, and she would finally be done with the semester. Had last night really happened? Had she really seen Selene? Clarissa had watched Selene not only kill another vampire, but feed on him as well. She could only imagine the feeling Selene had as she gorged on his blood. The goose bumps on her arms gave her a chill when she thought about Selene. The beautiful, dangerous, Selene. Alexandra was just as dangerous as Selene, but in a different way. Alexandra was smart, calculating and sexy. She pushed the line and made Clarissa feel alive when they had been together a century ago. Clarissa wondered where Alexandra was now. Had she stayed in Paris, living life as she had for decades? Or had she migrated to the U.S. like so many other vampires had done when Paris became overrun with their people. The U.S. was filled with possibilities and the early Coven had pressed for vampires to spread out when Paris and England had become too hot for them.

She had only been with a few women, choosing a solitary life over one filled with an endless parade of lovers that always died in the end. No, she was happy with the structured, micro-managed, driven life she had planned for herself. While it left little time for female company, it protected her from exposure to unwanted attention from what was left of the Coven. The Coven had found itself relegated to the empires of yesteryear. An obsolete idea whose time had come and gone when technology, capitalism and mobility started to dominate the culture. Few vampires acquiesced their autonomy to the outdated relic and fewer still remained under the control of the older dominant vampires. Perhaps the seekers had changed everything, acting more like out of control thugs than vampires. Their need for drugs and freedom made them leave the Coven, killing off some of the dominant leaders in exchange for the freedom that they so badly wanted and needed. No, now things were different and Clarissa, if truth be told, was glad for the change. If De Marcus hadn't died that night in the hay barn, who knows how her life would have ended up. One thing was for sure, she would still be living under his rule with no choice in the matter.

"Excuse me," said a man wearing a courier uniform. "I'm looking for a Ms. Graham. Is that you?"

Clarissa jumped at the interruption. "Yes... um, yes, I'm Ms. Graham."

"Great. Sign here please," he said, pointing to a line on the micro pad he held out.

"I'm sorry, but I'm not expecting anything. Can you tell me who this is from?"

"Sure." Looking down at the envelope, he read the name of the sender, "Knight-Pharmaceutical."

"Oh." Signing the pad Clarissa took the offered envelope, turning it over in her hands.

"Have a nice day."

"Thanks. You, too." Clarissa shut the door and sat down on the couch. Afraid to open the envelope, she held it up to the fluorescent light in her office. "God, please don't let this be a rejection letter."

Opening it, relief settled as she extracted a check

and a short note.

"Ms. Graham," Clarissa continued, reading it out loud, "I hope this will help with your event. Respectfully, A.J. Lockwood. Oh shit!" Clarissa couldn't believe her eyes. The check had more zeros than she had seen in a long time. Dropping the note on the desk Clarissa picked up the phone and dialed Carol's office.

"Hey, you're not going to believe this."

"Okay, what am I not going to believe? Wait let me guess. You went out on a date last night?" Carol giggled on the other end. "No, wait, you got laid last night?" The giggling continued on the other end.

"I'm going to hang up if you don't stop."

"Okay. Okay. So what did you get?"

"A check from, Knight-Pharmaceutical."

"No shit."

"No shit." Clarissa kept turning the check over and over in her hand, not sure if she should believe it was real.

"Well?"

"Well, what?"

"Well, how much?"

"Oh, are you sitting down?" Clarissa sat down on the couch, afraid she might faint once she told Carol.

"Yes, now spill, silly girl."

"One hundred thousand dollars." Shaking her head, she still couldn't believe the amount. "Can you believe it?"

"I'm coming right down. Don't move."

Clarissa still had the phone in her hand when Carol burst through the door. "Let me see. Let me see." Grabbing the check, Carol turned the check over and whistled, "Wow, I don't think I've ever seen a real check with that many zeros on it."

"I know. Can you believe it?"

"Are you sure it's real?"

Elbowing Carol, Clarissa looked down at the check still in Carol's hands, "Of course it's real. It came by courier just now."

"Wow," was all Carol could say as she stared at the check. "Was there a note or anything with it?"

"Yeah." Clarissa exchanged the note for the check, watching as Carol mouthed the note.

"You must have made some impression on this guy you saw at Knight-Pharmaceutical, yesterday?" Carol handed the note back to Clarissa. "This, Mr. Lockwood."

"I didn't see him. I saw some guy named, Kevin something. I'm actually kinda surprised. I didn't think our meeting went all that well."

"What do you mean?"

Shrugging her shoulders Clarissa continued, "Well, we were talking and then all of a sudden he got a call and had to cut the meeting short."

"Well this check says differently. Wow."

"I guess."

Clarissa looked at the check and then looked at Carol and started to laugh hysterically. "Wow," was all Clarissa could say as she and Carol sank further into the couch. The stress of funding the masquerade ball was off of her and she was relieved she didn't have to worry about it.

"Well I guess I better send Mr. Lockwood a note and thank him for his generous donation."

"Note? Are you kidding me? You better get your ass over and thank him personally. Besides..." Carol raised her eyebrows, "he might be cute and single."

Clarissa raised an eyebrow and frowned at Carol.

"Oh yeah. I forgot, you don't do testosterone. Well...."

Clarissa slapped Carol's arm. "You don't do men either. Remember, Mr. School Teacher?"

"Well, if Mr. Lockwood is handsome and single, I might dump Mr. School Teacher and switch to rich and young. Remember," Carol said raising a finger at Clarissa, "it's just as easy to love someone with money as it is to love someone without. A whole lot easier."

"And they say men are such dogs."

"Woof," Carol said, walking out of Clarissa's office.

Carol was right. Clarissa needed to thank Mr. Lockwood personally for the check. That much money deserved a personal thank you. Sitting down at her computer, she drafted a donation letter thanking Knight-Pharmaceutical for the endowment and reminding them that their donation was a tax deduction as well. Before sealing the letter, she dropped two VIP tickets into the envelope. Now, Clarissa didn't have to worry about the masquerade ball for a few years.

Chapter Twenty Two

The courier just called and said he delivered the check to Clarissa."

"Good." A.J. sat back in her leather chair and closed her eyes. "Any word from Brax or Selene?"

Kevin sat on the couch acting as if he didn't have a care in the world. A.J. wanted to jump across the desk and strangle him as she watched him playing with his phone. Her skin crawled thinking about how he had been able to deceive her all this time. It took everything she had this morning to sit across the table and talk to him about their "plan" to protect Clarissa. She had already talked to Selene when they exchanged cars back last night. She had informed Selene that she was to report to her and her only. All of this was just a ploy to get Kevin to relax. She didn't want to show her cards yet. No, she had plans for Kevin and they weren't going to be what he thought. He would pay for his treachery, with his life.

"Yeah, Brax is on Clarissa at the university and I sent Selene out to Clarissa's house to make sure no one broke in. Just in case. You know?" Kevin said shrugging his shoulders.

A.J. stood and walked to the window, pulling the shade lower. Thinking quickly, she responded, "I think we need to put Selene on Clarissa and Brax at the house. Selene looks more like a student. Brax will look like a gorilla looking for a forest."

"But A.J., what about—"

"Kevin. Do you have a problem with that?" A.J. stared at him and watched him shifting from foot to foot.

"No. I'm just saying if anything happens he's much more intimidating than Selene. That's all."

"Hmm, you might be right." A.J. saw Kevin relax a bit, thinking he had won. "But I want Selene at the university when Clarissa's there. Brax can take over from Selene when Clarissa's at home." Biting the inside of her mouth, she tasted blood. If she popped a pill right now Kevin would be suspicious. So A.J. took a long, deep breath and tried to relax. "Besides, hopefully whoever sent that assassin doesn't know he's dead yet." A.J. looked back out the window and continued, "maybe it will buy us some time."

A.J. sat back down at her desk and ran her hands down her black slacks, picking phantom lint off the crease. She wanted to look as relaxed as possible. She had a plan and now she needed to implement it. The phone rang and A.J. picked it up.

"Yes Gail."

"Ms. Lockwood. I have Dr. Mayfield on from research and development. He says there is an emergency in the lab."

"Thank you, Gail. Put him through." A.J. covered the receiver with her hand as she saw Kevin get up. "Stay. We aren't finished yet." A.J. watched as Kevin pretended not to listen to the one sided conversation. Clearly, he was paying attention. He hadn't gotten as far as he had in her organization by being stupid. If she had only known sooner, she would have been more careful about what she had said in front of him. Sighing dramatically, A.J. put the receiver back in the cradle and scrubbed her face.

"A.J., is everything okay?"

"I'm not sure, Kevin. Seems one of our employees has gone rogue. Dr. Mayfield thinks he has stolen a good part of the hemoglobin research. He can't seem to find the last critical research experiments and the notes on them. It seems the guy hasn't come in to work for the last week, complaining of the flu or something." A.J. turned to her computer and brought up a screen on the research department. "Kevin, do you know Walter Masten?"

Kevin looked like he was concentrating, moving his eyes across some phantom paperwork. "No, the name doesn't sound familiar. Is he a recent hire?"

"Not according to HR records." A.J. pointed to the screen and then looked back at Kevin. "I know I've asked a lot of you lately, but I need someone I can trust down in R&D figuring this out. Think you can handle it?"

"What about Clarissa?"

"Hmm, maybe you're right. Shit, this is going to cost us millions if he took that research." A.J. tried to look perplexed as she looked back at the computer screen. Taking a deep breath she let out a dramatic sigh, and laid her head back. She slowly started to drum her fingers on the arm rest of the chair. Clearly, she was trying to create as much tension in the room as she could. "I need to go down to R&D and see what I can find out. This might take a few hours, Kevin. Can you hold down the fort for me?"

"Tell you what. I'll go down to R&D and see what I can find out. You wouldn't know what to look for. I'm the one with the hemoglobin research background. It might not be anything, A.J. Who knows."

"Are you sure? It might take longer than a few

hours to go through all those records and experiments. But I need someone I can trust down there. As I said this could cost us millions, Kevin, if we can't come through with that new product." Standing, A.J. stood next to Kevin and slapped him on the shoulder. "I appreciate this, buddy. I don't know what I would do without you."

"Come on A.J. It's no big deal."

"Naw, I'm serious, Kev. You've had my back for a long time. Eighteen years to be exact and I can't tell you how much I appreciate it. I mean…"

"Okay, okay. You're making me uncomfortable. Geez, A.J."

"I'll have your calls forwarded up here. You know you can't get reception down in the bunker." A.J. watched as Kevin fumbled with his cell phone again and stumbled over his words.

"Well…I can…I mean…"

"What? You got a hot date and haven't told me about her?" A.J. chuckled opening the door to her office.

"No. No…I…I mean what if Brax or Selene calls?" Kevin palmed his phone and shoved it into his pocket.

"I'll have Gail take a message. If it's an emergency, I'll send someone down to get you. Thanks again, buddy. Hey, I'll walk down with you to the lab. I want to touch base with Dr. Mayfield and get some idea how long this will take. Man, I really appreciate you doing this, Kev. I see a big bonus in your future, buddy." A.J. knew she was laying it on thick, but Kevin just lapped it up. He was a pleaser and because of that he just couldn't say no, ever, to anyone. It would be his one fatal flaw.

A.J. waited as Kevin changed into his bio suit and went through the sterilization chamber into the lab.

"Hey, Kevin." Throwing him a thumbs up, A.J. pressed the intercom again. "Keep me updated."

"Will do." Kevin threw back two thumbs up and went past the second set of doors that would close him off from the rest of the world for a few hours, maybe even a few days, if A.J. played her cards right. A.J. went through the lockers and found Kevin's clothes. His cell phone sat on top of his stack of clothes and A.J. pocketed it. She would have to wait until she was in the privacy of her office to go through his list of contacts. Pulling the intercom phone, A.J. dialed Dr. Mayfield's office.

"Kevin's inside. You know what to do. Thanks. Let me know when it's done."

Slamming the receiver down, A.J. looked back into the lab and shook her head. It was too bad it was going to have to be handled this way, but A.J. knew she didn't have any other options if she was to keep Clarissa safe.

Clarissa entered the steel and glass structure for the second time that week and she still marveled at the interior lobby.

"Good Morning, Miss. Can I help you?" A glint of recognition struck the officer. "Oh, it's you. Back again, I see."

"Good Morning. How are you?"

"Well, I woke up alive today so it's a good day." It was clear by the way the man was smiling he was flirting with her. "You look much better than you did yesterday when you left. Are you feeling better?"

Clarissa smiled and wished she could flirt back but she wasn't built like that. She had watched Carol turn a man's head with just a few words, but she was more direct.

"I am feeling much better thank you. I'm here to see, Mr. Alexander or Mr. Lockwood."

Clarissa could tell from the look on the young man's face that she had said something funny.

"Well, Mr. Lockwood is a Ms. and I'm not sure she is available, but I did see Mr. Alexander this morning."

"Oh how embarrassing—" Clarissa pulled the note from her purse and laid it out on the desk. "Well, I guess I just assumed that the company was owned by a man. You can't tell from the name," Clarissa said, pointing to the note.

The young man picked up the note and smiled, "Yeah, I guess you're right. I would never have guessed this big company was run by a woman either. Easy mistake to make. Let me see if someone is available to see you."

Clarissa could hear the officer talking to someone as she looked around admiring the lobby again.

"Excuse me. Could you tell them I have a letter for Ms. Lockwood that I would like to deliver personally?" Clarissa informed the officer.

"Okay Gail, I'll send her up. See you at lunch." Clarissa felt herself get excited as the desk officer smiled at her. She would finally meet the person who had made the masquerade ball possible and her life a bit easier. "Ms. Graham, you can go to the fifth floor. Gail will be waiting for you there."

"Great, thank you so much." Clarissa smiled and made her way to the elevator. Yesterday it was the third floor, today the fifth. She was working her way to the top she thought, chuckling at her own silly joke. As the doors opened, an older woman stood waiting for her.

"Please follow me," she said with a sweeping gesture across another lobby. This one wasn't as stately as the one from yesterday, but the understated elegance was easy to appreciate. "Please have a seat and I will see if I can find Mr. Alexander or Ms. Lockwood. Can I get you anything while you wait?"

"No thank you. I'm fine." Clarissa thought again about what she would say to now, "Ms." Lockwood. She suddenly felt that the words she had rehearsed were inadequate for such a generous donation. How could she possibly thank someone who had practically saved the masquerade ball for the next five years? Anything she said would pale in comparison to the generosity of Ms. Lockwood. Clarissa's palms started to sweat and she felt her heart start to beat faster. She hadn't expected to be so nervous, but now faced with the possibility of facing her benefactor, she was downright scared. Clarissa closed her eyes and tried to relax. A deep breath, a soft sigh and Clarissa felt the tension leave her body. She tried to clear her mind, but the events of the night before crept to the front of her thoughts. What had happened was beyond strange. She knew she should be scared out of her wits, but she had been through hell before, and last night wasn't hell. Close, but definitely not hell. Her nice orderly life was practically upside down, but the delivery today had righted it somewhat. She knew she needed to figure out the who, what and why of last night, but right now she had business to take care of. She could think about last night later, after lunch, she told herself as she felt herself become nervous again.

A.J. heard the light tap on her office door.

"Come in."

"Ms. Lockwood, I can't seem to find Mr. Alexander. That young woman from yesterday is here waiting in the fifth floor conference room. She asked to see either you or Mr. Alexander, but I thought that since she had seen Mr. Alexander perhaps he could see her again."

A.J. felt her body tense when she heard Gail's announcement. Clarissa was here? What was she doing here?

"Did she say what she wanted, Gail?"

"She informed Larry at the front desk that she wanted to hand deliver a thank you letter."

A.J. hadn't anticipated that Clarissa would want to personally thank her for the donation for the masquerade ball. She felt a tingle run through her body as she thought about seeing Clarissa, but she quickly dashed those thoughts. It wasn't the time and she wasn't ready. But the possibility of talking to Clarissa gave her pause, however brief.

"Gail, can you tell her that neither I nor Kevin is available. Please tell her we're in a meeting and…" A.J. didn't want to seem insensitive, considering Clarissa had gone out of her way to come and thank her personally. Quickly writing out a note she handed it to Gail. "Gail, could you please give her this and please express how sorry we are that we are not available to meet with her."

A.J. had to see Clarissa a little more closely. Taking the stairs up to the fifth floor, she slowly opened the door from the stairwell and watched as Gail walked Clarissa to the elevator. She felt like the hunter as she watched Clarissa. Clarissa's smell drifted in the air and A.J.'s body reacted to the scent. She was beautiful up close and A.J. could barely control herself. Desire began to coil inside and she felt the tendrils of excitement course through her. She could hear Gail extend A.J.'s apologies and then she heard something she hadn't expected.

"I don't mean to pry, but could you tell me a little about Ms. Lockwood? She has been so generous and I would like to send her a thank you gift. Perhaps flowers, or candy. Something to show my appreciation."

"I'm sure that isn't necessary, Ms. Graham. I'm not sure there is much I can tell you about Ms. Lockwood. She is generous, so I'm not surprised by her gift to the university. I can tell you she is very fair with her employees as well."

A.J. watched as Clarissa smiled. Somehow she knew Clarissa wouldn't be deterred from her mission on finding out more about her. Clarissa had a dogged determination that A.J. had seen personally when they were together. Listening again, she heard Clarissa continue her line of questioning.

"Well, perhaps you can tell me if she likes the symphony, the theater or perhaps she has a favorite restaurant or vintner? I would really like to thank her with a personal gift that she would appreciate."

"Well…."

"Please, this has been the most generous gift we have ever received and I just can't be happy with a simple note and two VIP tickets to the masquerade ball. I am sure you understand my dilemma. Surely you've been in a similar situation with her generosity?"

A.J. knew she was trying to appeal to Gail's softer side. She didn't have the heart to tell her it wouldn't work. Gail had been with A.J. for almost as long as Kevin and wasn't a push over.

"Well, I can tell you, I honestly don't know what her favorite restaurant is or her favorite wine. Sorry. But, perhaps she would appreciate something personalized from you. If you have a favorite photographer or something simple, I'm sure she would appreciate that. She seems to love black and white photographs."

A.J. was shocked that Gail had noticed such a minor detail. She did, in fact, love the dramatic style of photography. She had several around her office and more in her penthouse. The drama of the black and white contrast reminded her of her past and it was a journey she took willingly. Perhaps it spoke more of how she saw her life, black and white with few areas of gray.

Pulled back to the two women, A.J. watched as Clarissa thanked Gail for her candor and quickly left. A.J. started to close the door when she heard Gail call her name.

"Ms. Lockwood?" Opening the door slightly, A.J. looked at Gail and then the elevator. "Don't worry, she's gone," Gail said, walking towards A.J.

"How did you know?" A.J. knew she had been discrete in her observance of Clarissa, but something had tipped off Gail.

"Perhaps it was the quick intake of breath when I mentioned the photographs in your office." A.J. watched Gail smile as they walked down the corridor. A.J. smiled back at the older woman and wrapped an arm around her shoulders.

"You are full of surprises, Gail."

Chapter Twenty Three

Clarissa fanned herself with the envelope from A.J. Lockwood. The faint scent of cologne wafted by her nose. While it wasn't familiar to her, she knew it was A.J. Lockwood's. Who else's could it be? Perhaps Gail's? No. She had smiled at Gail's common perfume when she first met the woman, something a lot of the older professors at her university wore. The cologne was fresh and inviting, alluring. Clarissa debated with herself on whether she should open the note or wait until she was alone. The pedestrian traffic around her was distracting and for some reason she felt the need to be alone when she read the note. If Ms. Lockwood had taken the time to write it, she wanted to take time to give it her full attention.

Clarissa's cell phone buzzed in her pocket and she quickly collected it and put the note in her purse. Carol's number streamed across the screen, causing Clarissa to smile at her friend's impatience.

"Couldn't wait could you?"

"What? I was worried. Can't a friend be worried?"

"Of course you can, but what were you worried about? Geez, it isn't like she was going to ask for the money back. Besides, I didn't even get to see her."

"She? Wait. You mean A.J. Lockwood is a she?"

"Yep."

"No Shit. Now, I really am sorry you didn't get to meet the infamous A.J. Lockwood. I bet she's some battle axe that eats kids for breakfast." Carol chuckled, "Oh, Clarissa, I'm sorry you wasted your time, but at least you got a big fat check anyway."

"Ever the optimist. Well, if it is any consolation, she sent me a note."

"What does it say?"

"I don't know. I haven't opened it yet."

"Why haven't you opened it?"

"I want to give it the attention it deserves, so I'm waiting until I get back to my office."

"Oh, well, I'll wait for you then. I want to see what it says. This is exciting, kinda like getting a gift you're just waiting to unwrap."

"Carol, you're being a little dramatic don't you think?"

"What?"

"Look, I'm almost back, so wait for me in my office and we can read it together."

"Okay, hurry. I can't wait to see what she says."

"Okay, Okay." Clarissa snapped her phone shut and laughed again. Carol was acting like a kid who just couldn't wait for Christmas.

###

A.J. opened the envelope and removed the two tickets first. She quickly read the short note thanking her for her donation and asking her to attend the masquerade ball as Clarissa's guest. Her disappointment quickly evaporated as she thought about the personal invitation to be her guest at the masquerade ball. She thought she might attend, but the invitation made it a certainty that she would. She had worried that she might have to cancel her plans to attend when things had changed so rapidly in the past couple of days. But now she felt excited at the possibilities of seeing Clarissa, talking to her and possibly sharing a dance with her. She would have to make sure her costume was appropriate for the time period, but most importantly, her mask needed to hide her identity until she was ready to reveal it.

A.J. pulled Kevin's cell phone from her pocket and began looking through the text messages. As she scrolled through them, she spotted a few from Brax letting Kevin know where he was. But as she continued further down, a text message from DM jumped out at her.

Kevin, Good Job. Finally. After all these years she is within my grasp. Call me for further instructions. DM

A.J. felt her body quake as she read the text. DM had known the whole time. But where was he and what was he waiting for? Clarissa wasn't safe anymore and now she needed to act fast or lose Clarissa forever. A.J. wrote the number on a piece of paper to give to Selene, then finished scrolling through the call list. Other than her number and Selene's, Kevin didn't get many calls. Lucky for her.

A quick call to Gail with instructions to find a costume for the masquerade ball and A.J. was set. She needed to talk to Selene and then make sure Kevin was handled and she would be ready to plan how she would approach Clarissa at the ball. It had to be subtle or it would scare Clarissa off. So much had happened to Clarissa in the last few days, A.J. was surprised she hadn't run already. How much Clarissa could take was beyond her. While she wasn't easily dissuaded, she had no history on Clarissa and could only guess what kind of torture she had to endure with De Marcus. A phone call later and Selene and A.J. would meet at a coffee shop close to campus. A.J. didn't want Selene too far from

Clarissa, just in case something happened.

As A.J. walked in, she spotted Selene. Selene's appearance hadn't changed in decades. Her long frame barely fit into the small chair. Selene stretched her long legs casually into the aisle of the coffee shop, causing anyone walking by to step over them. Clearly, she didn't care if she was impeding traffic. Selene was Selene and she didn't make apologies for being bold, aggressive or threatening. One look at her and it was clear by her body language, she wasn't someone to mess with. A.J. watched Selene flirt with a young, obviously college-aged girl, but never the less too young for Selene. Smiling at the girl, Selene slipped a piece of paper to the young woman before she walked away. A.J. didn't blame the young girl for flirting with the gorgeous woman. A.J. herself had fallen for Selene's dark looks and charming demeanor, but that was a century ago and A.J. didn't have time to stroll down memory lane today.

"Aren't you a little old for her?" A.J. said, pulling a chair out, turning it backwards and straddling it.

"Not really. I was turned when I was thirty, so that makes me, what, eight or ten years older than her." Selene's smile didn't reach her eyes, letting A.J. know she wasn't in a kidding mood.

"Yeah, if you don't add those two hundred years, or fangs, you could be great dating material around here." A.J. looked back at the young woman and hoped her thoughts of persuasion were working on the woman.

"Don't do that." Selene crouched forward at A.J.

"Don't do what?"

"Quit fucking with her mind. I felt it and I don't appreciate you mucking in my business."

"Look, you need to stay focused on the task at hand. After that, you can do whatever you want.

Besides, don't you have women at that club of yours?" A.J. had heard Selene owned a local bondage club, but wasn't surprised. Selene had owned one ever since A.J. had known her. Somehow it seemed appropriate, given Selene's propensity for violence and torture.

"Yeah, but not young beautiful women like that. Most women don't dabble with that stuff until they're much older. I like 'em fresh and untarnished." Selene winked at the girl as she returned and slid a hot cup of coffee towards Selene.

"You drink that stuff?" A.J. had never adapted to the taste of coffee. In fact, she had just adapted to an occasional meal and glass of wine. Scotch, now that made her blood warm. The earthy peat smell and taste made A.J. yearn for home and her farm. Shaking the memories off, A.J. got back to the business at hand. "Let's get back to business. So—"

"Where's Kevin?" Selene wasn't known for her patience decades ago and clearly she hadn't learned any yet, either.

"He's handled. He won't be an issue for us, but I don't know if he had a chance to relay any information to whoever he's working for."

"Are you sure Kevin was the leak? Maybe it was Brax?"

"Brax couldn't pour piss out of a boot, let alone know who he was going to be guarding. No, it was Kevin. He gave Brax his orders and he was the only one who had any idea Clarissa was around." A.J. cursed her trust in Kevin once more. If anything happened to Clarissa she would never be able to forgive herself, not now that she knew Clarissa was alive.

"Well, you know him best. But I'm curious. You're not usually this careless. Getting lazy in your old age?"

A.J. stared into black onyx eyes as she thought about Selene's statement. Had she lost her edge? She had been careful for decades, no centuries, protecting herself. It only took one well placed individual to split the seams of the well sown fabric that was her life. A.J. roughly caressed her chin as she thought about everything that had happened since finding Clarissa. She had almost lost her before she had even had a chance to talk to her. No, she had placed too much trust in the wrong person, but that would never happen again, not if she wanted to continue living.

"Not if I'm sitting here with you and he's…" A.J. looked down at her watch, "sitting in a freezer right now."

"Dead?"

"No, but he's on ice, so to speak. When the masquerade ball is over this weekend, I'll handle him. So no, I haven't lost my edge." A.J. wanted to make sure Selene didn't overestimate her worth and wanted to send a strong message, just in case anyone else was listening. Smiling back into the black onyx eyes, A.J. watched Selene nod her head in understanding.

"I put out feelers and if he talked to someone, I can't find 'em. So I have to assume he didn't have time to report back to his handler. Doing so would have put another assassin on Clarissa quick, and I haven't seen a soul, living or dead, anywhere around her." Selene leaned towards A.J. again. "Look, people like this don't wait for an opportunity, they create them. That's what happened last night. Brax wasn't on the case but two days before he reported that there was someone else following Clarissa."

A.J. looked up from her folded hands, her brow furrowed.

"You look surprised, A.J. What did you think I'd do last night after the first asshole attacked me? Sit back and wait for orders from a mysterious employer? I've known who you were and who the caged bird was. It's what I do and how I've stayed alive this long."

"I knew it wouldn't take you long to figure it out. I should have put you on the case in the first place." It hurt A.J. to admit she had made a mistake based on her past with Selene, but it was hers and hers alone to shoulder. "Let's get back to business. The masquerade ball is this weekend and I'm attending. I don't know how it's going to play out, but I'm willing to risk rejection to protect Clarissa."

"I don't think that's such a great idea, A.J. I think you need to play this right or you could risk losing what you value again, but this time forever. If you're not careful, she's gonna run and this time you won't find her."

"Look, I don't plan on a big confrontation at the masquerade ball. It wouldn't be prudent for either of us. Besides, we have a history and I'm hoping that she'll remember what we had."

"What kind of history?" A.J. could see the suspicion in Selene's narrowed eyes. What would she tell Selene? How would she explain their history and did she even need to? Selene worked for her, not the other way around.

"It's not important."

"It is to me. I need to know what I'm walking into now that I'm on the hook for two dead vampires. I've now made myself a target for whoever hired them and I'd like to know why."

A.J. tapped her lips with her index finger as she tried to control her agitation. She wasn't in the mood for questions she didn't want to answer. But more importantly, she wasn't sure she was ready to admit that

Clarissa had been her one and only true love. She also wasn't sure she was ready for the questions that would come when Selene found out she hadn't been the one to turn Clarissa, especially when she didn't have all the answers.

Standing, Selene tossed a few bills on the table and grabbed her jacket. "Look, I don't have time to try and squeeze a few answers out of you. I'm done."

A.J. stood and grabbed Selene's arm. "It isn't that I don't want to tell you. Well, it is that I don't want to tell you, but I don't know all the details. What I know, I'm guessing at," A.J. said measuring up Selene as they stared across at each other. "If you're done trying to play alpha dog to my alpha dog, I'll try and fill you in on what I know." A.J. guided Selene back to her seat and looked at her again.

"I'm listening."

A.J. let out a deep breath and looked around for a diversion. This wasn't going to be easy, but she needed to let Selene know what she had gotten her into. Pinning Selene with a stare, A.J. studied her face.

"I'm waiting."

"Clarissa and I were lovers in Paris centuries ago." A.J. rubbed her hands, as if doing so would warm them up.

"And?"

"She was human the last time I saw her."

"How is that possible? If you didn't turn her, then who did? Where is her master?" Selene's questioning glare made A.J. squirm uncomfortably. She knew those would be the first questions Selene asked. Heck, they were the first questions she had asked Kevin when he told her who the owner of the license plates was.

"Short version. She was sick and dying the last

time I saw her. Her parents thought I had made her sick, cholera, the plague, take your pick. Whatever was going around back then was lethal to humans and I wasn't sick. So obviously I made her sick in their minds. A Dr. De Marcus was hanging around her at the time, and he's the only one I can think of who would have had opportunity and motive. He hated that she loved me and not him. It bruised his ego, and I think at the last minute he turned her."

"So why is she single then? She belongs to him and he wouldn't just let her go out of the kindness of his heart. Not that I know him, but that first vampire's blood tasted old, so his master must be really old and most masters still subscribe to the old way. Domination, subjugation and control are still big with those old masters."

"I can't answer that. I have been busy trying to protect her and haven't had a lot of time to figure it out yet. Kevin looked into it and said De Marcus was dead, killed in an accident in England. But the only records are in the Coven and I don't have time to travel to Europe to go through them. I had to trust Kevin. He did tell me where and what Clarissa was doing, so he had some integrity," A.J. said, hoping she sounded convincing. But even as she said the words, she wasn't sure she could even convince herself. Kevin had thrown a grenade right in the middle of her well laid out plan. Now, she had to figure out what was left of it and if it could be salvaged.

"I need you at the masquerade ball with me on Saturday night. I have two VIP tickets so you won't stick out like a sore thumb. Besides, if you're outside and I'm inside, we should be able to keep her safe without her knowing it." A.J. waited for a reaction from Selene, but only got a frown. "What?"

"I don't like playing dress-up. It makes it too hard to tell who the players are."

"And?"

"I'm not wearing a dress."

A.J. started to laugh at Selene's implications. She had never even thought of asking the very butch assassin to dress in women's clothes. The thought of Selene in women's attire made her think of a drag queen, which only caused her to laugh harder. The laughter echoed through the coffee shop causing people to turn and look in their direction.

"Knock it off, A.J. I'm not kidding. I am not dressing up in a dress so come up with another idea. I can sit in the car and watch the dance from there, but I am not wearing a dress."

"Selene, you would look like a woman playing a guy dressed in drag. No offense, but the thought never crossed my mind. Besides, you can call Gail, my secretary, and tell her I want her to set you up with a costume. Okay?"

"Fine," huffed Selene. She wasn't accustomed to being laughed at, and when people did, it usually cost them their life.

Wiping a tear from her eye, A.J. felt sorry for the beautiful woman. It must be hard to be a trained killer one minute and then think you might have to wear a dress the next. Oh well, the job would be over soon, hopefully, and Selene could go back to her indulgences at her club. Until the next time she was needed. A.J. discussed her plan with Selene, going over every detail of the night. There could be no missteps this time. They both needed to be sharp, or it could cost Clarissa her life.

Chapter Twenty Four

Wow, you look gorgeous, Honey." Carol whistled her approval as Clarissa turned in her new ball gown. She had worn the same one for the past three years and had decided that this year she would splurge and have a new one made.

"You like it?"

"Well, let's just say if this was a different time and I was a different gal, I would do you." Carol had a way about her that if someone didn't know her, they would make different assumptions about her occupation.

"Oh, swarthy language. Careful, you just might turn my head." Clarissa slapped Carol's hand away as she tried fingering the gown. "Besides, I can't wait to see what you dress Mr. Sex Ed. in. I'm sure he'll be the one on the short leash."

"Well," Carol hesitated, looking anywhere but at Clarissa, "he isn't going."

"What? What do you mean he isn't going? You didn't invite him or you broke up with him already, as in isn't going?" Clarissa watched as the question lingered in the air while Carol fidgeted with her purse. "Carol, what's going on?"

"Oh, we broke up. I don't even know why we broke up, but we just did." Carol wiped an errant tear before it trailed down her cheek.

"Oh, Carol. I'm sorry. What happened?" Clarissa pulled her long gown behind her as she wrapped her arm around her friend's shoulder. "I'm sure it's just a misunderstanding. Don't you think?"

"Look, Honey. I know the difference between a misunderstanding and being dumped and he dumped me." Snapping her finger she finished, "just like that. One minute we're talking in bed, the next thing I know he's telling me he's not good enough for me. You know that 'it's not you, it's me' bullshit."

Clarissa wished she could feel bad for Carol, but she had thought the guy had moved too fast on Carol anyway. "Well, look on the bright side. There'll be lots of available men at the ball so you can dance your way through them to find Mister Right." Clarissa hoped Carol wouldn't take it the wrong way.

"Well, I'll just settle for Mr. Right Now. I'm beginning to think Mr. Right just doesn't exist. Besides, he was cold all the time." Clarissa frowned at Carol's comment.

"Huh?"

"Yeah, he was always cold. Said the doctor told him it was poor circulation and it would get worse as he got older. I always had my thermostat set at seventy five degrees when he was over. At least now my heating bill will be lower." Carol shrugged off the comment and went back to fingering Clarissa's dress. "Maybe I need to get a new dress, too."

Clarissa thought about what Carol had said. The bite marks earlier in the week, the cold body and now that she thought about it, Clarissa had never seen Carol's boyfriend. *Strange, Carol had always paraded her new boyfriends through the university,* thought Clarissa. Something wasn't adding up. She wanted to ask Carol more questions, but thought better of it when she saw Carol wipe her eyes again. Clearly, Carol was taking it harder than she let on. A tug on Clarissa's arm brought her back to the present.

"Hey, did you hear what I said?"

"Oh, sorry. No, what did you say?"

"I said maybe you can introduce me to Ms. Lockwood at the ball." Carol smirked, wiggling her eyebrows.

Maybe Carol wasn't having as hard a time as Clarissa thought. Looking at Carol suspiciously, Clarissa shook her head, "I don't think so. Besides, your gate doesn't swing that way. Remember?"

"Well, maybe my sexuality is fluid and my fluid needs to be changed," Carol said, as she looked through the rack of dresses. "Besides, remember when I said it is just as easy to love a rich man as a poor man? Well, maybe it's just as easy to love a rich woman as a poor man. Hmm?"

Clarissa slid the dress off her shoulders and handed it to the seamstress with a nod. "Thank you. I'll pick it up Friday." Grabbing Carol's elbow, she pulled her out of the shop. "Come on, Ms. Fluid, we are not having this conversation. Besides, you need time to settle, not settle for something that isn't you."

"Oh," a dramatic sigh escaped Carol as she followed Clarissa towards her car. "I know. I'm being silly. It wasn't that I really liked him. Besides, I just met him a few weeks ago. He was just passing time. If truth be told, he was starting to get weird."

"Weird? Weird, how?" Clarissa was now interested in finding out more about Carol's phantom boyfriend.

"You know how men can be. Weird." Carol turned and faced Clarissa as Clarissa unlocked the car. "One time he sucked on my neck so hard I thought he would break the skin. When I screamed, he jumped off the bed and apologized like crazy telling me it would never happen again. Then, other times, he would just sit and watch me do things, while he stroked his belt. You know, weird stuff."

Clarissa frowned at Carol, "What do you mean 'stuff'? What kinda stuff?"

"Oh come on. Stuff. You know…" Carol wiggled her eyebrows at Clarissa, "stuff."

"Oh." Carol's meaning suddenly dawned on Clarissa, "you mean masturbation stuff?"

"Oh, Christ, we're in public, Clarissa. Someone might hear you." Carol looked around causing Clarissa to mimic her actions.

"Oh, right." Clarissa blushed realizing what she had just said. Clarissa slammed the car door and turned towards Carol. "Okay, so what other weird stuff did he do?"

"I don't know," Carol said, shrugging her shoulders. "Now that I think about it, maybe I'm just being silly. Besides, it's over now so who cares. Right?"

Clarissa had a bad feeling about Carol's boyfriend, but she wasn't sure how she would get more information out of her without it being obvious. At least he was out of the picture now. She needed to come up with a plan to find out more information about him. Something just wasn't right. She had learned a long time ago to trust her gut, and right now her gut was telling her something was very wrong. Especially after what had happened two nights ago in her own backyard. She couldn't be too careful now.

Let's get some lunch. My treat." Clarissa knew a glass of wine with lunch and she would be able to pry just about anything out of her friend.

"Okay, if you're buying. I'm hungry."

Clarissa never noticed the car that pulled out behind them as they left the parking lot.

An hour later, Clarissa and Carol were laughing and toasting the end of Carol's weird relationship.

"So, you never told me how you met this guy," Clarissa said casually.

"Oh, I was out walking my dog after work. He was at the dog park reading a newspaper and watching everyone with their dogs. I sat down and the next thing I knew he was asking me out." Carol shrugged.

"Wow. Sounds smooth."

"Yeah, I guess. I never thought about it really. He teaches, I teach. We had a lot in common." Clarissa watched as Carol swirled her wine glass and watched the amber liquid swirl up the sides. "It was easy. We met after work, had wild sex and then laid around and talked."

"How come you never brought him around? You always bring your boyfriends around to show them off." Clarissa hoped it didn't sound condescending, but she had a feeling.

"I wanted to, but he was always busy with school stuff and he usually came over at night, after work. I tried to get him to come with me when you invited me to dinner the other night, but he ended up getting sick or something and called at the last minute to cancel. Otherwise, you would have met him."

"Huh." Clarissa lifted her glass and toasted, "here's to shitty boyfriends and great friends. May there always be plenty of the latter and fewer of the first."

"I'll toast to that. Here, here," said Carol, finishing

her wine and setting her glass down with a thud. "Thanks."

"For what?"

"For being there for me. I know I can be a pain sometimes, but I'm glad we're friends."

Clarissa looked at Carol and wished she could tell her that their friendship might come to an end soon, but she just didn't have the nerve. Besides, she was fond of Carol so maybe, maybe she would stay friends with her after she left. Clarissa wished she could tell Carol her suspicions about Carol's ex-boyfriend, but maybe it was better this way. He had at least had the decency to leave before anything bad had happened to Carol. Or worse yet, what if he had met Clarissa. They would both know the other's secret, and then what? No, Carol was lucky it had ended the way it had as far as Clarissa was concerned. Besides, Carol always found something, or someone else, to take her mind off her troubles and the ball would do just that.

"So, you never said if you heard from Ms. Lockwood about attending the ball."

"Oh, yeah. Her secretary called to confirm that she would be attending, alone."

Clarissa's student worker had gotten the call earlier in the day and informed Clarissa. Clarissa was surprised by the new development. Not that Ms. Lockwood would attend, but she would be attending alone. Clarissa had thought that Ms. Lockwood would be bringing a date so the news of her lone attendance excited Clarissa for some reason. Now, Clarissa would be able to spend a few minutes alone with her benefactor, giving her the time she needed to thank her properly. She had gone shopping the night before, looking for something special for the woman and had found what she hoped would be the perfect gift. It sat wrapped in her office. Clarissa would present it to her at the ball, but she wasn't sure if she wanted to do it in front of an audience or in private. The anticipation was almost too much for her as she thought about the gift. She had gone to a local gallery looking for a black and white photograph to give Ms. Lockwood. As she strolled through one gallery in particular, she had accidently seen the photo hanging on the wall of the gallery office. There was something about the photo that propelled her back to France when she was young. The countryside was just as she remembered it, gently rolling hills and a farm house tucked away just inside a grove of trees. The contrast of the trees and the grass was amazing, but even more amazing was that the photo was taken at dusk. The moon, just barely seen above the forest, brought out the path leading to the forest, tree trunks catching the moonlight as it cast shadows around the farm house. Clarissa had bargained hard with the owner, finally paying handsomely for the photograph. The owner had no idea who the photographer was or when the photograph was taken, but assured her that it was worth what she was paying for it. A gentle tugging and a question brought Clarissa out of her daydream.

"Hey, where are you?" Carol asked as she poured some more wine for each of them.

"Oh, sorry. I was just thinking about the photograph I purchased for Ms. Lockwood."

"Hmmm, daydreaming about tall, dark and gorgeous?"

"How do you know what she looks like? For all we know she could have a hump on her back and be old and wrinkled. Besides, a woman who runs a company like Knight-Pharmaceutical is probably driven and a workaholic, not to mention she probably goes home to a husband and two point five kids."

"How does someone have two point five kids?" Carol questioned Clarissa.

Slapping Carol's arm, Clarissa laughed at her joke. "Funny. You can ask her when you see her since I know you'll be dying to see what she looks like. Anyway…" Clarissa let her sentence hang without finishing it. If she was honest with herself, Clarissa was dying to meet the woman who had just made her life so much easier. How lucky could she have been to decide to go to Knight-Pharmaceutical first, instead of one of the other donors on her list?

"Fine, I'll ask her myself tomorrow night. Hmm." Carol said, crossing her arms and pouting.

Chapter Twenty Five

Selene sat in the dark booth watching Clarissa and another woman have dinner. Clarissa was as beautiful as Selene remembered. Even though Selene had only had one night with her, it was a night she had never forgotten. It was rare that a woman asked for another woman to do the things Selene had done to Clarissa, but she had known immediately that Clarissa was in need the minute she had walked into the club. Selene had felt Clarissa's blood lust coursing through her, the demon warring inside Clarissa's body calling out to Selene for release. And Selene had been happy to oblige Clarissa's requests. It was what she was good at. Watching Clarissa now, Selene wished she had spent more time with her when she had it. But that was then and this was now. Whoever wanted Clarissa dead had almost succeeded and Selene wasn't about to let them get a second chance.

Selene watched Clarissa interacted with the woman sitting next to her. It was clear to Selene they were friends. In fact, Selene had seen the woman coming out of Clarissa's office at the university.

"Carol..." Selene whispered, remembering the name Clarissa had called after her as she left her office, "something. Hmm."

Selene hoped her feeding the night before dulled her energy and that Clarissa wouldn't be able to sense her in the restaurant. Selene smiled as she observed

Clarissa in a more relaxed state. Two nights before, she had felt Clarissa hiding in the tree and wondered how the woman had held her composure as she watched the events play out. Clearly, Clarissa had changed since the last time they had seen each other, but instinct was instinct and a vampire feeding usually was just enough to set off another vampire's primal instinct. The more Selene thought about the previous night, the more she wondered about A.J. as well. She had seen both Clarissa and Selene. The energy coming from them both had to be overwhelming for Alexandra and yet she, too, had been in control the whole evening. Knight-Pharmaceutical was paying her, so perhaps A.J. was working on something that took care of her urges. She would have to ask about that the next time they were together, perhaps at the ball the following night. Selene doubted, though, that she would get the chance, remembering that whoever was trying to get to Clarissa was still a threat and, until that threat was eliminated, this was all business.

Parts of Clarissa's conversation drifted to Selene's keen hearing. It was clear by the conversation that the other woman's boyfriend had dumped her, but something caught her attention.

"You know, now that I think about it, we never went out during the day. Like I said, he was always busy on the weekends during the day. We mostly went out at night."

"Hey, do you have a picture of him?" Selene heard Clarissa ask. Clearly she was thinking the same thing Selene was, that he might be a vampire. It would be risky on his part to have a relationship with a human but it wasn't unheard of. It just didn't last. It usually either ended up that the vampire left, afraid of accidental exposure, or the vampire killed their lover by accident.

Listening more closely, Selene wondered if the woman had a picture. If so, then it probably wasn't a vampire. A seeker or night walker couldn't be seen, but if it was a day walker then all bets were off. Even vampires were evolving, at least some.

"Let me see if I have his picture on my phone. I tried to snap one of him once and he got pretty pissed. So I tried to sneak one of him to show you." Selene watched as the woman thumbed the screen of her cell phone. "Let's see. Here it is."

Selene stood and walked towards the bathroom hoping to get a peek at the phone as she walked past.

"Hmm, that's funny. All I see is the elbow of his jacket and shirt. Darn, I thought I sneaked one of him." While Carol tilted the phone towards Clarissa, Selene was able to catch a quick glimpse of the photo, but there wasn't anything to identify the man. "Nope, I guess I don't have one. Sorry," the woman said as she finished thumbing through the photos.

"That's all right. No biggie, Carol," Clarissa said, finishing her wine. "You ready to go? We have a big night tomorrow night."

"Yeah, let's get out of here. All this wine is making me tired. Mind if you give me a ride home?"

Selene heard Clarissa agree and then watched as the two women walked arm in arm out of the restaurant. Pulling her cell phone, she dialed A.J.

"Hey, we need to talk. Call me back." Selene didn't mince words. Stuffing the phone back in her pocket, she pulled her hat far down on her head and followed Clarissa out and to her own car.

"Clarissa, why don't you spend the night and tomorrow? You can go home, pick up your things and we can meet at the university to help finish set up."

Selene watched as the two women continued arm in arm to Clarissa's car.

"I don't know. I have Neff at home and she might get worried." Clarissa snuggled closer to the woman.

"Aw, come on. It's so darn late I'll worry about you driving all the way home."

Selene hoped Clarissa would take the woman up on the offer. It would give her some time to take care of some business she had neglected and talk to A.J. about the earlier conversation about the woman's boyfriend. With Kevin out of communication with the world, and the killing of the two guys two days before, it was doubtful that whoever hired the assassins would have had time to hire new muscle. It was clear after talking to A.J. that this plan had taken years to develop and it would take more than a few days for the guy Kevin worked for to get someone briefed and following Clarissa. To be on the safe side though, Selene would get one of her guys on Clarissa, but not before she got A.J.'s approval for the switch out. The vibration of her cell phone caught her attention and she stepped into the shadows so she could still watch Clarissa.

"Timing is everything," Selene said as she looked around to make sure no one was following the two women.

"What's up?" A.J. sounded breathless.

"Oh, did I catch you at a bad time?" Selene said, the innuendo hanging in the air.

"Knock it off. I'm just working out. You called earlier. Everything alright with Clarissa?"

"Yeah, she's leaving with a co-worker…" Selene paused catching the last bit of conversation between Clarissa and the woman. "It sounds like she is going to be spending the night at her co-worker's tonight. I'm going to bring one of my guys over to babysit while I run some errands. That okay with you?" Selene heard A.J.'s breathing slow down and pause for the briefest of moments. "Look, A.J., I need to take care of some business and get that damn costume from your assistant. Now if you want to come over her and sit and watch the house, I'm fine with that. But I need to take care of my own business. I didn't plan on being away this long. It's either that or I walk for good. Your choice?"

"You trust this guy? I mean, he works for you, right?"

"No, I'm his master and I trust him. He takes care of certain things for me when I can't, but right now I need to take care of some personal stuff. By the way, it seems that Clarissa's friend might have been dating a vampire. Just a guess right now, but it has all the markings of a night walker."

"No shit. What does he look like?" Selene could hear A.J.'s heartbeat pick up at the mention of the boyfriend.

"I don't know. From what I gather, he dumped her last night. But she was describing some of his dating habits and he is either one twisted son of a bitch or he's a seeker or vampire. Too coincidental if you ask me."

"Interesting. Is he still hanging around?"

"No, he dumped her so I doubt he would be hanging around. Guess he isn't returning her calls or anything. Sounds like he was getting cold feet, so to speak." Selene chuckled at her own joke.

"Funny. How long will you be off the site?"

"Shouldn't be more than a couple of hours. Besides, I doubt Kevin's boss has had any time to bring in someone new and brief them. He probably is still trying to get hold of Kevin. I figure it will take him a day or two to come up with a new game plan when he can't get hold of Kevin."

"Maybe." The tension in A.J.'s voice cautioned Selene not to press her luck tonight.

"Tell you what, A.J. I'll put two of my guys on Clarissa. That way there's double coverage and, trust me, no one wants to mess with these guys. Not even you."

"I'm trusting you, Selene. If anything happens to her, you pay like Brax did. Do I make myself clear?"

"Yep. See ya tomorrow night." Selene slammed the phone down closed and got into her own car. No one threatened her. No one, and the fact that she had just let A.J. pissed her off. Smiling, she remembered the punch A.J. had taken the other night after she killed Brax. *Well she knows I still got it so....*

Chapter Twenty Six

A.J. was getting antsy as she waited for her car to arrive. Looking back at her reflection in the mirror, she smiled at the striking figure standing before her. Pulling her long black hair back into a pony tail, she studied her reflection again. Then, letting it fall loose, she looked again. Up or down? She couldn't decide which would look better. Wanting to make a statement to Clarissa, she had chosen wisely for her outfit. To fit her long frame she had selected a deep purple velvet shirt and a form fitting black leather doublet that accentuated her full breast and narrow waist. The high collar of the doublet framed her neck and face perfectly accenting her square jaw line. Even the colors A.J. picked were carefully selected. She wanted to make an impression on Clarissa that she wouldn't forget.

Looking down, she was glad she had selected the deep purple velvet Venetian pants rather than the traditional trunkhose they wore during that period. The pants fit her like a glove and gave her a slimmer look than the bags that the seamstress had shown her. She shuddered as she thought about how fat her ass would look in the sacks. She also declined the stockings that men usually wore and went with a pair of knee length black leather boots. The final negative came when the seamstress tried to convince her that if she truly wanted to be in costume she should wear the cod piece. Laughing, A.J. swiftly and sternly declined the offensive leather swatch. She wondered what men were thinking when they decided to attach something so disgusting to their trousers, but then again she was sure it had everything to do with their manliness. *Fools!* She thought.

She felt her skin tingle as she thought about finally seeing Clarissa up close. But what would she say to Clarissa? Nothing, of course. Clarissa didn't know who A.J. was really. To Clarissa, A.J. was the generous donor that had helped fund her ball. She had no idea that she would be standing in front of Alexandra, her lover from her distant past. A.J. could feel the tendrils of doubt coil in her stomach and start its insipid journey to her head. No, A.J. would control her demons tonight. This was her one chance to try and delicately reach out to her one true love and she wouldn't lose that chance. A.J. reached for her tin of capsules and stashed them in the pocket of her pants. Hopefully, she wouldn't need them tonight, but she wanted to be prepared, just in case. The last few weeks had been a rollercoaster of emotions and tonight was the culmination of that ride. A knock on the door caught A.J.'s attention. Selene stood at the door in a costume A.J. was sure was appropriate for Selene's personality.

"Guess you couldn't resist the village rogue look, huh?" Selene stood in front of A.J. in a classic renaissance shirt of royal blue, black leather pants and knee high boots that tied in the back. Wrapped around her waist was a rapier belt holding a rather sharp looking sword that A.J. was sure wouldn't be allowed in the ball.

"Well aren't you the noble man or should I say noble woman," Selene said, bowing in a low grand gesture. "I see you spared no expense, Mi Lord."

"You don't actually think they'll let you take that thing in, do you?" A.J. questioned, pointing to the sword.

"Well, if I was going in they probably wouldn't. But since I am watching from the outside, I'm not going to worry about it. Besides, I see you have a bit of protection of your own." Selene pointed to the sheathed dagger peaking out of A.J.'s boots.

"It's an adornment, I assure you."

"Yeah, well, you're going to have to practice that a whole lot more if you want them to believe it. Mi Lord." Selene made another sweeping gesture to the door and bowed her head obediently. "After you."

A.J. grabbed her half mask from the entryway table and looked down at it. The harlequin geometric pattern was painted to match the purple velvet of her shirt. She thought the purple diamond on only one side reflected her dual life and complemented her outfit well.

"Did you get one of these, Selene?" A.J. asked, holding up her mask and looking at Selene in the mirror's reflection. "I definitely don't want anyone to be able to identify you if something happens tonight." Smiling at Selene, she continued, "But your roguish good looks would be hard to miss, so try to be careful. I'm sure it will be hard to keep your mind on business 'cause if I were a guessing woman, there will be plenty of eye popping candy there tonight. All those young university girls with their tight bodices will be hard to resist." A.J. wagged her eyebrows at Selene. "So try." The playfulness was gone from A.J.'s voice as she closed the door behind them.

"I have mine in the car. It isn't quite as grand as yours, but I'm sure it will do for the evening." Selene opened the door for A.J. and climbed into the back seat facing her.

"Have you set everything up at the ball?" A.J. questioned Selene. The lights of the city flashed by as they got closer to a night A.J. hoped would be one that fantasies were made of.

"Yep. But how are you going to tell her? I mean it's been a long time, A.J., and from what you told me she doesn't even know you're alive, let alone here."

A.J. nervously rubbed her lips with her gloved hand. Selene was right. How was she going to approach Clarissa? She had thought about it over and over again and the same scenario came up, rejection. Clarissa probably thought A.J. was the same person Clarissa had known when she died, or didn't die but was changed. She didn't know what De Marcus had said to poison Clarissa against A.J. so she was going into this blind. A.J. tried to relax. Hopefully the large donation to the ball would be the starting point she needed to talk to Clarissa in private. From there she would slowly reveal herself to Clarissa. It might take days if things didn't go well tonight, but she was sure Clarissa would want to find out about the elusive A.J. Lockwood.

Chapter Twenty Seven

Clarissa fidgeted one last time with her dress, smoothing out a crease. She had waited for this night all semester, and it was finally here. The Renaissance Masquerade Ball took a year to plan and had grown into quite a fundraiser for the university. As it grew, so did its popularity with the community and the university. Each department dean and administrator attended. Originally, she had started it as a way for the students to learn about Renaissance life. Each student picked their favorite writer, sculptor, noble or someone who lived during that time and dressed appropriately. Now, it was a full-fledged dance, with a band, food and the opportunity to masquerade accordingly. It seemed that most people liked the anonymity the masquerade afforded them. She often found herself wondering who was with whom, only to find out later someone had a scandalous rendezvous that evening and no one suspected. She worried that the President might cancel each time someone was outed after the event. He made it a point to tell her what a great time he had and how he looked forward to the next year.

Making one last pass through the ballroom, she felt her excitement heighten at the coming night's events. She rarely had a date for the event, finding it too cumbersome to host and be someone's dance partner also. The energy in the room was electrifying. She couldn't put her finger on it, but she felt as if she was ready to vibrate out of her skin. The tingling she felt could only be described as, sexual, watching the guests begin to arrive. Tonight's ball included some of the most charitable donors the event had seen to date. Donors had the option of entertaining in a separate room, reserved just for them, or mingling with everyone else. The invitation made it clear. A mask was optional, but almost every guest opted for a mask of some sort. Quite a few of the women made it a point to try and outdo each other's mask. Eventually, they would be preening like birds, each greeting the other in the finest feathery, sequins and velvet she could afford. The men were not to be outdone at this event, either. The event had its fair share of Kings, musketeers, noble men and the occasional crusader. There was so much velvet and brocade stretched across hefty thighs, she was surprised a fire or two hadn't started with the rubbing that took place as the men walked.

She assigned the students their tasks for the evening, and she made one last round along the perimeter of the dance floor. The guests were arriving at a steady pace and making the several bars, strategically placed in the ballroom, their first stop. A few maids and peasants had started dancing with the nobility standing and watching the entertainment.

"Clarissa, the ballroom looks wonderful, as usual," said a regal looking gentleman.

"Why thank you, Dean Marsh. I am glad you approve. And you are looking very regal this evening. Is that a new crown?" Clarissa tried not to sound too patronizing to her boss.

"Why it's nice of you to notice. My wife bought it on that bidding website. She said I needed something new to wear this time." He pulled at the lapels of his coat. "She got this as well. How do you like it?"

"Hmm. Blue suits you. It is definitely your color." Clarissa smiled making a show of admiring his rather large expanse of a jacket.

"Well, if you will excuse me, Dean. I see one of the donors over there and I would like to thank them for attending and for their contribution. Have a wonderful evening and please give your wife my best, won't you?"

"I will. Hurry off now and make sure that generous donor knows how much we appreciate his support," Dean Marsh said, making a motion of shooing her away.

Clarissa hesitated for a moment wanting to correct Dean Marsh, but rethought her decision. He wouldn't care whether the head of Knight-Pharmaceutical was a man or a woman, just as long as they kept donating to the university.

"I'll do my best," Clarissa said, walking towards the door.

Clarissa made it to the archway of the hall and she felt herself suddenly become lightheaded. Not wanting to make a scene, she retreated to a dark portion of the hall to conceal herself. Her skin tingled and she felt the hair on her neck straighten as she sat in a brocade chair under the stairs. Assessing herself, she realized she didn't feel sick. Just the opposite, she felt as though a lover had caressed her, softly, alongside her neck. Her chest tightened as she felt the sensation again. This time, a stroke ran along her breasts. Her nipples tightened against the brocade fabric. She had opted not to wear a bra tonight, due to the tight fit of her dress. The bustier that was sewn in was more than enough support, but now she wished she had opted for one more layer of fabric to cover her quickly hardening nipples. Sitting straighter, she arched her back in hopes of alleviating some of the tightness in her chest. It only added to the pressure on her already sensitive nipples. A deep breath, followed by another, and she stood hoping to regain her composure. She needed to be alert and fully functioning tonight, but this was more than she needed. Standing, another sensation rippled through her. Now she couldn't tell if she was over-stimulated from the excitement of the evening, or if it was something else. She was starting to feel like she did when she left the bar weeks ago and that wasn't good. *No, it has to be all the excitement,* she told herself, *it is all that pent-up excitement and energy that comes with this event,* she reasoned.

Slowly, she forced herself to relax and focus on what needed to be done and that was greeting the arriving guests. The night was early and she had lots of work to do before she could fully relax. Entering the entryway of the ballroom, she felt the soft caress against her check again. Looking around, she tried to see if she recognized anyone. Anyone like her, but she didn't see a familiar face. Not that she would have been able to, with all the feathers and masks adorning the guests.

"Good evening, President Woods. Thank you for coming." Clarissa smiled demurely, bowing her head slightly.

"How did you know it was me, Clarissa?" President Woods shook the offered hand firmly, before introducing his partner. "My wife, Shirley."

"Pleasure to meet you, Mrs. Woods. Well, sir, you are a rather tall man, and it would be hard to miss you, even with your mask." Clarissa smiled and swept her hand towards the ballroom.

"Enjoy your evening, sir." Turning towards his wife, Clarissa spoke softly, "you better watch out for him, Mrs. Woods. He looks rather dashing tonight." Clarissa winked, shaking her hand.

Clarissa stood there for a few moments more, realizing there would be no way for her to know who the donors were with their masks on. So, she made her way to the donor's private room. There, she would be able to thank them personally and introduce herself to any new donors who might be attending. She had stashed the gift she purchased for Ms. Lockwood behind the bar, hoping she would have a private moment to give it to the woman. She could hardly contain her excitement at the thought of finally being able to meet her benefactor. She had to remind herself that Ms. Lockwood was a professional and not someone to be gushed over. Now Carol, Clarissa knew, would gush all over the woman, making a scene that would take a lot of apologizing on Clarissa's behalf to fix. No, Clarissa would handle Ms. Lockwood privately.

Entering the room, she looked around and found no one. As she turned, something caught her eye on the marble table by the window. A rose. That hadn't been there when she set the room up earlier. Walking over, she noticed a card laying across it, addressed to her. Picking up the card, she felt a soft breath caress her neck. Turning, she anticipated seeing someone behind her, but there was no one. Returning to the card, she gently spread the flap open and the delicate scent of perfume drifted from inside the envelope. The fragrance was familiar and yet it wasn't. Slowly, she pulled the card free from the envelope, its face blank. Opening it, the recognizable ink of a fountain pen wrote a simple note in French. Without a second thought, Clarissa read the French easily. Something she hadn't done in decades:

Clarissa,

Votre beauté est davantage que les seuls mots peuvent exprimer. J'espère que vous accepterez cette rose simple comme expression de mon intérêt en finissant par vous connaître.

Respect

Clarissa,

Your beauty is more than mere words can express. I hope you will accept this simple rose as an expression of my interest in getting to know you.

Regards,

Clarissa turned the card around to see if it had a signature, but there wasn't one. Looking at the writing, she felt a vague prick of recognition, but couldn't place it.

Clarissa picked up the rose and inhaled its heady aroma, looking around once more to see if anyone lingered in the room. Clarissa closed her eyes, caressing her lips with the rose, and breathed in the soft floral scent. Her eyes popped open, and she looked down at the rose. It wasn't just any rose from a flower shop. This rose was one of her favorites found only in France when she was a child. The *Alba semi Plana*, a white rose with large petals had been in France since the sixteenth century. *Coincidence*, thought Clarissa as she remembered picking the beautiful flower for her mother when she walked in their garden. She had cherished those moments with her mother, and realized she missed her. Remembering wasn't a good thing. Not now, not when she had so much to do tonight. Who would have known this was her favorite rose? It had to be a coincidence. No one knew her favorite flowers, and she never got that close to anyone anymore. Clarissa took a sharp breath as she remembered seeing the same rose in the stained glass feature at Knight-Pharmaceutical. Lately, her life had been a series of coincidences, and she didn't like it. But right now she couldn't think about it all. She had a job to do and then she would try and put an order to those coincidences. As she looked around the room one more time she felt the energy again, the tingle mixed with electricity coursing through her body. *Something isn't right, something is very, very off,* she thought as she made her way to the door and back to the ballroom.

A.J. stood on the terrace watching Clarissa place the card back into the envelope and tuck it into her bodice. The rose earned a place tucked securely behind her ear. Standing in the shadows Clarissa hadn't seen her, but A.J. knew she felt her. She had slowly caressed Clarissa's neck in her mind, knowing she would feel it. They had been that connected before, and she was glad to see that they still were. A.J. adjusted her doublet and ran a hand over her hair smoothing it back. Signaling to Selene to park the limo, she slipped her mask over her face. On the one hand, she hoped Clarissa didn't recognize her. Yet on the other, she hoped for the possibility to sweep her off her feet and that the short note and rose had set her up for just that.

A.J. pulled her invitation to the ball from inside her jacket and watched others make their way through the receiving line. The line was long and slow with each guest being announced and welcomed with a personal thank you and small party chatter. From her vantage point, she could watch as Clarissa stepped to the back of the line and waited for each guest, shaking their hand and welcoming them with an enchanting smile. A.J. handed her invitation to the announcer and watched Clarissa as he announced her arrival.

"Ms. A.J. Lockwood."

###

Clarissa felt one of her students, Shirley, tug on her sleeve and lean over to whisper in her ear.

"Professor, I think that's the donor we have been wondering about. The one that made the hundred thousand dollar gift, renewable every year if certain conditions were met, remember?"

Turning her head towards the announcer, Clarissa tried to sneak a peek at the elusive donor. Her mask hid any possibility of being recognized so Clarissa turned her gaze back to the patron in front of her smiling sweetly. Her hand trembled slightly as she shook his.

"Thanks, John, for coming. We appreciate your support for the event. Please let me know if there is anything you need tonight." Clarissa felt her hands tremble more as she released his.

Slowly, guests made their way down to Clarissa until finally; she was face-to-face with her anonymous donor.

Shirley spoke-up first, "Welcome tonight, Ms. Lockwood. This is Professor Graham, the hostess for this event. Can I say how much we appreciate your support for the ball? I would love to thank you personally if you have time later in the week."

"Shirley, please. I am sure Ms. Lockwood is a busy

woman," Clarissa said, as A.J. stood directly in front of her. "Thank you for your support this evening. You don't know how much we appreciate it, especially in this economy." Clarissa felt a charge run through her body as A.J. clasped both of her hands in hers. Her eyes meeting A.J.'s, she felt herself being pulled into a warmth she hadn't experienced in centuries.

"Are you alright, Ms. Graham?" a low rumbling voice asked.

Clarissa's head was swimming. She felt herself begin to tremble as the electricity wound its way through her body. Arching an eyebrow, she looked back at A.J. and smiled weakly.

"I'm sorry. Do we know each other?" she asked, trying to release her hand from the strong embrace. *I am being held, aren't I?*, she thought, closing her eyes and taking a deep breath to steady herself.

"No, I don't think we have met, here." A.J. reluctantly released Clarissa's hand, a slow smile crossing her face. Clarissa noticed her twinkling blue eyes and felt like she was being enchanted by the exchange.

Clarissa let her gaze roam over the statuesque woman standing before her. The purple and black accentuated her features in such a way that Clarissa could almost imagine what lay behind the harlequin mask. The tight leather left little to the imagination and her gaze traveled lower wondering what lay beyond the velvet and leather. A blush crept up Clarissa's neck and she lowered her head looking at her own gown, trying to avoid A.J.'s gaze.

"I couldn't help but notice your rose. It's beautiful." Trying to redirect the conversation somewhere else, A.J. looked at both women.

"Someone left it for her. Romantic huh?" Shirley

piped in before Clarissa could answer.

"Indeed. Very romantic." A.J. smiled at Shirley.

"Yeah, we're trying to figure out which guy it is," Shirley said, looking around the room. "I told Ms. G he'll probably show up when she least expects it."

"Well, I hope that it isn't someone dangerous, don't you?" A.J. said, looking directly at Clarissa.

"We have security everywhere. So if someone does something stupid, we'll get 'em." Shirley's animated demeanor made A.J. chuckle.

"I am sure Ms. Lockwood would like to mingle. I noticed you're alone, but there were two tickets in the envelope. Will you be meeting someone here?" Clarissa suddenly found herself disappointed at the possibility.

"Yes, I hope to. Well, thank you, ladies, for the engaging conversation. I look forward to speaking with you another time. If you will please excuse me, I think I'll find a drink." A.J. smiled and bowed slightly towards Clarissa. Slowly, she raised Clarissa's hand to her lips and gently placed a kiss near her knuckles and then turned it over and kissed her wrist. "I hope the night is a great success." Turning, A.J. walked towards the crowd that was forming in the ballroom.

Clarissa felt as if her skin were on fire from the touch. The softness of Ms. Lockwood's lips lingered on her wrist and she felt herself sway a bit.

"Professor, are you alright? Should I get you some water?" Shirley's wide eyes and shocked expression almost made Clarissa laugh.

Steadying herself, Clarissa found it hard to respond. Her body ached for another touch of those lips and yet she didn't know why. As she turned to watch Ms. Lockwood walk in to the growing crowd in the ballroom, she quietly answered, "No, I'm fine."

"Wow, I've never seen someone kiss a woman's hand like that. Let alone another woman. That was hot! Gosh, I wonder what she looks like under that mask."

"Shirley!"

"What? I'm just saying, with a killer body like that, hopefully she isn't a paper or plastic kind of girl."

"What? Paper or plastic? What in heaven's name do you mean?" Clarissa exhaled shaking her head.

"You know, as in bags, paper or plastic. The kind you put over someone's head when you have sex with 'em. You know, 'cause it would kill the moment."

"Oh my god. Are you kidding me? Okay, stop already. I can't believe you."

"What?" Shrugging her shoulders, Shirley laughed, "I'm just joking. Besides, did you see that body? She is a goddess, and I want to worship at her alter."

"Okay, that's enough, Ms. Hormone. I expect you to behave tonight. Understand?" Clarissa said, giving Shirley a disapproving glare.

"Fine, I'm just saying—"

"Stop now, or leave. It's your choice." Clarissa glanced at the retreating back of their newest donor and smiled. Clarissa had to agree, what little she could see was definitely sending something through her. Clarissa's body thrummed again remembering the softness of Ms. Lockwood's hands as they pulled her slightly towards the woman. The softness of her lips as they caressed her wrist. The blue eyes, though, had sent a chill through Clarissa. She felt as if she had been lost in them before. The square jaw and long black hair gave few clues to what laid under the mask, but maybe tonight when she presented Ms. Lockwood with the gift she had purchased, Clarissa would see her unmasked.

Chapter Twenty Eight

A.J. disappeared into the crowd and turned back to watch Clarissa unobserved. She had practically attacked Clarissa when she kissed her hand. She had felt herself start to lose control when Clarissa's perfume drifted up into her nostrils, clouding her ability to think clearly. A.J. couldn't believe she had done something as intimate as kiss Clarissa's wrist, and right in front of everyone, too. This was going to be a long night if she didn't regain control of herself and soon. The room was starting to swell as A.J. made her way to the bar.

"Scotch, neat," she informed the bartender. Hopefully, a drink would relax her and she wouldn't have to resort to her "safety" pill. Swirling the amber liquid, A.J. remembered the softness of Clarissa's wrist. It had been a long time since she had kissed a woman there, and the last woman she had done that to was standing fifty yards away from her. A.J. was starting to feel penned in, like an animal going to slaughter. The noise, the bodies and all that blood pumping around her was starting to assault her senses. She needed air and quick before something unplanned happened.

A.J. noticed a door at the other end of the room, the room Clarissa had been in earlier. So, she weaved her way through the crowd, reaching it just as she felt a hand on her shoulder stopping her progress.

"Excuse me, but aren't you Ms. Lockwood of

Knight-Pharmaceuticals?" A masculine voice asked as he turned her towards him.

A.J. cringed. She had almost made it without a problem, but no such luck. Smiling her best smile, she looked up at the rather tall man standing before her. "Yes, yes I am. How can I help you?"

"Well, I would say you already have." Sticking his hand out to shake, he continued, "I'm President Richard Woods. President of the university?"

"I see. Nice to meet you, President Woods," A.J. said, shaking the president's hand. She wasn't in the mood to chit-chat so she didn't say anything else.

"I wanted to personally thank you for helping Professor Graham with your generous donation for this event. I know you've made healthy contributions to our science labs and we are looking forward to making great strides in the research you're funding. So…" Clearly A.J. wasn't helping further the conversation and President Woods wasn't much for platitudes so he stood for a minute more before continuing, "Well, I just wanted to say thank you again, Ms. Lockwood."

"If you'll excuse me, President Woods, I am finding it a bit stuffy in here and I'm afraid that I might pass out. Now that wouldn't look good, would it?" Walking past him, she went to an open window and gulped several deep breaths before she felt calm. She hated being rude, it wasn't something she did regularly, but she was afraid that she wouldn't be able to control herself much longer if she didn't get away from all the bodies squished together and all that blood pounding in her ears. The energy in the room was almost more than she could bare and add touching Clarissa to the equation and she was on overload.

"Psst."

A.J. practically jumped out of her skin when she heard the sound.

"Relax, it's just me." Selene edged out of the darkness of the shadow and peered into the room. "Anyone in there with you?"

"No. It's clear. What's up?"

Looking at A.J.'s glass and then back up at A.J. she asked, "Hey, why don't you bring me one of those. That bar over there is fully stocked and I'm thirsty. You don't want me going out and finding something to drink, do you?"

Smirking at the darkened Selene, A.J. responded, "No, I don't want you finding something to drink, or someone to keep you company. Here, take mine." A.J. handed the drink through an opening Selene had cut in the screen. "Could you please not damage the property here?"

"What?" Selene shrugged her shoulders then reminded her, "You just gave them one hundred thousand bucks. You don't think they can replace a screen? Geez." A.J. watched as Selene leaned further into the shadows. Suddenly A.J. heard a spurt and then a cough.

"Geez, what is this shit? It tastes like ass. You drink that crap?" Handing A.J. back the drink, Selene wiped her mouth on the cuff of her shirt. "God, when did you start drinking ass? Yuck."

"Knock it off. It isn't that bad. Besides, it's an acquired taste."

"Yeah, I guess you lick enough ass you can acquire a taste for it."

A.J. raised her eyebrows and pinched her lips together. Selene was starting to get on that last nerve she had saved for the stupid people at the party. Now she would waste it on Selene if she wasn't careful. "Look, you want something else to drink or are you just gonna bitch?"

"Red wine." Selene raised her nose in the air and sniffed.

"Oh, knock it off. God, Selene, you're so dramatic."

"Someone's here." A.J. saw Selene's back straighten and all joking was gone in her eyes.

"Where?"

"I don't know. I'll be back. You better go find Clarissa, now."

A.J. practically ran to the door and scanned the room looking for Clarissa. The crowd had grown and now it would be harder to find her if she wasn't at the front receiving guests. Looking at the entrance, the receiving line had ended and only a few security people stood there. Another scan of the room came up empty. A.J. needed another way to find out where Clarissa was and fast. She closed her eyes and let her mind start to look for her.

###

Clarissa worked her way around the large dance floor and to the bar at the far end of the room. The dance floor was so crowded that people were starting to bump into each other and the vibration of the music coursed through Clarissa's body as she stepped past a huge speaker. Letting her eyes roam the room, she searched for one mask in particular, but it was the proverbial needle in a haystack. While no one had the purple and black geometric mask, everyone had something on and it was harder than Clarissa thought it would be searching for A.J. Finally, the band played a softer, slow song, and Clarissa's heart started beating slower, too. A hand on her shoulder stopped her dead in her tracks.

A low throaty voice caressed her ear. "Ms. Graham, would you do me the honor?" A hand extended as she turned towards the sultry invitation. Taking the offering, Clarissa looked up into the purple and black mask she had been searching for.

"Ms. Lockwood, I'm not sure I should. I mean…" Clarissa stammered as A.J.'s touch sent a chill through her body. "I mean as the hostess, I'm responsible for the guests and well…"

"I understand."

Clarissa watched A.J. turn and start walking towards the doors of the hall. "Wait."

She couldn't believe she almost let A.J. leave. Clarissa planned for this moment for the past two nights and now A.J. was right in front of her asking her to dance. What was she thinking? Slipping her hand into the crook of A.J.'s arm, she halted her progress to the door, "I would love to dance, but I have to warn you, I'm not that good," lying, she smiled. Clarissa hoped that she could convince A.J. to follow her into the VIP lounge so she could convey her thanks and give her the small token of her appreciation.

Clarissa felt herself pulled into A.J.'s tight embrace and gently guided around the dance floor. Many had decided to sit this one out and so the swelling ranks of dancers had dwindled to just several pairs. Clarissa felt as if thunder were rumbling through her body, her hips making closer contact with her partner.

"Ms. Lockwood—"

"Please, call me A.J."

Clarissa looked up into the mask that hid her

dance partner's features watching her eyes crease slightly in the corners as she smiled at Clarissa. A touch on her lower back sent tingles throughout Clarissa's body, and she closed her eyes absorbing the energy. Nipples hardened as Clarissa was pulled closer into A.J.'s embrace. Her body was reacting so easily to A.J.'s touch she thought she might have to pull away to relieve the pressure, to douse the fire that was coursing through her. Yet, Clarissa couldn't move. She found herself expertly guided around the dance floor, her feet barely touching the floor, or so she thought.

"Your rose, it's beautiful. I've only seen it one other place..." Clarissa heard the soft intake of breath as A.J. gently sniffed the rose. "It looks beautiful on you, Ms. Graham."

"Please, call me Clarissa." Clarissa smiled back at her dance partner, slowing getting lost in beautiful soft eyes.

"Of course."

Clarissa felt as if her skin was on fire everywhere A.J. touched her. Closing her eyes she felt as if someone was caressing her, a soft stroke brushing the side of her breast and then her cheek. As she melted into the caresses, Clarissa's body started to respond. Her clit tightened and then hardened, her legs trembled and a tremor shook her body. She started to feel lightheaded, her body reacting to the gentle sensations. A slight stumble caused her to grasp A.J.'s strong arms to steady herself. A soft, low moan escaped Clarissa's lips as she rested her head on A.J.'s broad shoulder.

"I'm sorry, I don't know what's come over me," she whispered softly against her dance partner's neck.

Clarissa felt A.J. release her tight hold on her body. Putting some distance between them, A.J. whispered.

"Clarissa, has anyone told you how beautiful you look in that dress?" Clarissa blushed at the question and lowered her head. "I'm sorry. I didn't mean to embarrass you, but you're breathtaking."

"You're very kind, thank you."

The question had been asked in French and Clarissa responded, without realizing, in her native tongue. Surprised, Clarissa looked back up into A.J.'s eyes, and then touched the rose in her hair. Confused, she waited. For what, she wasn't sure, but something was very familiar in the way A.J. held her. Slow tendrils of energy started to surge through her body, A.J.s warm breath falling on her neck. A thought crept into her mind, *please don't be afraid.* Clarissa jerked her head up and stared into the smile that lingered on A.J.'s lips. She had heard the voice and yet nothing was spoken out loud. It had been years since she had heard another voice like that, in fact centuries. A panic rolled through Clarissa's body, she needed to get out of there and yet she felt trapped, almost secure, in A.J.'s arms. Clarissa was thankful that her mask hid the panic that she felt, yet she was sure if A.J. studied her long enough, her eyes would give her away.

"Please, allow me to escort you to the lounge. I think you need some air. Besides, I believe you have something for me? Yes? After that, I'm afraid I must leave."

Clarissa felt herself being guided towards the VIP lounge, but yet she didn't try to struggle. As panic started to shred her logical mind, her heart raced at the idea of being alone with A.J. Lockwood.

Chapter Twenty Nine

A.J. had heard the soft moan Clarissa released when she caressed her. She wondered if their connection was still intact and the moan confirmed it, but she chastised herself for speaking to Clarissa in French. It had shown her hand and perhaps Clarissa had figured out she had left the note and rose. Pulling Clarissa into the room, A.J. closed the doors and leaned back against them watching Clarissa try to steady her breathing. At least A.J. wasn't the only one trying to compose herself.

Clarissa was the first to speak, trying to break the tension in the room. "Would you like something to drink Ms. Lockwood?"

A.J. winced at the use of her formal name. Clearly Clarissa was trying to distance herself from what had happened outside.

"Hmm." A.J. turned the lock on the door before advancing towards Clarissa.

"We have a fully stocked bar. I mean it's the least we can do for such a generous donation as yours. Perhaps a glass of wine or perhaps—"

"Ms. Graham." A.J. stood in front of Clarissa reaching for her hands.

"Clarissa. Please call me Clarissa." Clarissa refused to meet A.J.'s glance and A.J. felt the tension return to Clarissa's body.

"All right, Clarissa. I apologize for my comments

on the dance floor. I've offended you." A.J. took her hands and held them tightly in her own. She wished Clarissa hadn't worn a mask so she could see her face. It had been so long since A.J. had seen her that she wasn't sure she could wait much longer. A.J. guided Clarissa to the couch, never letting go of Clarissa's hands. "I don't know what's come over me. Perhaps, it's being around so many people, the music, or the lovely company, but again I apologize for my inappropriate comments. However, you are very striking in that dress." A.J. felt Clarissa try to pull her hands free, so she let them go. She didn't want Clarissa to run away before they had a chance to talk.

"Ms.—"

A.J. lifted a finger and touched Clarissa's lips. "Remember? You said you would call me A.J." A.J. looked at Clarissa imploringly.

"A.J., can I offer you something to drink?"

"If you'll have something with me? Then I'll leave you alone to do your hosting duties." Smiling, Clarissa nodded and then went to the bar retrieving two glasses and a bottle of champagne.

"I hope this is alright. I had it delivered special for our honored guests." Clarissa handed the glasses to A.J. then tried to open the champagne bottle with little success.

"Please allow me." A.J. popped the champagne easily and slowly filled both glasses and watched as Clarissa tried to return her smile. It was clear to A.J. that she was going to have to talk fast if she wanted to reconnect even just a little with her former lover. A.J. sat once again and offered up her glass in a toast. "Please, allow me. Thank you for dancing with me and for an enchanted evening."

"I think I should be the one to thank you. If it weren't for you, we wouldn't be able to have this event. So," Clarissa tipped her glass towards A.J., "I'm in your debt."

A.J. swallowed the amber liquid slowly allowing it to rest on her palette and give her time to study Clarissa. Clarissa lowered her glass and twirled the stem between her fingers studying the swirling liquid. A.J. cleared her throat and watched soft pools of green look back at her. The tip of Clarissa's tongue darted out, wetting her top lip. If she didn't know better, A.J. would have guessed that Clarissa was flirting with her, but she recognized the nervous reaction. Sitting so close to Clarissa was starting to have an effect on A.J.'s body. Her heart raced and the demon that had been dormant was starting its slow ascent throughout her body. It was hard not to notice Clarissa's pulse speed up, sending off waves of sexual energy. A.J. crossed her legs hoping to stave off the tingling that had started to spread to her clit. A.J. took another sip of the sour champagne hoping that it would dull her over-stimulated senses.

"Do you have scotch back there by any chance?" A.J said, nodding towards the bar. "I'm not much of a champagne drinker."

"Of course, please allow me."

A.J. took advantage of the opportunity to study Clarissa again when she walked away from her. She looked almost the same as she had when A.J. had first met her in Paris. Her soft brunette hair was up, but stray strands hung in ringlets around her face. Her long slender neck took A.J. back to a time when they had first kissed.

Alexandra stood behind Clarissa, pointing to features on her country estate. Clarissa's perfume, mixed with the heat of the night, gave Clarissa an alluring, almost hypnotic aroma. Alexandra heard a flutter from Clarissa as her lips brushed against the slender neck. It was almost as if she was offering Alexandra an opportunity and yet Alexandra knew it was an innocent act.

"I'm sorry, I couldn't resist. Your beauty is overwhelming me, and I couldn't control my actions. Please—"

Clarissa turned and pressed a finger against Alexandra's lips.

"Shh."

Alexandra lowered her lips to those that beckoned for a kiss. The softness sent Alexandra reeling as she deepened the kiss. Clarissa's tongue speared into Alexandra's mouth causing her to gasp, but only stopping for a second before she returned with her own gently probing kisses. Alexandra cupped Clarissa's face, her fingers slipping into her hair and releasing it from its confines. The strands fell loosely around Clarissa's face, framing it seductively. Alexandra molded her body against Clarissa's as her thumbs stroked soft, delicate cheeks. It took everything she had not to lower her lips to the throbbing vein under her palm and taste Clarissa, but she had promised and the promise was getting harder and harder to keep. Pulling away, Alexandra looked in the green eyes that swam with an undercurrent of lust. She watched as Clarissa turned her head and sucked in a thumb, sending a jolt through Alexandra's body.

"You're playing with fire, my love. You're delicate lips beg me to do other things and I've already gone further than I wanted. Please spare me further transgressions. I'm not sure I'll be able to control myself if we continue." Alexandra lowered her forehead to Clarissa's and took a long, slow, deep breath.

"Alexandra..." just hearing Clarissa say her name made her knees weak. "Surely, we both knew this day would come. I've thought about it for weeks."

Alexandra felt a feather light kiss on her palm and then Clarissa pressed her hand to her breast. "I ache for your touch. I've thought of nothing else when I'm alone. Please release me from my internal torture. Please."

Alexandra saw the pleading in Clarissa's eyes and trembled at the request. Would she be able to just stop when Clarissa was satisfied or would she take it too far and let her demon loose to do its own bidding?

"Please."

A.J. felt a tap on her arm as she wandered back from her memory. A short glass was held in front of her and she looked up into Clarissa's puzzled eyes.

"Are you all right, A.J.? You looked as though you were a million miles away just now."

How could she put into words where she had actually gone without driving Clarissa away? How would she explain her own presence here, at the masquerade ball? Taking the glass, she smiled and took a long sip. The liquid burned as it went down, but she needed to set her mind back on course.

"Thank you." A.J. noticed a wrapped item sitting next to Clarissa on the couch. Looking at it and then back to Clarissa she took another sip of the single malt scotch. "Well, I should leave you to your other guests. I've taken far too much of your time." Standing, she felt Clarissa's hand gently tug on her sleeve.

"Before you go, I've wanted to say thank you appropriately. I hope you don't mind." Clarissa motioning to the couch. "Please won't you sit for a moment longer?"

The gentle request sent a chill through A.J. and

she licked her lips and took a deep breath. She was afraid she didn't have much time before either she or Clarissa was fighting the change. Reaching into her pocket she extracted her tin of safety pills and popped two and slid them under her tongue. A questioning glance made A.J. respond.

"Ah, I have a condition that I need to take medication for. Nothing serious," A.J. said sitting back on the couch. "So, I assume what you have there is for me?" A.J. questioned.

"Well, the last time I was at Knight-Pharmaceutical I asked your assistant about getting something for you as a thank you for the generous donation you made to the university." Clarissa fidgeted with an errant string on her dress before she looked back up at A.J. "She said that you enjoyed black and white photography so..."

A.J. grasped Clarissa's hands to steady them and stop the fidgeting, but it only caused her body to tighten when she slowly started to caress Clarissa's palms. "And so you have?"

"Well, I stumbled into a gallery. Well, not really stumbled, but I happened to see this photograph and it touched something in me. I know that sounds strange, but it spoke to me. Reminding me of another time in my life and well..."

"Clarissa," A.J. lifted Clarissa's chin and continued, "is that the photograph?" A.J. asked, looking at the wrapped item sitting next to her.

"Yes. Please accept this with my humblest thanks. I hope it speaks to you, the way it speaks to me." Clarissa said. A sudden reticence descended over her when she passed A.J. the wrapped photograph.

Tearing through the wrapping a slight gasp escaped her lips.

"It's beautiful," A.J. said, stiffening when she recognized the landscape. She looked back at Clarissa wondering if she realized where the photograph was taken. It was close to where they had both lived in Paris. Perhaps Clarissa was testing A.J.? Waiting for something further from Clarissa and seeing nothing, she whispered, "It's stunning, just stunning, Clarissa."

Clarissa smiled while A.J. pulled the photograph closer to inspect it. The photographer had to be a vampire, the dusky tone of the photograph and then lack of civilization gave away its origins.

"Do you know who the photographer was?"

"No, the gallery owner didn't know, but assured me it was worth more than the purchase price."

Quickly turning towards Clarissa, A.J. questioned her again, "I hope you didn't pay too much for this? I would never forgive myself if you're left penniless because you purchased a gift for me."

"I assure you, A.J., the college pays its faculty well enough that I could afford the photograph. Besides, I wanted to show my appreciation. I hope I have." Clarissa smiled demurely at A.J. The desired affect wasn't lost on A.J.

"You have. Now, may I make a small request?"

Chapter Thirty

Selene peeked in through the screen and watched as A.J. and Clarissa talked. She had finally talked to someone associated with the Coven, and now Selene needed to let A.J. know what she found out. It was clear, looking at the two women on the couch, that something deeper was transpiring, and Selene hated to break up the reunion. Sticking her finger through the screen, she wiggled it at A.J. hoping it would catch her attention before she had to do something a little drastic.

"Come on, look over here ya big lust bag." Selene watched A.J. stare into Clarissa's eyes, her gaze never wavering. A few more fingers through the screen and she practically had her hand through it. Waving it back and forth, Selene still couldn't capture A.J.'s attention. Extracting her hand, she saw Clarissa cover her heart and swoon slightly. A.J. quickly knelt next to Clarissa and wrapped her arms around her.

"Smooth, Romeo." Selene felt her pulse quicken when A.J. threaded her hands into Clarissa's hair and kissed her. "Some women have all the luck, and I'm the one who's supposed to stay focused. Right."

Clearing her throat, Selene retreated back into the shadow of the porch and waited until A.J. was finished, which turned out to be quickly since both women had heard Selene. She rested her back against the wall as the voyeur in her tingled.

"Selene."

A.J. was at the window, the tone of her voice definitely bemoaning her displeasure at being interrupted.

"Sorry, Romeo, but we need to talk, now." Selene looked into the room and noticed that Clarissa looked more like a scared mouse than a dismayed lover. "I just got off the phone with someone at the Coven, and you're not going to like what I found out. She okay?" Nodding her head at Clarissa, Selene noticed A.J. didn't look over shoulder.

"I was just getting ready to find out, 'til you interrupted."

"Well, when you leave she has to come, too. She isn't safe anywhere, anymore." Selene looked into A.J.'s eyes and wished the screen and the darkness didn't hide her expression. She would have to rely on her ability to be persuasive in convincing A.J. that whatever her plans for a slow reconcile would have to be sped up or dashed permanently. "De Marcus is alive."

"What? Fuck!" Selene watched as A.J.'s knees weakened and she grabbed the sill for support.

"Look, we can protect her, but she needs to either leave the party with me or you tonight. Your choice." Selene saw Clarissa get up and start to walk towards A.J. "She's coming. I'll be in the car, waiting. She has you to protect her in here so you don't need me. But she needs to leave with one of us tonight." Looking at A.J. it was clear she was unsettled by the news. "Do you understand what I'm telling you, A.J.?"

"Yeah." Shaking her head she whispered, "give me about thirty minutes."

"A.J."

"Selene." The menacing tone slid over Selene and

she let it slide.

"Okay." With that, Selene was gone.

A.J. grasped the sides of the window and took a deep breath. Once again, De Marcus had ruined her plans with Clarissa. A.J. had to think fast or her world would be upside down again because of him. A soft touch in the middle of her back caught her attention.

"A.J., I'm sorry. I know that wasn't the reaction you wanted. I mean, I would be lying if I said that I wasn't attracted to you, but I barely know you. I feel like I've met you before but—"

"Clarissa, please don't apologize. It's my fault. I'm pushing things too fast. I'm used to getting what I want and, well…" A.J. let the words die on her lips turning and reaching for both of Clarissa's hands. "Time is not our friend at the moment."

A.J. smiled and pulled Clarissa away from the window. She didn't want anyone hearing their conversation, but more importantly she didn't want to risk Clarissa's safety if someone was waiting for an opportunity. A.J. watched as a puzzled expression crossed Clarissa's face.

"I don't understand."

"Please sit down and let me explain." Confused, Clarissa sat on the couch. A.J. knelt in front of her. "Clarissa, I've looked for someone like you my whole life. In fact, many years ago I thought I had found someone like you, but she was taken from me." A.J.'s thumbs caressed the backs of soft hands as she looked down at them.

"Oh, A.J. I'm so sorry for your loss."

A.J. reached up and started to untie Clarissa's mask. Clarissa tried to stop her, but A.J. smiled and whispered, "Please."

She hadn't forgotten how beautiful Clarissa was, but it had been so long since she had seen her this close, she wanted to cry. Holding back tears, A.J. reached up and framed Clarissa's face with her hands. *You're so beautiful,* thought A.J., gently stroking the beautiful face with her thumbs.

"Who are you?" Clarissa's pleaded.

"I'll explain everything, if you promise me you won't run." A.J. watched Clarissa's heart beat speed up. She could feel Clarissa tense under her touch and ran her hands down the frightened woman's arms. Grasping her hands, she continued, "Have you ever loved someone so much you would give your life for that person?"

Clarissa nodded her head and looked down at their joined hands. Whispering, she said, "I have. Once, a long time ago, but things changed and there wasn't anything I could do about it." A small tear trickled down Clarissa's face, unsettling A.J.

"Clarissa, I need you to do me another favor. Take my mask off for me." Clarissa sat and looked at her. Another pleading whisper escaped A.J.'s lips, "Please, don't be afraid."

Time seemed to stand still while A.J. waited for Clarissa's hands to do her bidding. She watched Clarissa bite her lower lip and then, finally, reach up to the ties that kept A.J.'s mask in place. A.J.'s heart was pounding so loudly she was sure Clarissa could hear her own fear. She could take anything right now, but rejection. Never in her wildest dreams did she think she would be sitting in the same room as Clarissa. So a few minutes of apprehension was a small price to pay to reconnect with her one true love. As the mask started to fall, A.J. lowered her head and raised Clarissa's hands to bury her face in the soft caress of her palms. Gentle kisses covered the delicate fingers and she started to cry. She felt Clarissa's fingers cup her chin and raise it.

"Please don't cry, A.J. I'm sure you're...." The words trailed off when Clarissa got her first glimpse of A.J.'s face. "Alexandra."

Chapter Thirty One

Gulping for breath, Clarissa felt as though she had been punched in the stomach. How could it be? She had cradled the crying face of Alexandra Locke and now staring at her were the most beautiful, sad blue eyes. The silence was stifling and all Clarissa could think about was running away from this murderer. Afraid to move she sat still as a statue, scared that if she didn't Alexandra might hurt her. And yet, the pain in Alexandra's eyes told a different truth. As tears streamed down Alexandra's face, Clarissa resisted the urge to wipe them way. She was afraid that if she touched her lover from the past, she might melt into her arms, and yet this was the woman that had killed her family. Clarissa's emotion battled within her, the longing for Alexandra to touch her, kiss her, as she had done in the past, was at war with the pain of losing her family at Alexandra's hands.

"You murdered my family. Why?" Clarissa's soft tone hid the undercurrent of emotion that was starting to well up inside her.

"What?"

Clarissa was taken aback by the shocked look on Alexandra's face. She hadn't prepared herself for a meeting with Alexandra, ever. Now she was face to face with the killer she had always known Alexandra to be.

"You heard me. Why Alexandra? Why my family? Was your grief at losing me so strong that you had to take it out on them?" Clarissa stiffened with each word trying to control the turmoil she could feel working inside her body. If she changed now, she didn't care. She was face to face with a monster and perhaps it would take another monster to exorcise Alexandra from her mind completely. "I loved you like I've never loved before or since. I gave everything to be with you and that is how you repaid me, by murdering my family?"

Alexandra bowed her head, resting her hands on each side of Clarissa's legs. Clarissa felt the rage flow off Alexandra as she watched her hands begin to tremble. Confused, she once again reached down and lifted Alexandra's chin to face her. She wasn't going to let Alexandra get away with trying to intimated her or leave without an explanation. She, too, had strength, and she wasn't afraid of Alexandra Locke. While she hadn't sought her out for revenge, she also knew that this meeting would never have taken place if she had her way. Clarissa had learned to deal with her hatred for Alexandra. It was tucked into nice little box she kept packed away in the back of her mind. It was the only way she survived it. But now it seems the box wanted to be open and she could feel the hatred spilling out of what was now an open wound.

"Answer me," Clarissa said with so much venom it slapped Alexandra across the face. And then she couldn't hold back. Fists pummeled Alexandra with such fury that A.J. only sat there stunned by the punishment. Blow after blow assailed her and yet she took them. Clarissa's onslaught slowed when she realized that Alexandra wasn't defending herself. A stinging slap across Alexandra's face brought clarity to Clarissa and she immediately recoiled. Shamed by the attack, she lowered her head and whispered, "Answer me."

###

A.J. sat stunned at the accusation. The beating she could handle, but the accusations floored her. Her tongue had lost all ability to function and she just stared into angry green eyes that looked like they would stake her where she knelt. Trying to put two and two together as quickly as she could, a slow rage began to build in A.J. De Marcus. He had once again taken everything she loved and tainted it. Even now, he had wormed his way back into what should have been at least a reunion between friends. But no, he had taken even that away from her. Well, this time he wasn't going to win. A.J. would do whatever she needed to convince Clarissa that not only did she not kill her family, but that she still loved her with every fiber of her being. She rose and sat on the couch next to Clarissa and watched Clarissa recoil from her touch. Pulling her hands back, she clasped them in her lap trying to control the tremors that worked through her body. Clarissa being so close was starting to stir her lust and she didn't need that competition with her head right now.

"I don't know what lies you've been told, but I never touched your family. I knew how much they meant to you. I even respected their wishes when they banished me from seeing you as you lay dying. I wanted to be there with you, to comfort you when you took your last breath. I wanted my face to be the last thing you saw when you passed from this world and into the next. But it wasn't meant to be, thanks to De Marcus." A.J. took a long deep breath steadying herself for what might come next.

"Why would he lie to me? Assuming he's the one

that told me?"

"Why would I? I thought you were lost to me, passed on to the next world, never to be seen again. I left the night before you died. I went to my country house and grieved for years. I closed myself off to everyone and everything. I was practically ruined by my grief and I didn't care. I had lost the one true thing that mattered to me, you." A.J. straightened, looking around the room. She didn't have much time and now she needed to convince a woman who thought she had killed her family that the safest place was with her. This wouldn't be easy, but she didn't have a choice.

"When did you know I was alive? How long has it taken you to put your plan into action?" Clarissa was throwing accusations around like spitballs and A.J. was trying to figure out what she was accusing her of now.

"What are you talking about?" A.J. was confused, and she needed Clarissa to clear up that confusion and quick. Time wasn't their friend.

"The assassin that was sent to kill me the other night. That was you, right?"

The accusation was like a punch to the gut and A.J. leaned her elbows on her knees trying to steady her breathing.

"I just told you how much you mean to me and you think I'm trying to kill you?" Running her fingers through her hair, she worked to control her rage. "Sorry to break the news to you, but I'm the one protecting you." Standing she began to shake with rage. "I fucking can't believe you would think I would have anything to do with hurting you." Reaching into her pocket she pulled out her tin and popped two more pills. She was spiraling out of control and it was getting harder and harder to keep her wits about her listening to the lies being thrown at her. "I saw you at that bar, with that… that butch or whatever she was. I couldn't believe it." A.J. paced the floor, running her hands through her hair recounting the night to Clarissa. "I followed you on my motorcycle. When you got home I called a friend and gave him the information to track you down."

With her back to Clarissa she continued speaking to the wall. It was easier on her head and her eyes. She wanted to run. For the first time in her life she wanted to be anywhere but right here next to Clarissa. A.J. could feel the daggers piercing her back, her shoulders dropping in defeat. Had Clarissa bested her? Would she really give up so easily and let Clarissa walk out of her life again, for good? Time was a cruel mistress, and A.J. would have plenty of it to think of all the things she should have said to the beautiful woman she dreamed of when she needed hope.

"I didn't know he was working for the enemy, until the other day." As she turned looking at Clarissa time stood still for a brief moment, their eyes meeting. Centuries fell away and memories flooded them both. But then the wall was put back firmly in place right where it had been only minutes ago.

"Enemy? What are you talking about, Alexandra?" Clarissa's expression gave little away to A.J., walking back and looking at her lover imploringly.

"De Marcus, he's alive, and I can only think of one person who wants to hurt both of us. He is the only thing linking you and me together."

"That's impossible. He died in England. He fell out of a hayloft and onto a combine. The woman he was with saw it all." Clarissa grabbed her head and shook it, "That's…that's impossible, Alexandra, he's dead." The fear in Clarissa's eyes gave A.J. pause. What had he done to Clarissa to make her so frightened? It didn't matter. She was safe now and A.J. was going to do what she should have done centuries ago. Kill De Marcus.

"Listen to me. We have to go now. I can protect you, but you have to leave with me." A.J. pulled Clarissa up and turned, but was quickly stopped when Clarissa jerked back.

"Wait. I can't leave now. I have the ball, and I have to make sure everyone is taken care of. Stop, Alexandra, you don't understand." Waving her hands around, "This, this is my responsibility. I have to take care of things around here."

A.J. grasped the bobbing head in her hands, stopping Clarissa from continuing. "You don't understand. If we don't get out of here you won't have to worry about…" A.J. flung her hands around and gestured to the room, "any of this. Get it? You'll be dead. Look, you can tell everyone that I'm sick and that you need to see that I get home. Me being the 'big' donor and all. I'm sure your President Woods will beg you to take extra good care of me." A.J. looked as the fear of death came to realization in Clarissa's expression. "Clarissa, people could die if De Marcus shows up here. Do you understand? And it would be on our heads. I don't think I can live with that, can you?"

A.J. pulled Clarissa to the door and waited while she unlocked it.

"No, I couldn't live with that. I'll find President Woods and then we can go."

"I'm coming with you. Trust me, I can be very convincing. Besides, I just need to put the thought in his head and we're out of here."

"That was you talking to me on the dance floor, wasn't it? The caress on my face and along my…" The words died on Clarissa's lips as she touched the side of her face. "The rose that was left for me, you did that didn't you? Now it all makes sense. It's been you all this time, hasn't it?"

"Clarissa, I wanted more time to get to know you again. To be able to reveal myself to you and not frighten you away, but now I'm afraid we don't have that luxury." A wave of energy hit A.J. and Clarissa as soon as they hit the dance floor. Too many people and not enough room were overloading their senses and making them vulnerable.

"Alexandra, there. I see President Woods over there." A.J. followed Clarissa's finger and found the tall gentleman speaking to someone.

"Clarissa, we need to go. Now." A.J.'s tone gave no room for discussion, pulling Clarissa in the direction of the front entrance. Suddenly, A.J. felt Clarissa being pulled in another direction.

"Oh there you are. I've been looking everywhere for you. Oh, who is this gorgeous woman?"

"Carol. I don't have time to talk. This is A.J. Lockwood and I'm afraid she is feeling sick. Can you cover for me? I have to take her home." Clarissa hoped the excuse would do the trick, but Carol lingered, holding Clarissa firmly.

"Oh, right. You need to take her hoooome." Carol winked at Clarissa and then whispered, "I think I would change my fluid for her. Have fun." She winked again, and let Clarissa's hand go.

"Nice to meet you. Perhaps another time, Carol." A.J. winked, knowing she was playing into her game pulling Clarissa to the door.

"I can't wait," Carol called out to the departing couple. "Oh, by the way, Mr. Sex Ed. decided to show up after all. We can exchange all the juicy details Monday."

A shudder went through both women as A.J pulled Clarissa into the crook of her arm and looked around for her car. There was at least one other vampire, other than them and Selene in the area. A.J. wasn't exactly ready to engage it without knowing who it was first.

"Get in. Hurry." A.J. practically shoved Clarissa into the car just as it start moving. Slamming the door, Selene appeared to pop out of the shadow.

"Selene!" Both women gasped at the same time.

Stunned, A.J. looked at Clarissa and questioned, "You know Selene?" Then looking back at Selene, "You knew you were protecting Clarissa and didn't think I needed to know you knew her?"

"Look, don't get your panties in a bunch, assuming you're wearing any. It was a long time ago. Besides, it isn't my history to tell." Selene winked at Clarissa and smiled. "Good to see you again, kid. You okay?"

Both women turned their gaze on Clarissa as she let out a staggered breath, "I hope so."

Chapter Thirty Two

Selene handed both women a glass each filled with red wine and let out a sigh stretching her legs out between the two women sitting across from her. Her eyes moved from A.J to Clarissa and then back to her employer. The tension in the limo was palpable and seemed to constrict both women's throats, so Selene spoke first.

"What happened in there?"

"De Marcus was in there." A.J. took a sip of the wine and grimaced, then looked at Selene.

"What?" Clarissa looked at Selene and then they both looked at A.J. when she choked on her drink.

"Scotch please. This tastes like ass." A.J. smiled and raised an eyebrow at the bodyguard.

"Hmm, some people have no taste."

Clarissa touched A.J.'s arm when she handed the glass back to Selene. "Wait, De Marcus was at the ball. Are you sure?"

"He was the one talking to President Wood when we were leaving. Didn't you see him?" A.J. accepted the scotch and took a long deep sip hoping the burn would trail down her body ridding her of the desire to kiss Clarissa. Now that they were safe and on their way to A.J.'s penthouse, the tension was leaving her body in droves. All she had to do now was convince Clarissa she wasn't the murderer Clarissa thought she was. *Easier said than done*, A.J. suspected. She knew she had her work cut out for her and hoped she might be able to illicit Selene's help to convince Clarissa of that fact.

"I knew I felt someone there. I just figured it was you two. Shit." Selene looked out the window and watched the street lights pass, thinking about all the ways she was going to kill De Marcus, that was if A.J. let her.

"Who's Mr. Sex Ed?" A.J. said, directing the question to Clarissa.

"What?"

"Carol said Mr. Sex Ed was there. Who is he?" A.J. now looked at Selene, each sharing a knowing glance before they looked at Clarissa.

"Oh, that's Carol's ex-boyfriend. He dumped her the other day so I'm surprised he even showed up. No biggie."

"De Marcus." Selene and A.J. said in agreement.

"What? No way. Are you sure?" Clarissa cringed thinking about how Carol had described their past sexual encounters. "We have to go back. She has no idea what she is getting herself into."

"No." A.J. said, taking another sip of Scotch and looking back at Selene.

"Alexandra, you don't know what a ruthless bastard he is. He'll hurt her." Clarissa grabbed A.J.'s arm and pulled A.J. towards her. "He, will, hurt, her. She's my friend. I can't let that happen. Stop the car." Frantic, Clarissa grabbed the door handle and started to open the door. Jerked back into her seat, she felt A.J.s body pressed against hers while strong arms encircled her.

"Look, my only concern is you right now. If he wanted Carol dead, he would have done it a long time ago," A.J. whispered into Clarissa's ear, guilt sending a chill through her for enjoying the feel of Clarissa's body pressed against hers. "I think he was using her to try and get to you and since you never saw him, he can't be sure it's you." A.J. felt Clarissa relax against her as she loosened her embrace hoping she was right in her logic and De Marcus.

Selene watched the two women and wondered how long it would take for them to become reacquainted. *Smooth A.J. smooth.*

A.J. looked at Selene and raised an eyebrow. *Knock it off.*

"I'll send Selene to Carol's house tonight to make sure she gets home okay. Will that ease your mind, Clarissa?"

"I suppose, if that's the best I can get."

"No, you can get a lot more if you want, but it's what I'll do for Carol to make sure she's safe."

A.J. nodded at Selene to make sure they both understood what Selene needed to do. "Make sure Carol's okay. Leave the rest to me."

"You're the boss, A.J."

###

A.J. and Selene stood by the side of the limo discussing the next steps needed to both protect Clarissa and take care of Kevin and De Marcus.

"She doesn't look too happy, A.J." Selene said looking at Clarissa in the limo.

"Yeah, well, it seems that De Marcus told her that I killed her whole family in my grief over her death." A.J. slid a hand through her hair then pulled at the collar of her costume.

"Oh shit. No wonder she never tried to contact you."

"What do you mean? You don't think I killed her family do you?" A.J. stepped closer to Selene and waited for an answer.

Looking into blue eyes that betrayed the pain they were in, Selene shook her head. "No A.J., I don't think you could do something so despicable, but if she thought you killed her family she would want revenge. Wouldn't you? So, if she found you, she would do the honorable thing and avenge the death of her family. Or die trying."

"I'm gonna kill that bastard. Did you see her reaction when we mentioned De Marcus? I thought she was going to come unglued right then and there. He was an evil son of a bitch back then, but I never thought he would turn Clarissa. He had lots of other women, so why turn Clarissa?"

"For the same reason he wants her now, you."

"Me?" A.J. and De Marcus had always been rivals with the women, but there were plenty to go around so she never gave it much thought. In fact, her taste ran much gentler than his, so they rarely competed for the same breakfast back in Paris.

"A.J., the Coven records are full of accounts of his brutality. They want him dead and the only reason they don't do it is because he's an elder. They looked the other way when he faked his death. The word was, as long as he didn't contact them he was dead to them, too. It seems, he was sick of the Coven and their constant intrusion into his life. They didn't find out for a long time that he had faked his death. So, now they want that dirty business taken care of." Selene grabbed A.J.'s shoulder and pulled her closer, "Someone knows what he's been up to, and now they want answers. So you're not the only one looking for him now."

"You mean they know about the attempts on Clarissa's life? But how?" A.J. didn't like how this was sounding. The more that happened the more twisted things were becoming.

Shrugging her shoulders, Selene bent her head and whispered, "Someone made a call. Now the Coven is worried what little clout and respect they have will start to be eroded if he kills his slaves and they didn't do anything about it. They're still old school like that, lucky for you."

"Fuck them. I don't follow their rules anymore. I take care of what's mine and I don't need their help or their Coven." A.J. was fuming at the idea that the Coven would assume she needed their help. She had walked away from that patriarchy a long time ago and she wasn't about to get down on bended knee again. Just because someone was trying to kill the one person she had loved to the death, well almost to the death.

"You know he probably wants you dead, too, A.J."

A.J. knew that De Marcus would have to kill her to get to Clarissa, but she didn't care. She wouldn't give up Clarissa that easily, not now that she had her back in her life. A.J. just needed to convince Clarissa this was where she belonged.

"That goes without saying. It's the only way he would get to her, if I'm dead." A.J could see Clarissa starting to fidget so she finished her instructions to Selene, "Look, go back to the university and keep an eye on Carol. Make sure she gets home tonight, alone. No strays following her home, if you know what I mean. Call the police on the asshole if you have to, but make sure she gets home safe. I'll have Clarissa call her in an hour, so that should give you plenty of time to get him arrested or something."

"Then what?"

"Then, we meet in the morning and deal with Kevin." A.J. said one last thing before she got back into the car. "Put someone on Carol. I don't want Clarissa worried about her friend. Then try and find out who called the Coven. I need to know, friend or foe."

Selene watched the car's light fade pulling her cell phone out of her leather pants. "I think I need to change first." A quick dial and she connected with her contact, "Hey, I need you to do me a favor. Call Sgt. Gilmore and tell him to meet me over at the university. Thanks"

Chapter Thirty Three

A.J. rubbed her palms watching Clarissa try to ignore her. She felt like a school girl with her first crush as she tried to think of something to say. What could she say to the woman who thought she killed her family? Each passing street light threw light into the limo. A.J. caught glimpses of the woman she had fallen in love with centuries ago. A tributary of tears etching their way down Clarissa's face pulled A.J. from her hesitancy.

"Clarissa?" A.J. moved closer, but didn't touch her, "Why are you crying?"

Clarissa looked at A.J. and sighed, "Memories. They're the bane of our existence, aren't they? I mean we live forever, meet so many people on their journeys through life and they become a thread in that fabric we call our life. I know it sounds like I'm trying to be so circumspect, but I can't help it, Alexandra. I don't know what to believe right now. I hope you understand." A.J. watched Clarissa bite her lip. Another habit she recognized from the "old" Clarissa when she tried to control her emotions. "So do I call you A.J. or Alexandra?"

A.J. reached out, gently pulling Clarissa's hand into hers. Running a finger over the knuckles and down her fingers, A.J. waited, but Clarissa didn't resist the touch. Whispering, she said, "I'm sorry about your family, Clarissa. I..." A great weight seemed to settle on A.J.'s shoulders as she kept her eyes on Clarissa's fingers. Threading her fingers through her lover's hand, she cradled it between her own and sighed, "I was so lost in my own grief that I never thought about the pain that your parents would go through in losing you. I should have stayed close. Perhaps, I could have protected them. Prevented what happened." A.J. remembered Clarissa's little sister, Michelle, with her blonde hair and green eyes constantly following her around. While there was no love lost between A.J. and Clarissa's father, she understood his passion to protect his family and the need to provide for them. What De Marcus must have put them through A.J. could only imagine and it was probably ten times worse than what she envisioned.

"If what you say is true, how would you have known what he intended?"

A flood of memories assaulted A.J. as she fell back into the grief she felt when she thought Clarissa died. She had gone to her country home, closed the drapes and languished inside. Every remnant that reminded her of Clarissa she burned, killed or soiled. A.J.'s plan was to die a slow, agonizing death through starvation. She starved herself to the point of almost being comatose. Her one saving grace was her servants who stayed on despite being ordered to leave. Lucas, her personal servant, had offered his own life to save hers and still she refused the gift. Lingering at death's door, Lucas slaughtered a lamb and drained it of its life saving blood. He took advantage of her delirium and tricked her into consuming the blood. Months had turned into years before A.J. could force herself to resume some sort of normalcy. But to survive, A.J. knew she needed to leave France and probably never return and to never think of Clarissa again. One was easier to accomplish than the other.

"I would never have known, Clarissa. When you died, I died, too. I tried never to think of you again. Trust me when I tell you, it would be decades before I was successful in forgetting your perfume, the way your hair smelled, or the way you smiled when I kissed you." A.J. felt Clarissa's grip tighten at the revelation.

"Well, you've seemed to have done well for yourself in spite of everything." The bitterness that crept into Clarissa's voice was subtle, but not biting, yet.

"I've done a good job at compartmentalizing my life, Clarissa." A.J. stopped stroking the back of her hand and looked into her eyes. "I have boxes of your memories stored away in the back of my mind, waiting to be unpacked some day. Perhaps, today's that day?" Before Clarissa could say anything A.J. finished with her own biting retort. "Besides, you look as though you've done well for yourself, Professor Graham."

"Life goes on, so they say."

"So they say."

A.J. swung the door wide and made a sweeping gesture for Clarissa to enter. Cautiously, Clarissa walked into the dark, cool space.

"Let me get the lights."

The room barely came alive as soft lighting accented different features of what was obviously the living room. At first, Clarissa was impressed by the huge building A.J. called home, then she realized that she was here for all the wrong reasons. Her life, her very existence, now depended on A.J. Lockwood. She shuddered at the thought and then felt a gentle hand touch her back, guiding her to a leather chair.

"Can I get you something to drink? Do you eat?" A.J. looked embarrassed as she motioned to the frig, "I mean, food or...well, you know." Shrugging her shoulders she leaned against the bar. "I don't know how long it's been since you've taken care of your need, or how you do it, but I can offer—"

"I don't drink human blood. I haven't in a long time." Clarissa blanched at the thought of biting another human to satisfy her needs. Urges were something else, and she knew how to handle those.

"I'm sorry. I didn't mean to imply anything. I merely was offering to...I mean I don't feed anymore either. It's rare, I mean." A.J. ran her hand up and down her arm nervously trying to explain herself.

"Then how do you survive if you're not the blood sucking killer I once knew?" Clarissa stared at A.J., waiting for her to fly off the handle. She knew she was provoking her and she wasn't sure why. But she was somewhere between caring and hating at the moment and right now it was easier to hate A.J. than care about her. To care meant to forgive and she still wasn't sure she believed A.J.'s version of the truth about her family. "I'm sorry, I didn't mean that." Scrubbing her face she relaxed back into the soft leather and closed her eyes, "Yes I did, I meant it to sound that bad."

"I've never killed to live, only to survive, to protect my own and keep what was mine, Clarissa. Perhaps you have me mistaken with that animal that brought you over." A.J.'s skin prickled at the accusation and her temper flared. "Besides, if I was that animal, you would be my slave and not his."

Clarissa opened her eyes to find A.J. gripping the sides of the chair she sat in, staring down at her.

The look in her old lover's eyes bore no malice, no hatred, just pain. Pain, Clarissa was sure she had caused when she made A.J. promise not to turn her all those decades ago, only to find her living here in the world A.J. thought she was alone in. Clarissa stared back into the murky darkness of A.J.'s soul and saw the wanting she had seen before in her lover's gaze. A tingle coursed through Clarissa at A.J.'s nearness. She could feel the soft breath against her face and she turned away as she tried to distance herself from the need that flowed off of A.J. in waves.

I never stopped loving you. The thought drifted into her mind.

"Stop it, Alexandra. I won't let you control me like that. Invade my mind without my permission." Clarissa stood pushing A.J. back, but A.J. grabbed her hands and held them to her chest. The beat of A.J.'s heart surged between her fingers.

"Tell me you don't love me. Tell me you believe that I would hurt your sister, Michelle." A.J. grabbed Clarissa's head, forcing Clarissa to look at her. "Look into my eyes and tell me you think I'm the same as De Marcus. Tell me and I'll let you walk out of here and never bother you again, but tell me you believe that." A tear and then another, followed by more, slowly released themselves as A.J. waited for Clarissa's answer. "Is it easier to tell yourself that I'm a monster? Is that how you've survived all this time, Clarissa?"

Clarissa reached up and grabbed A.J.'s hands and pulled them from her head. She had thought about a night like tonight over and over again. Now faced with the opportunity for the confrontation she dreamed about, she was at a loss for words. Had she truly believed De Marcus when he told her Alexandra killed her family? Or had she just given up and lived his lie? It was easier, wasn't it? To believe the reason Alexandra hadn't saved her from De Marcus was that she was running from her own evil deed. It all had seemed so clear at the time and now Clarissa knew in her heart she was wrong. Alexandra hadn't abandoned her, in fact, it was the opposite. She had abandoned Alexandra.

Clarissa's heart sank at the sudden realization. Life had taken turns that could have put her closer to Alexandra yet she purposely had taken a different path. Clarissa dropped A.J.'s hands and walked to the window. The lights flickered as rain began to tap against the window. From the penthouse Clarissa could see for miles and yet the fog in her mind kept her from seeing anything, only feeling A.J.'s pain. She rested her forehead against the glass and sighed. She had been running for a century and now she could walk out of the penthouse and into De Marcus, if A.J. was right. Or she could face her demon and deal with A.J. The choice had to be made, now.

Tell me. Strong arms wrapped around Clarissa and held her tight. *Tell me you don't love me. Tell me that Paris was just my imagination. But tell me something, Clarissa.*

Chapter Thirty Four

Selene watched the ball start to wind down. She had fit in perfectly at the dance. Walking around, winking at the occasional wandering eye, but never taking her eyes off of Carol. She had to laugh. No one had thought to take her rapier away from her and she fingered the ball of the hilt, leaning back into the shadows watching. The room had a tension in it Selene recognized. The sexual tension of those about to be freed, the drunken laziness of those about to pass out and one undeniable frenzy about to be released. Scanning the room, Selene's gaze moved from face to face. The lateness of the evening had induced everyone to take their masks off and in doing so, it allowed Selene easier access to search for De Marcus. Carol remained without an escort the remainder of the evening and Selene was worried that A.J. might have been mistaken about seeing De Marcus.

A sudden chill hit the room and Selene felt it settle in her bones. A master vampire was close by. She rarely encountered the cool energy of a master and she shuddered as her skin felt like needles were stabbing her. Selene needed to control her own body right now or it would give her away and the advantage to De Marcus. Sgt. Gilmore hadn't arrived yet so there was little she would be able to do if she did find De Marcus. Another cold stab went through her and she felt her knees might buckle at the onslaught. Spying Carol by the bar now talking to a couple, Selene barely caught the conversation. Something about grades and finals mingled with other conversations floating above the dance floor. Selene needed some air, but leaving Carol alone wasn't an option so she needed to think fast.

"Excuse me, Carol isn't it?" Selene touched Carol's arm and apologized to the couple standing across from them.

"Yes, can I help you?"

"Might I have a moment of your time?" Smiling at the couple again, Selene quickly escorted Carol to a door off the bar.

"Yes, yes of course. Is everything okay?"

"I wanted to let you know that it seems a few people have seen a suspicious person walking around the grounds. I don't think it is anything to worry about, but I thought I should let you know since Professor Graham isn't here."

"Oh, my. Yes thank you...and you are?" Carol offered her hand for a handshake and then looked at the rapier hanging from Selene's belt.

"Oh, Professor Grahamn didn't tell you? I'm with the private security team she hired for the event. You can call me Selene." Selene shook the offered hand then looked down at her weapon. "Oh it's just a prop. Professor Graham wanted me to fit in with the crowd. She didn't want to draw attention to Ms. Lockwood and the security detail she hired to protect her."

"Wow, I guess she didn't want anything happening to our 'big' donor did she?" Carol threw up a set of air quotes as she smiled at Selene.

"No, I guess not."

Selene felt the frigid cold slice through her again. Falling to one knee, she gasped as if she had been punched. She heard Carol gasp and then a deep baritone voice greeted Carol.

"Carol, darling, there you are. I've been looking all over for you." Selene looked up to see an average looking man sweep Carol into an embrace, his eyes never leaving hers. "What are you doing out here, darling?"

Selene answered knowing Carol would blow her cover. "I'm sorry. I was having some difficulty." Selene started slurring her words hoping Carol would play along. "Seems I over indulged a bit and well...I think I'm a little tipsy. She was just helping me to my car. Isn't that right, Carol?" Selene stood and swayed over to Carol and flopped into her, pushing her away from De Marcus. "I–I–I think my car is over there." Pointing in the opposite direction from the hall, Selene grabbed Carol's arm and pulled her towards the parking lot. "This way, Mi Lady. I believe my horse is this way." Selene giggled and staggered a few more steps pulling Carol along. "She'll be right back, kind Sir. Won't you, Carol?"

Carol looked down at the staggering Selene, "It's okay, John. Go inside and save a dance for me. I'll just get her to her car and she can sleep it off."

Selene let her head sway but she never took her eyes off of De Marcus. The cat and mouse game would have to wait until Selene had Carol somewhere safe.

"I'll be waiting for you inside, darling," De Marcus boomed, walking towards the loud music spilling out of the hall.

Selene pushed Carol towards a few trees in the parking lot and then stood up.

"What the hell?" Carol pushed Selene back, her hands on her hips. "What's the big idea?"

Selene pulled Carol into the trees and then looked

back to where De Marcus entered the building.

"Listen to me very carefully." Selene squeezed Carol's wrists to get her attention. "That man you just talked to is a trained killer. I don't know what your relationship is to him, but you need to leave now. Get in your car and find somewhere to go. Do not go home. Do you understand me?" Selene hoped her tone would scare Carol. Just in case it didn't, Selene now loomed over Carol imposing her full self over the petite woman. "He's why I was hired. Do I make myself clear?"

"Wait, I know him. John might be a bit strange but he has never hurt me before. Besides, I don't even know you." Carol tried to pull away, but Selene tightened her grip and pulled her back closer.

Staring into Carol's eyes she tried one more time. This time her tone was as menacing as it could be. "If you walk back into that room I can't guarantee your safety. Now, you can wait until the police get here or you can," Selene was so close, Carol's hair fluttered as she spoke to the visibly frightened woman, "get your ass in your car and get the fuck out of here. Comprende?"

Carol started to shake when Selene released her vise-like grip. Even in the darkness Selene could see the color drain out of Carol's face. Clearly she had made an impression on the clueless woman, but it was for her own good, reasoned Selene.

"Wait, I have—"

"No, no waiting. No arguments. You have a spare key?" Carol nodded continuing to shake. "Good. Call Clarissa in an hour. Tell her where you are and when things are under control here she'll call you to come back. Take the weekend and go on a road trip." Pulling Carol back as she started to wander off, she added, "but do not go home. He'll find you and kill you. I'll walk you to your car to make sure you get out of here. Go out the back way so he doesn't see you."

Selene watched tail lights fade into the darkness before she started back to the hall. Clearly, Sgt. Gilmore was taking his sweet time in getting to the university, so Selene texted him again to speed up his progress. Selene dropped to her knee again, the result of another frigid slice working its way through her body. As she was gasping for air, a pair of polished black boots stood in front of her.

"Well, perhaps you can tell me where Carol has wandered off to." Selene felt herself being pulled up by her hair. She tugged her head back but De Marcus had a firm grip buried in her black locks. Just as she stood, her rapier tip pricked De Marcus' throat.

"Perhaps you should reassess your tone my friend. I believe you have me mistaken with someone else." Selene pushed the tip of her blade a bit further into his neck. De Marcus smiled at Selene, exposing his fangs. "I don't frighten easily." Her grip tightened on the handle of the rapier as her fingers lengthened and her own fangs dropped. She could feel her body start to morph, the crunch of bone echoing in her ears. Her blood started to surge pulling her head free from his grasp. A step back and she extended the distance just enough to push her sword further into his throat.

De Marcus raised his hands and surrendered his position, briefly. Selene had underestimated his bulk as she looked at him further. His cape had covered his body effectively, hiding rather large arms and a broad structure that looked more like a brick building than an athletic man. She watched as he looked around the area. His eyes darted about, searching she was sure, for an avenue of escape. She needed to keep him focused on her until the police arrived.

"Don't even think about moving, De Marcus."

"Do we know each other? Perhaps in another life?" De Marcus licked his lips and smiled again.

"No, I assure you we've never met, especially not like that." Selene knew what he meant watching his gesture.

"Well then perhaps," his gaze roamed down her body and then back to her face, "in another way."

"Really? Please."

A shiver of disgust rolled through her at just the suggestion of any intimacy between the two. De Marcus twitched causing Selene to drop her shoulder just enough that the pressure of her rapier eased. He lunged at her, causing her to twist to the side, but he caught her shoulder with a glancing blow. His nails left three deep scratches across the front of her chest. Regaining her footing, she watched De Marcus lick her blood from his fingers.

"Oh, young blood." He said mockingly.

Selene's body surged and blood pounded in her ears. She took a deep breath and centered herself before she answered. "Enjoy it 'cause that's the only taste you get."

"We'll see," he taunted again. An arrogant smile lingered.

An explosion of movement brought the two together. There was a swishing of the rapier as it cut air, then flesh drifted through the air. A solid thud of a punch landing and an audible expulsion of air echoed. Another thud, the rapier cutting through cloth and the quick movements ended just as fast as they had begun. Selene found herself thrust upward at the end of De Marcus' arm. Her breathing was quickly being cut off, but her sword was buried to the hilt in De Marcus' chest. His grasp on Selene's neck gave way as he reached for her hand on the rapier.

Selene tumbled forward sending De Marcus onto his back, cushioning her fall. Landing on top of De Marcus, she felt a shooting pain in her arm. He had sunk his fangs into her forearm and held her against him.

"Release me, you son of a bitch," Selene shouted, pulling her arm from his clenched teeth.

Selene could see the blade of her rapier had bent and stuck out behind De Marcus's shoulder. Grabbing the handle she began to wiggle it back and forth opening the wound wider. While the blade was close to his heart, it wasn't a fatal wound. Nonetheless, it would keep him down for a few days. She continued to yank on the blade, blood soaking his white shirt. The action finally caused De Marcus to release his grip on her arm and he began to scream.

"I'll kill you, you bitch."

"Stop screaming or I'll continue to open you like a Christmas pig." Selene jerked the handle again to emphasis her point.

She could feel De Marcus try and toss her off, so she reached down and pulled the dagger she had hidden in her boot and pushed it into his throat. The tip instantly drew blood and she licked his throat. A tingle rushed through her when his blood hit her. She felt her body tighten and surge again. Setting her fangs to his jugular, a pair of red and blue lights caught her attention. Her back up had arrived.

Chapter Thirty Five

A.J. held Clarissa as they stared out into the night. The city looked different tonight. Maybe it was just having Clarissa in her arms, but there was a hopefulness tonight. A.J. felt her former lover relax in her arms. She sighed resting her cheek against Clarissa's head. How long would Clarissa let A.J. hold her? A.J. thought about all the things she wanted to say to her, about all the things that had happened since their last meeting. She wanted to carry Clarissa into the bedroom and reacquaint herself with her lover, but. There was always a but.

"Perhaps you would like to take a shower and change into something more comfortable?" A.J. released her, turning Clarissa to face her, finally. "I'm sure I can find some sweats that would fit you. Would that be alright?" A.J. asked, studying Clarissa's face. A quick nod and a shy smile would have to suffice. "Okay. Um, my guestroom is that way." A.J. pointed to the right. "I'll bring you some clothes and you can shower in there. Fresh towels are in the cabinet, along with a toothbrush and a few other items you might need."

"Look, I don't want to keep you from anything. I mean, it's night and I'm sure you have stuff you probably need to take care of."

A.J. stopped and looked back at Clarissa. "What are you implying?" A.J. saw Clarissa visibly shake when she heard A.J.'s tone.

"I'm just saying that, well, you know."

"No, I'm afraid I don't. Please elaborate, Professor Graham, on your meaning of 'stuff'. I'm sure you, as the literature professor, have an excellent command of the King's English, so please enlighten me." A.J. pulled Clarissa to the couch and sat down. "I fear, perhaps, you have an impression of me that's no longer valid." A.J.'s stilted cadence and tone clearly left little to wonder how angry she was at the moment.

"I'm sorry. I can see that I've upset you. I just—"

"Tell me what you think I am, Clarissa." Her controlled anger seethed just under the surface and A.J. was having difficulty masking it. "This is a discussion that we should have now and not later. I don't want there to be any misconceptions or lies between us." Grasping Clarissa's hands she slowly reiterated, "Please, tell me who you think I am."

"I'm sorry, Alexandra. I just...." The comment died on her lips as she stared down at their joined hands.

"You keep apologizing, but you aren't saying anything, so let me. I don't sleep during the day. I sleep at night. I don't hunt or kill humans and I don't drink their blood." A.J. pulled a tin case out of her pocket and opened it. "When I feel the need, I pop one or two of these and put them under my tongue. The affects are immediate. They're concentrated blood capsules and have pretty much helped me control my life for years now." A.J. put the container on the coffee table. "I enjoy a good meal and I like a good Scotch. I can be out in the sun, but I chose this city because of the fog that lingers near the coast. I don't like the desert, for obvious reasons, and I move every ten to fifteen years."

Looking at Clarissa, A.J. wondered what she was

thinking. Did she believe her or did she still believe the lies De Marcus had told her. She could only hope that the flame that burned in her heart continued to burn in Clarissa's. If not, then the future would hold no hope for A.J. She had already decided that days ago. Moving closer, A.J. tilted Clarissa's gaze to meet her own.

Her tone softened, growing husky as she continued, "Since I saw you, I've thought of nothing else. I had hoped to court you like I did when we were back in Paris. The donation to the ball was to be my entry back into your world." A.J.'s lips hovered over Clarissa's. Watching Clarissa close her eyes she softly kissed her lips, lingering briefly. "I am still enchanted by your beauty and I would be lying if I told you I didn't want to make passionate love to you right now." Releasing Clarissa, A.J. took a deep breath and stood, "Now, I'll find those sweats for you and deposit them in the bathroom."

A.J. rolled her shoulders and took several deep breaths. She felt like a school girl who just had her first kiss on the playground. Her nipples hardened being close to Clarissa and her heart pounded in her ears. She contemplated closing the door and masturbating, but even that wouldn't be enough to release her body from its fragile state. She wanted Clarissa and she knew only Clarissa could release her from the agony she was in. A.J. wanted her to come willingly, so she would wait. Forever, if she needed to, but she would wait.

Clarissa caressed her lips, still feeling A.J.'s kiss lingering. The softness reminded Clarissa of their first kiss, the possessive way Alexandra had kissed her that long ago night in Paris. If only they could return to that time and place and live life differently. Clarissa knew now she would have made a different decision back then. She had been so selfish when she told Alexandra she didn't want to be a vampire. But Alexandra had never forced her to change her mind. She had left the decision in her lover's hands and had abided by Clarissa's wishes.

De Marcus was different. He had taken what he wanted, relying on her parents' innocence. As she lay dying, De Marcus had convinced her father to let him treat her. He had been persistent in his pursuit of Clarissa and she often wondered why he continued. She had seen the way he looked at Alexandra and wondered if they had been lovers, but Alexandra had only dismissed the idea, telling Clarissa they had history and not to worry. After De Marcus turned Clarissa, he boasted how he had taken the very thing Alexandra had wanted. It was only fair, he said, since she had cost him his rightful place in the Coven. He never said much beyond that and soon after died, or so she thought.

A hot shower, a glass of wine and Clarissa would feel better. She was sure of it. Clarissa realized looking down at her dress that Carol had helped her with all the buttons on the back. Now, she was in need of assistance to get the darn thing off. Embarrassed at her predicament she called for Alexandra, but got no response. She tapped lightly on A.J.'s door but still nothing. Tapping again she opened the door and started to say something, but before she could say anything she saw Alexandra naked, rummaging through a drawer. Her strong, tight body was just as beautiful as she recalled. Alexandra's firm breasts barely swayed while she shuffled things around. Clarissa licked her lips thinking about all the times she had tugged them with her teeth and then soothed them, running her tongue over the taunt tips. Lowering her gaze, the sight of Alexandra's firm ass made Clarissa blush remembering the times she laid next to Alexandra caressing it. She finished her assessment just in time to see Alexandra staring back at her in the mirror.

"Oh, sorry. I guess you didn't hear me." Clarissa quickly slammed the door shut and clutched her chest. The sight of Alexandra's naked body sent instant tremors through her and made her tingle, raw desire pooling between her legs. Clarissa felt herself blush thinking of Alexandra naked. Feeling a bit lightheaded she bent over gasping for breath. God, Alexandra was still beautiful. The quick look had given Clarissa enough to know Alexandra still had power over her. Her hand trembled as she brushed a lock of hair out of her face.

What am I doing standing here? If she finds me here waiting, what will she think? That I'm a wanton hussy, that's what she'll think.

Clarissa made a mad dash to her own bathroom and slammed the door. She didn't have to wonder if Alexandra still excited her. No, that question had just been answered. Now, she had to deal with a new demon. Its name, desire.

Chapter Thirty Six

A.J. stood dumbfounded. Had Clarissa been standing at the door the whole time, watching her? There was no mistaking the look she had given A.J. either. Lust, pure lust had met her eyes when she looked at Clarissa. A.J. heard a door slam at the other end of the penthouse and threw some sweats on.

A.J. slowed her breathing when she knocked on the bathroom door, "Clarissa? Clarissa, open the door." A.J. pressed her ear against the door and listened. Gosh, how juvenile, she thought, waiting then knocking again. "Clarissa, did you need something? I didn't hear what you said back there." Motioning to no one, she shrugged her shoulders again. Geez, what am I doing?

A click and then a billowing cloud of steam rolled out a crack in the door. "Sorry, I didn't mean to bother you, Alexandra. I just needed some help with the buttons of my dress. I can manage. Thank you." Clarissa tried to shut the door, but A.J. pressed her shoulder against it.

"Nonsense. Let me help you. Besides, I have some sweats for you." A.J. pressed harder, the door budging slowly. Slipping her arm through, A.J. handed Clarissa the bundle. "See?"

Taking the clothes, Clarissa released the door, coming face to face with A.J. A.J. focused on the blush claiming Clarissa's heaving breasts. The steam in the room only added to the obvious discomfort both were feeling. Clearly, the heavy dress was starting to weigh more as the steam saturated it. A.J. smiled, and then twirled her finger commanding Clarissa to turn around. With expertise she hadn't relied on in decades, she started to unfasten the brocade buttons. Each button revealed the softness of Clarissa's neck, then her tender shoulders. A.J. stopped suddenly, a tattoo exposed as she slid the dress down further. It was clearly tribal in nature and had a form to it that left A.J. struggling to figure it out. The blackness in deep contrast to Clarissa's pale white skin gave it an ethereal look. A.J.'s finger traced the spinning tines of the tattoo as it swirled into the circle. Clarissa's muscle under the tattoo tightened while A.J. continued to trace its gentle curves.

"It's beautiful," said A.J., feeling a kindred spirit with the markings. "What does it mean?" A.J. finished the buttons, the dress pillowing at Clarissa's feet. Her gaze followed the billowing fabric slide down the perfectly shaped hips and legs. The lack of a bra didn't help A.J.'s libido as Clarissa covered her breasts. Stepping out of the dress, A.J. scooped up the heavy costume and tossed it on the makeup table. The question momentarily forgotten, A.J. watched the beautiful body unfold before her. The steam had started to collect on Clarissa's naked form. A single drip between her shoulder blades beckoned A.J.'s tongue to follow the trail it was making down Clarissa's back and down between a firm ass. Overwhelmed with desire, A.J. busied herself pulling pins from Clarissa's hair, watching it slowly cascade down her back and absorb the wetness that had pooled. Need was starting to build in A.J. and she watched her hands shake as she fingered the soft locks. Clarissa's head fell back into A.J.'s hands and a slight moan escaped her lips. The sound sent a tingle through A.J., reminding her of the moans of pleasure she had elicited from her lover in the past. To be breathing the same air Clarissa did was almost more than A.J. could've ever dreamed of. Now, she was disrobing Clarissa, seeing the beauty that she had thought was lost to her. A step closer and A.J. would be entwined with her lover. It took everything she had to keep her distance. It wasn't will power, but a cold, heart wrenching fear that if she touched Clarissa this intimately, she would vanish.

The softness of Clarissa's voice pulled A.J. back into the moment. "It reminded me of a joining, of kindred spirits on the same journey meeting and connecting. Obviously the sharpness of my life is represented by the spikes. The other strokes are those that are trying to tear that life apart."

A.J. looked down at the spiral of life as it intertwined with the others. The description left her speechless and made her wonder what Clarissa had been through at that time in her life to need such a permanent reminder of the event. Her finger trailed around the spiral and then out one of the tines and then back into the spiral again and then out and back in again. It reminded A.J. of the Wiccan triple spiral, the symbol for life, just more tribal. Clearly, Clarissa had added the tearing of that life to two of the tines but one tine had no tearing symbols attached to it. *Perhaps it should stay a question?*, thought A.J. as she cleared her throat.

"Ask me," Clarissa said, pulling a towel off the rack to hide her nakedness.

"I didn't say anything." A.J. looked down into endless pools of green. Clarissa's eyes had always captivated A.J., just as they did now. She struggled with herself, wanting to pull Clarissa into her body, to feel her strength under her touch.

"I heard you. You said 'perhaps it should stay a question,' so ask me." Clarissa's smoldering gaze was hypnotic so A.J. did as she was bid.

"Why are there no tears on the other tine?"

"It represents the one time in my life when I didn't have to endure pain or fear or loneliness, the time I had with my family. It's the one pure time in my life." Reaching up she laid her hand against A.J.'s face and caressed it. "I've always had them with me. I just had to look over my shoulder to see it. It was too painful to see it every day. To look at the loss, and remember the love." A.J closed her eyes. Feeling the gentle hand against her face almost made her weep.

Turning into the palm she laid a kiss on it. She felt Clarissa's soft breath against her face before she felt the kiss. A.J. pulled Clarissa into her body, molding herself against the petite, lean frame. Careful not to push, A.J. just held her, hands safely positioned on Clarissa's hips. Clarissa's arms encircled her waist. Clarissa's fingertips burned a path across A.J.'s skin, stroking the muscles along her spine. She reached up and pulled A.J. into a fiery kiss. A.J.'s body tightened and desire pooled between her legs, as she lifted Clarissa off her feet. A.J.'s head spun as the kiss deepened. A delicate tongue probed her lips. As if on command, A.J. parted her lips and immersed herself in Clarissa's exploration. A.J. leaned back against the wet wall and slid down to the floor, still clutching Clarissa. A.J. broke the kiss, struggling to take a deep breath. Desire spurred her further as she caressed the long porcelain neck, her tongue staking claim to the pulsing vein that lay beneath it. A whisper barely broke through A.J.'s consciousness continuing her path back up to Clarissa's lips.

"Alexandra, please…" Clarissa's voice, heavy with desire, pleaded. "…I'm not sure that I can—"

A.J. snapped out of her self induced haze, "I'm sorry. I don't know what I was thinking." Trying to stand, A.J. felt a hand push her back.

"Stop." Clarissa cupped A.J.'s face in her hands and steadied her. "I was going to say, I don't know if I can stop. I don't know if I want to stop." Translucent pools of green started to shift into a darker, urgent green. Clarissa was struggling with herself. Trying to maintain her composure, her body begged for release. "I've hurt you tonight and I'm the one that's sorry. I'm sorry for ever believing De Marcus, for believing that you'd hurt my family." A finger stopped Clarissa's lips, but she pulled it down and continued, "for never coming to find you. I've wasted all of these years with bitterness and anger, and thoughts of revenge."

Standing, A.J. pulled Clarissa even tighter to her body, her lips next to her ear. "Listen to me. Every breath I share with you is a gift, one I don't want to take for granted. Tomorrow will take care of itself, so let's take tonight to explore and reacquaint ourselves with each other. Let me make love to you. Please?" A.J. knew she sounded pleading, but it was all she had right now. The strong, independent woman was left at the ball. She had humbled herself to Clarissa in hopes of reconciling with her and she wasn't ashamed of it. But tomorrow she knew what she needed to do, so tonight she needed to right her world with Clarissa. She needed to show Clarissa she hadn't forgotten about her, that the monster Clarissa thought she was had never existed. Not then, not now and not ever.

A.J. felt Clarissa wrapped her legs around her waist, gently rocking her hips against A.J.'s rock hard abs underneath the sweat shirt. The walk to A.J.'s room was painstakingly slow and arduous. Each thrust against A.J.'s body, an exercise in patience. Grabbing Clarissa's ass A.J. pulled her up and kissed her. A.J.'s tongue demanded entrance and wouldn't be denied. Feeling as if she would swallow Clarissa whole, A.J. lowered her lips to the pulsing vein and started to caress the throbbing underneath. Moans had replaced the pleading and A.J. tried to move faster, but spied the couch and decided to nestle Clarissa into its leathery palm. The bedroom would be for another time.

Clarissa peeled the damp sweatshirt off A.J., stroking the lean muscles. Her fingers traveled up and down A.J.'s arms. A shiver, replaced by goose bumps, betrayed A.J.'s desire. Everywhere Clarissa touched made her feel like she was on fire. The slow burn was replaced by a rampaging torrent of flames as they whipped through A.J.'s body. She slipped between Clarissa's legs and pulled her against her. Slick wetness coated A.J.'s stomach and the heady smell of desire wafted to her nostrils. A.J. could barely control her own need as it pooled between her legs. Her hands went to Clarissa's breasts and pinched one and then the other nipple, which hardened at the contact. Rolling one between her fingers, she heard Clarissa moan and then gasp as she did the same to the other one. Dipping her head she licked the hard nipple, and then sucked it into her mouth. Rolling it with her tongue, she gently bit the tip and released it.

Moving on to the other breast, her lips continued their exploration of Clarissa's body. A.J. slipped her hand between Clarissa's spread legs and stroked the soft hair. Beneath her, A.J. marveled at the way Clarissa's body greeted her. Its openness, its fragility made A.J.

want to protect it. Its willingness to yield made A.J. hesitate for a brief moment, giving pause to what was about to happen. Suddenly, she felt Clarissa's hand on hers, pulling it towards her wetness.

"Don't stop, Alexandra."

"I don't plan to." A.J. lowered her mouth to the wetness. She wanted to savor every detail, just in case tomorrow had other plans for them. A.J. shuddered when her finger slid into Clarissa, a barely audible hiss escaping her lover's lips. She felt Clarissa's hands on her head as her tongue slowly and methodically flicked at the hard clit. Time seemed to slow as Clarissa's body rocked back and forth on her finger. Wetness coated A.J.'s palm as she added another finger to the gentle rhythm her hand had settled into. Her heart raced as she felt Clarissa's muscles contract around her fingers. She knew Clarissa was almost ready to orgasm. Sliding her fingers to Clarissa's opening, she stopped and looked up.

"I want you to feel me, to taste me when you come."A.J. crawled up next to Clarissa. Her hand still encased in Clarissa's wetness, she lay beside her lover pulling Clarissa on to her. Slowly, she began to work herself into Clarissa again, each stroke deeper and harder than the first. Clarissa's body responded, arching against A.J., changing as she wrestled with herself.

"Let it go, Clarissa. Don't fight it. Here…right here," A.J. said, exposing her neck. "I want you to have all of me, heart and soul, my love." A.J. felt a prick, then sharp fangs biting down on her neck. "That's it. Fuck." Both women's bodies changed form as they orgasmed together. Out of control, A.J. felt her sharp nails rake down Clarissa's back as she rocked through another orgasm. The endorphins of pain heightened each woman's orgasm as they both gripped the other. Clarissa released her hold on A.J. and placed a small bite on her breast. A small drop of blood pooled and then was quickly licked away. A.J. slipped her fingers into Clarissa's hair and pulled her head back exposing a throbbing jugular. A.J. hesitated as she watched Clarissa's essence call to her.

"Alexandra, please take me," Clarissa pleaded as her fingers raked down A.J.'s body. Clarissa lowered her neck closer to A.J.'s lips and pleaded again, "Please."

Fangs broke through the soft, pliant skin and blood gushed with each throb of Clarissa's heart. A small stream of blood slipped down A.J.'s face as she sucked at Clarissa's offering. Her orgasm ripped through her as she tried to control her instincts. She could easily suck the life out of her lover if she wasn't careful. She hadn't worried when Clarissa had bitten her. She had controlled the situation by adding pain to the equation when she raked her nails down Clarissa's body, causing her to release A.J.'s neck. But she would have to take control again, since she could easily over power Clarissa and lose her forever.

The blood lust was intoxicating. It had been decades since A.J.'s last actual feeding and a century since she had fed off another vampire. Underneath, she felt energized. A renewed life pulsed through her body. Another orgasm and she flipped Clarissa under her. She let her gaze take in the vampire that was Clarissa. Clarissa was on fire, every inch of her vibrated with an energy that merged with A.J.'s own. Her eyes had changed from a soft, light green to a deep almost emerald green and her body was wound tight. A.J. knew that the hooded eyes that stared at her did so without seeing anything. Continuing to bask in Clarissa's essence, A.J. relaxed her hold on the petite form that lay under her. The last vestiges of an orgasm quietly worked its way through A.J.'s body. Softness replaced the hard muscles.

A smile lingered on Clarissa's lips as she welcomed A.J. into her body. Quickly and without effort Clarissa slipped from under A.J. as she languished in the aftermath of an orgasm. Lowering herself, she rubbed her hard body against A.J.'s own lean form. Slowly, deliberately she slid A.J.'s sweat pants down her long legs. As she crawled up A.J.'s body, she once again rubbed against soft skin of her lover. A.J's tight ass tucked neatly against her front. She licked up the exposed back, sliding her hand into A.J.'s long dark locks. A.J. felt her head gently pulled back and a whisper in her ear.

"Your turn," Clarissa purred. A tongue swiped across the two puncture marks in A.J.'s neck causing a tingle to roll through her body. A.J. lay pinned underneath Clarissa. As she tried to roll Clarissa, A.J. was surprised by her strength. "Whoa there, Sweetheart. Where do you think you're going?" The cocky tone was followed by the gentle rocking of Clarissa's hips against A.J.'s ass. This was a side A.J. had never experienced with her lover and she was pleasantly surprised by her body's reaction to the dominance. A.J. dominated other women, she was never dominated, but now she found the idea of this new Clarissa had promise.

Feigning surrender she smiled and flicked a tongue against a fang. "What did you have in mind?"

"Hmm," Clarissa murmured against A.J.'s neck, "It's been a long, long time since I've been this excited. I'd hate to waste it. Wouldn't you?" Her hand raked down A.J.'s back leaving four bloody scratches. A.J. felt herself respond to the pain, writhing under the quick path Clarissa had taken to her wetness from behind. The growl buried deep in her throat was unleashed as Clarissa stroked her further.

"Turn over. I want to watch you." Clarissa lifted her body off and waited until A.J. lay facing her on the couch.

A.J. once again complied with the simple command. The need to please was too great to protest against. A.J. felt Clarissa deliberately flick her hard clit back and forth before squeezing it. Another growl, this time from Clarissa, hummed in A.J.'s ear followed by a swipe of a tongue rounding her ear lobe before it was nipped by her fangs. The bite produced a drop of blood that was quickly licked away as the stroking continued.

The pain fueled A.J.'s need and she knew it wouldn't take much to send her over the edge, if she was lucky. The room swirled as A.J. tried to focus on Clarissa's hand. She felt as if she had been on a two day binge, the taste of human blood was like a recovering alcoholic having their first drink in years. She wanted more, more Clarissa, more sex and more pain, but probably not in that order. Her energy spiked and her skin pricked when Clarissa slapped at her wetness. The smell of blood with raw sex saturated the air in the room. Taking a deep breath, A.J. tried to outlast the orgasm that was about to roll through her body, but it only gave her a brief reprieve. Why she was denying herself this last euphoric moment was beyond A.J.'s reasoning. She knew that once she had shared Clarissa's blood they would be tied beyond mere thoughts and words. The love they shared would bind them for life. The bite would heal their fragile relationship and each time they shared blood, their bond would strengthen.

They would be bonded at their souls and yet she tried to stave off the inevitable a moment longer. Waiting a few minutes more for a moment she never thought she would have was torture she would enjoy. Their first time together would always be this night, this moment, this very essence and she wanted it to last, forever.

Hard, short strokes brought A.J. to the edge. She felt Clarissa move down her body, spreading her legs wider. A warm tongue lapped at her wetness, almost sending her over the edge. Her tenuous hold was slowly slipping from her grasp. With each stoke of Clarissa's tongue against her clit, she felt her muscles tighten around strong, commanding fingers. An orgasm started to build, her skin forming goose bumps as the orgasm spread throughout her body, and then an explosion of colors blinded her. Clarissa moved up the tight body, her lips sliding easily against sweaty skin. Small tiny nips against her skin kept A.J. wound tighter and tighter. Face to face now, A.J. could still see the unmistakable gaze of lust in her lover's eyes. Her heart beat echoed in her ears and A.J. felt the onslaught of another orgasm take control of her body. Lips pressed against hers and she welcomed the tongue that pressed further. Grabbing Clarissa's head she kissed harder. Her body arched into the rough strokes, her muscles not quite able to capture the fingers that pushed her into the black abyss of her mind. Holding Clarissa's fingers to her, she felt her body finally clinch them and hold their further progress. She couldn't pull herself from the darkness that had enveloped her yet. She wrapped her mind in it, like a warm cocoon that sheltered her from the outside. To end their love making would bring her back to a reality she wasn't sure she was ready to face, so she lay there, Clarissa nestle on her breast, Clarissa's hand buried in her wetness and blackness surrounding her. Her mind was blank, knowing that whatever she felt or thought Clarissa would also.

"What are you thinking?" Clarissa pulled her hand from A.J. and licked a tip of a finger.

"Nothing," A.J. answered honestly.

"I know. But why?" Clarissa rested her chin on A.J.'s chest and watched her.

"It's easier to think of nothing than to think about what's just happened."

"I don't understand. Are you sorry for what just happened?" A.J. could feel Clarissa's anger start to surface.

"No, not at all. I'm just trying to enjoy it, feel it, not analyze it. Does that make sense?" A.J. pulled Clarissa's body tighter against her own. Turning so Clarissa's back was against the couch, she stroked her lover's face and lay a gently kiss on her lips. "I want to feel this moment, immerse myself in it and make sure I have it tucked securely in my heart." Her thumb stroked down Clarissa's lips, followed by another kiss before she spoke again. "We are bonded, you and I. Our souls, our blood and our lives are one. I belong to you and you to me. As vampires, we share a connection no other has with us. You didn't have that with De Marcus, did you?"

Clarissa's dropped her eyes. "No, what I had with De Marcus I never want with anyone."

A.J. raised Clarissa's face, staring into the soft green she had seen earlier. Her heart ached for the pain she saw there. She wouldn't push Clarissa tonight, but some day Clarissa would share her past with A.J., and she already had an idea of what would be said.

"I love you."

###

Selene would have killed De Marcus and been done with, but it wasn't her call and A.J. hadn't said she could. Lucky for him the police arrived in time to save his sorry ass. She rubbed her arm where he had bit her and grimaced. He had a debt to pay and she hoped A.J. would give her the opportunity to collect. She had left her sword buried in his shoulder with strict instructions that it shouldn't be taken out for at least a few days. The pure silver blade had been a gift, a gift she wished she could have kept, but it was more useful at the moment buried in the vampire than hanging on her office wall. While Sgt. Gilmore wasn't one of them, he was sympathetic to a fatter paycheck. Selene gave very detailed instructions on how De Marcus should be handled, explaining that as long as he left the sword buried in De Marcus's shoulder he wouldn't be a problem. The leg irons and hand cuffs were for Sgt. Gilmore's protection and if they were removed…well she had done her due diligence in alerting the officer.

Selene wished she could relax, but she knew well enough that De Marcus would eventually escape his confines. It was only a matter of time. Hopefully, it would give A.J. the time she needed. Selene rubbed her arm again as the bite throbbed with each beat of her heart. The rush she felt was starting to wear off and she was feeling hung-over. A flick of her hand opened her cell phone and she hit speed dial.

"Hey. We need to talk." Selene rolled her neck and felt a kink work its way out with a pop. "Yeah, I'll see you in about an hour. I need to stop home and take a quick shower and grab something to eat." She paused, listening to the voice on the other end. "Fine, I'll see you in the morning." Looking down at her watch, she saw that dawn would come in about four hours. Enough time to catch a quick cat nap or maybe a little entertainment, if she was lucky. Closing the phone she looked around at the partygoers who were starting to leave.

I haven't seen that much brocade in a long time. She shuddered as a rotund man jiggled past her. *Yuk!*

Chapter Thirty Seven

A.J. tossed the cell phone on the bar and walked over to the huge windows that looked over the city. Bracing her arm against the cold glass, she welcomed the cool sensation as it stroked her body. Looking out without really seeing, she tried to weave each thread of the night's events back into a fabric she could understand. In only a matter of hours she had gone from elation to devastation and back to elation. No, elation wasn't the right word, as she looked for a word that would describe what had just happened between her and Clarissa. She played out the events of the night in her mind. She remembered the look on Clarissa's face when she revealed herself. Fear, no anger. At least that's how A.J. felt. It wasn't exactly the homecoming she had hoped for. Then she thought about how devastated she was when Clarissa had accused her of killing her family. How could Clarissa even think she would do something so vile, so spiteful? Whatever A.J. had been through in the past century was nothing compared to what Clarissa had gone through. A.J. had made her peace with Clarissa's death, coming to terms with the fact that she would never have another meaningful relationship, ever. She wouldn't put herself through that pain again. But Clarissa had carried the pain of her family's death with her every minute of every day, and she had blamed A.J. The fact that De Marcus had planted such a poisonous seed in Clarissa showed how evil he was. He knew she would never seek A.J. out, ever. His secrets would be safe and A.J. would never know Clarissa was still alive. But he had planned for even that possibility by planting Kevin within her organization. He had thought of almost everything. Now, she needed to be just as vengeful. A.J. knew what she had to do with Kevin and if she was lucky he would lead her right to De Marcus. Death was too good for De Marcus, she reasoned. She wished she could make him suffer the way he had made Clarissa suffer all these decades.

Walking back into her bedroom, she leaned against the door jam and watched Clarissa sleep. She smiled at the vision before her. She felt like she should be pinching herself to make sure it was real. A.J. had lost hope of ever finding love again. Not only had she found love, but she had found it with the one woman in the world who had set the sun for her so many centuries ago. Clarissa stirred. A.J. knew she would wake soon so she climbed in beside her and snuggled against the warm back.

"You have a heated blanket, too," Clarissa murmured as she turned into A.J.

"Uh huh," A.J. whispered into the head that lay on her breast. "You, too?"

"Yep. I love it." Clarissa said, looking up. "So what now?"

"What do you mean?"

"Well…" looking sheepishly at A.J., Clarissa caressed the warming body beneath her. "Where do we go from here?"

A.J. hesitated, rolled Clarissa on her back and kissed her lover before she answered. "Where do you want to go from here?"

"Honestly?"

"Yes, honestly." A.J. felt her heartbeat speed up at the answer she knew was coming. She steeled her body from reacting as she watched Clarissa fidget with her bottom lip.

"I need to take care of my cat, Nefertiti." Clarissa smiled at A.J.'s surprised look.

"You need to take care of your cat?"

Cocking her head to the side she smirked, "What did you think I was going to say?"

"Well," A.J. smiled, relieved that she hadn't heard something that would damn her soul to an eternity of hell. "Honesty again, right?"Clarissa nodded. "I thought you might run. I thought you would still blame me for the death of your family."

A.J. watched as Clarissa closed her eyes and laid her head on A.J.'s breast. A.J.'s fear was palpable and she knew it. But they had to address the issues at hand, otherwise they would either be working at cross purposes or they would continue a circular conversation. Forward was the only direction they could take at this point.

Running her fingers through the soft locks of hair, A.J. tried to relax as she thought about the conversation they needed to have. The intimacy that they were sharing was hopefully laying the foundation for what would be the start of their relationship. What she now had with Clarissa she would never have with anyone else, ever, and she didn't want there to be any secrets between them. Pulling Clarissa tighter to her, she cleared her throat and started what A.J. hoped would be a clearing of the air between them.

"Clarissa, I hope you believe me when I say I didn't kill your family?"

Clarissa nodded her head, but didn't look up.

"Look at me and say that. Please."

Clarissa rose from A.J. and sat crossed legged in front of her. Pulling a blanket around her nakedness, Clarissa kept her eyes down as she picked at something on the blanket.

"If you can't look at me and tell me you believe me...then we can't be together." A.J. threw the half-hearted ultimatum out. Sitting up, she faced Clarissa not bothering to cover her own nakedness. Waiting, she stopped Clarissa's fidgeting by placing her hand over Clarissa's.

"It's not that at all, Alexandra. I'm ashamed of myself. I'm ashamed to say that I believed a man who beat me, betrayed me and then left me to survive on my own. I carried his lie closer to my heart than your love for me. I'm ashamed to say that I survived not by being mad at him, but by thinking of revenge on you." Grabbing A.J.'s hands, Clarissa continued her explanation, "How can I look at you now and not hate myself for what I knew was a lie, even then?"

"Please, my love, don't let this tear at your heart." A.J. wiped a tear from Clarissa's face that had started what would be a journey for many more. "It's in the past, and we should leave it there."

Grabbing A.J.'s hand, Clarissa placed a kiss on the palm then turned it over and placed kisses on the back before placing it on her chest, over her heart. A.J got up and wrapped herself around her lover, pulling her onto her lap.

"We'll work through this, but only if you choose to be with me. Otherwise—"

Clarissa placed a finger on A.J.'s lips, stopping her from continuing.

"We are bonded together, our souls are one now. To lose you would be like losing my arm. While I could live without it, it would be difficult and I don't plan on living like that. Do you?"

A.J. pulled Clarissa closer, and whispered, "No. You have filled my heart beyond words."

A.J. hoped that when she told Clarissa what she had to do next, it wouldn't change her mind about her. They would never be free if she didn't take care of her business with Kevin and De Marcus and time wasn't their friend. The sooner she did it the quicker they could get on with their lives. But before she did that, she needed a few things settled between them.

"Clarissa, I have business I need to take care of and I want to be honest with you. Kevin has betrayed me and I need to handle it." A.J. continued to caress Clarissa's back as she spoke. "I'm not sure what will happen, but I won't lie and say there isn't a possibility that he could die today. It's up to him."

Looking down into Clarissa's eyes she didn't see fear or judgment, only sadness. If there was a different path, A.J. would be the first one to take it. However, Kevin had made his choice and set his path when he decided to work for De Marcus. It was set and it left A.J. with few options. Her reputation in the Coven would be compromised if she didn't make him pay for his actions. As for De Marcus, his path was set the minute he changed Clarissa. His future only held death, his own.

"Selene will be here in the morning. I think we should talk about what will happen then. Don't you?"

A soft caress told A.J. that whatever happened, their future was cemented together. A.J. explained the twisted path her life had taken since she had seen Clarissa in the bar weeks ago. Telling the story only made A.J. madder as she pieced together all the deceit that had taken place right under her nose. Kevin had played on her trust and made himself invaluable. A slow process to be sure, but to a vampire who had forever, it was just a grain of sand in the large hour glass. A.J. explained that Kevin was being held at Knight-Pharmaceutical. She was sure by now he had an idea of what was happening, but in a few hours he would know his fate. Watchful eyes held A.J.'s as she explained what she had to do next.

"I hope you'll understand why I have to do this." A.J. looked down at their hands hoping Clarissa would never have blood on hers.

"Alexandra, I spent a century judging you only to find out I was wrong. I have to trust your judgment on this. If it wasn't for you I wouldn't be alive right now." Clarissa kissed A.J. again, but this time she lingered hoping they could have a few more hours together as they waited for Selene. "Have I told you how beautiful you still are? I'm so glad you haven't changed. I often dreamed about you." A finger trailed down A.J.'s arm, and reignited the smoldering fire that had been banked. "Your soft skin, that sexy smile you have when you look at me." A.J. couldn't help herself but smile as she looked at Clarissa. "That one, that sexy pout you have when you're trying to be tough."

Fingertips grazed across A.J.'s bare breast and her nipples puckered immediately. A tingle shot through her body as she tried to control her breathing. Closing her eyes, A.J. felt her lover palm her breasts as nipples hardened with the lingering touch. Pulling Clarissa on top of her, A.J. laid back down on the bed. Clarissa's body easily slid against her own taunt muscles, the movement so sensual. A.J. ran her hands over the soft curves of her lover's body, memorizing them again for the second time that night. She wanted to explore every inch of Clarissa's body like a sculptor memorizes their work of art. Slowly, deliberately, she felt each contour, every muscle as it tightened with pleasure. She continued to follow every curve as it led to the next sensual spot. Clarissa rubbed herself against A.J.'s body, the way water flows around a reed, gently bending around the reed as it makes its journey.

A.J. felt herself balancing precariously on the edge of the abyss again ready to tumble back into the enveloping warmth, but this time she would take a companion on her journey. Sharp nails made small strokes down Clarissa's back, blood barely coloring the flesh. Arching her body into A.J.'s, Clarissa's moan slowly worked its way into a growl as she shuddered against A.J. A firm ass pushed up and gave A.J. just enough room to slide her hand between Clarissa's legs. Her clit wasn't hard to find. The engorged clit stood out between her silky, soft lips, begging to be stroked. Desire flooded A.J.'s body and she was sure the minute Clarissa climaxed, she would, too. Gently, her thumb pushed the hood back as she stroked Clarissa's clit. A.J.'s body jerked with each stroke and soon she could feel Clarissa's wetness all over her fingers. It was just the invitation she needed. Stroking the clit one last time, she slid two fingers into Clarissa, who was now pleading for relief. Her own need ran parallel to Clarissa's, matching her shudder for shudder, breath for breath. She pulled Clarissa's head to her and buried her tongue deep into the wanting mouth. Her fingers slid deep at the same time her body jerked and strained against the onslaught of Clarissa's orgasm. Pumping into her lover, A.J. slowed her hand to a rhythmic tempo that matched her own need. Falling back, she pulled Clarissa into the dark abyss as she climaxed again and again. Her tongue tasting her own essence from their earlier love making further pushed A.J. into contentment. A.J. felt Clarissa jerk one final time and then dissolve into a heap on top of her.

A long, slow sigh released the last of the tension from A.J.'s body. How had her life changed so completely in just a few short days? Decades of torment dissolved into the fabric of the past, becoming stains, the only reminder they had been there.

Chapter Thirty Eight

Peeling her costume off, Selene stepped into the streaming shower hoping to wash the last few days' events from her mind, as well as her skin. She stood under the steady stream of hot water, letting the shower's hot pulses punish her body and take over her thoughts. What she wanted now was a clean slate but she knew that wouldn't be possible. Killing was easy. It shouldn't be, but sometimes things had to be done. So maybe a clean slate wasn't possible. She would have to settle for a new chapter then, slipping the last few days into a box, which she tucked away in the recesses of her mind. Selene knew that she would never leave the job half done and right now De Marcus was unfinished business she and A.J. needed to have a conversation about. Grabbing a soft towel she wiped the mirror and looked at her reflection. She had fallen into the life of an assassin quite by accident. One minute she was enjoying life in the town called Jamestown, the next she was a ruthless killer. Hearing Clarissa accuse A.J. of murdering her family brought back Selene's own murderous rage. She tried to never think of her family, the pain too great. But Selene's mind wandered back to the night that would change her life, literally forever.

Selene begged her father for the opportunity to go to college, unheard of at the time, but her father had resources and money wasn't an issue. So she attended college, preferring her studies to marriage. She had convinced her father that she would be an asset to any man after she completed her studies. Eventually men stopped calling and Selene was able to finish and work in the family business. As America grew her father thought a new start, in a new land would bring great opportunities. So, she had come to America with her family for a new beginning. They had barely finished the modest home they lived in when a traveler came by one night and asked her father for lodging. He had offered their barn to the dashing young man, telling him that with a house full of women, it was the best he could offer.

The urge to meet a possible husband had sent her sisters aflame, something Selene couldn't understand. Her two sisters had put together a basket, thinking the traveler might be hungry and, of course, it gave them the perfect excuse to visit. They had gathered their courage and asked her, as the elder sister, to be the lookout. Selene watched as her sisters went to the barn. Sneaking behind them, she sat in the shadows outside the barn and watched as her sisters flirted with the traveler. After sitting for a few minutes, the young man had practically pounced on her sisters, ripping them to shreds. Selene remembered screaming as she ran for the house. Before she had taken only a few steps, he was standing over her covered in blood. His gaze kept her transfixed, unable to move, or to warn her parents. Picking her up, he remarked how lucky he had been to find such accommodating lodging with a meal plan. The last thing she remembered as he bit her was the sound of a shotgun firing.

Selene woke to find herself lying in a pool of her and her father's blood. His throat had been ripped open. She shuddered looking into eyes staring at nothing.

Running into the house, she found her mother laying in blood soaked sheets, a gurgle escaped her lips. Run, was all her mother had the strength to say before she died.

The days that followed were a blur. The settlers had buried her family as she laid bed ridden and traumatized from the horrendous event. The people of Jamestown assumed a pack of wolves had killed the family. For Selene, the terror would revisit her again when her body began the process of changing. The need for blood soon became so overwhelming she roamed the forest at night for small animals, gorging on their blood and stayed hidden during the day. She eventually realized she had become what the traveler was, a vampire.

Selene wished she had the courage back then to take her own life, but as instinct took over, the will to live overwhelmed her. Selene felt her body break out in a sweat reliving the memories long buried. The man who turned her didn't assert his rights as her master. In fact, he had left her for dead, probably assuming she would die without his guidance, or worse, that the people in her community would kill her when they found out what she was. Decades would pass before she found the man who had taken her family. When she did, she killed him without even blinking an eye. That was another time, tucked away in another box that didn't need to be opened just yet. Selene ran her fingers through her hair and dressed. Slipping on her shoulder holster, she tucked her knives in the sheath behind her back. Then, she slipped her jacket on and settled herself. Business was business.

A.J. sat in the darkened room and reflected on

what she had to do today. Watching Clarissa sleep, she wished she could crawl back into bed and stay there for days making love to the beautiful woman. They had a lot of catching up to do, but business had to come first this one and only time in her life. Kevin's betrayal stoked the anger that lay just beneath the surface. It waited to be released, to be given free reign and she let it simmer as she waited for Selene to arrive. He would pay for endangering Clarissa, probably with his life. There was no other way as far as A.J. was concerned. Then there was the matter of De Marcus. A.J. hoped that Selene had him tucked safely away and had not killed him. His death would be slow and agonizing. He deserved no better than to watch his life slowly drain away. Then A.J. could put the past behind her and move forward with Clarissa. A buzzing brought A.J. from her thoughts. Selene had arrived.

"Come on in," A.J. said, pulling the heavy door open. "You look like shit."

"Well, good morning to you, little Miss Mary Sunshine. Aren't you the picture of tranquility?"

"Ouch. Someone didn't have their morning coffee, did she?" A.J. watched as Selene rubbed her forearm grimacing. "What's wrong with your arm?"

Selene slipped her jacket off, raising her arm to A.J. "Seems your lover's ex-husband likes to bite. He bit me last night when we tussled." Selene rubbed the bandage again trying to ease the ache that had set in.

"Tussled?" A.J. raised her eyebrows at the word.

"Okay, after I buried my rapier into his shoulder."

"You didn't kill him, did you?" A.J. suddenly felt deflated thinking about how she wouldn't have the pleasure of watching him die.

"No, he's safely tucked away, but I don't know how long that will last," Selene said as she looked around the room. "So… what did you do all night?" Selene wagged her eyebrows at A.J.

"Knock it off. Tell me what happened when you went back to the ball." A.J. handed Selene a cup of coffee, then sat on the sofa.

Selene recounted everything that had happened from her encounter with Carol to the fight she had with De Marcus.

"Where is Carol now?" A.J. knew Clarissa would ask when she woke her. Hopefully, the woman was smart enough to listen to Selene, but A.J. was worried Carol would put herself in harm's way trying to protect to Clarissa.

"I don't know. I put the fear of God into her though. So, if she's smart, she's in some flea bag motel waiting to hear from Clarissa." Taking another sip of the steaming brew, Selene continued, "I told her to wait and Clarissa would call her."

A low growl rolled through A.J. It was getting messy and she hated messy. She would have to tell Clarissa to be light on details when she talked to Carol. The less she knew, the safer Carol would be until they sorted out this mess.

"Alright, let me tell Clarissa we're leaving." A.J. wanted to get things over with fast. Kevin was just a loose end now that needed to be tied up. With De Marcus safely tucked away, she didn't need him anymore.

A.J. stood in the doorway looking at Clarissa. After all the lost time, she couldn't get enough of watching Clarissa sleep. She looked peaceful lying in A.J.'s bed. It was a shame she couldn't just crawl right back between those legs and lose herself again. Soon it would be finished and she could take Clarissa away from all of this and get reacquainted with her lover, again. A moan slipped from Clarissa's lips as A.J. tapped her shoulder.

"Clarissa. Clarissa, Honey." Lowering her head to Clarissa's ear she inhaled her scent. The mixture of sex and sweat wrapped around her head and she felt herself swoon. A tingle coursed through her body when Clarissa wrapped an arm around her neck.

"Hmm, is it morning already?" A soft kiss on A.J.'s neck made goose bumps on her skin.

"Yes, but you don't have to get up. Selene is here and I need to go take care of that business we talked about. Okay?'

An eye slowly popped open as Clarissa pulled A.J. down for a kiss. "You have to leave right now?"

"Trust me, I wish I didn't, but the sooner I take care of this the sooner we can get on with our lives." A.J. pressed Clarissa down into the bed and kissed her thoroughly. "Please, don't leave the penthouse. Okay? As long as you're here, you're safe. No one can get in as soon as I set the alarm." A.J. wished she had time to go into the extensive security system, but the sooner she took care of Kevin, the sooner she would be back. "Promise me you won't leave." A.J. rested her head against Clarissa's, her hands cupping the soft face. "Please?"

Suddenly, Clarissa was awake, "What about Carol? Oh, my gosh. I completely forgot about Carol."

Jumping out of bed, Clarissa almost ran into the living room before A.J. could stop her.

"Whoa there, Honey." A.J. pulled her back into her before she got to the door. "You don't want Selene to see you like this, do you?" A.J. smiled stroking the naked breast pressing against her.

"Oh." Clarissa blushed as she looked down her naked body. "Right."

A.J. relayed the night's events to Clarissa and told her what Selene had said to Carol.

"Oh, she must be scared out of her mind. She thinks her boyfriend is a killer and he's after her." Clarissa buried her head and started to cry. "It's all my fault. I put her in danger. If I hadn't come here she wouldn't be running for her life right now."

A.J. wrapped her arms around Clarissa and rocked her. "Stop. You didn't know De Marcus was alive, let alone following you. Come on, worry about the things you can control and not the things that you can't. Look at me." A.J. tilted Clarissa's chin up and kissed her. "Call Carol, but don't say too much. Tell her she can come home at the end of the week. That should give us enough time to take care of De Marcus. Okay?" A.J. smiled, hoping she was right.

"Okay. When will you be back?"

"It shouldn't take long." A.J. kissed her lover again, desire warming her again. "I better go."

"Be careful." Clarissa gave A.J. a bittersweet smile.

Chapter Thirty Nine

The tension in the car was palpable, each woman lost in her thoughts about what was coming. A.J. almost felt sorry for Kevin, almost. He had allied with the wrong person, and now he would pay for such an alliance. A.J. thought about all the ways Kevin might try to wiggle out of his current predicament. She would give him a chance to explain his actions first, but she knew he would tell her what he thought she wanted to hear. Would she have to resort to torture or would he willingly tell her what she wanted to know about De Marcus? One thing was for sure, today Kevin Armstrong would cease to exist. It would send a very clear message to De Marcus, he was next. It was one thing to lie, it was another to betray someone. Honor amongst vampires was a given, it was what bonded them as a coven. You didn't steal another's slaves, you didn't kill without reason and you took care of your own business. Perhaps those were antiquated ideas. The new vampires, the seekers, were coming into existence with no master, no honor and were ruthless. They killed without reason and lived like there was no future for them. Yet, the two vampires Selene had killed were old school, from the coven, and they refused to give up their master, preferring death to dishonor. She smiled knowing they had done the honorable thing as far as she was concerned. Their master would be proud of their sacrifice for him. However, De Marcus didn't deserve such undying loyalty. He had disgraced the coven, himself and his own family when he killed Clarissa's family. She would like to be judge, jury and executioner for him.

"Here, take two of these and put a few in your pocket," A.J. said, handing Selene the tin holding her safety pills. "I don't want you spiraling into a blood lust when we question Kevin."

Selene raised an eyebrow at the comment. "I think I can handle myself, A.J. Thanks anyway."

"When was the last time you fed, Selene?" A.J. didn't take her eyes off the road holding out the tin. When no answer came forth she continued, "That's what I thought. Pop two and slip 'em under your tongue. Then put a couple in your pocket."

A.J. watched as Selene picked one up and turned it over and over in her hand. She didn't need Selene going off half cocked today. De Marcus had bit her and she knew that the injury would color her judgment. Depending on how long he had latched on, his saliva mixing with her blood could have an adverse reaction. Selene had been around long enough to know that so A.J. didn't worry.

"Trust me, A.J., I know what you're thinking, but De Marcus wasn't able to hold on for that long. He didn't mix with my blood. Besides, I had a little snack at home." Wagging her eyebrows at A.J. she hoped she was putting A.J.'s fears to rest.

"I'll feel a lot better if you take the capsules." A.J. wouldn't be deterred. She didn't need to worry about two vampires in the room. One who wanted to kill and one who would most certainly do whatever it took to live.

"Fine." Selene snapped the capsules and tossed

them into her mouth. The reaction was almost immediate as Selene felt her skin tighten and her heart speed up. "Shit, what is in these things?"

"Good huh? Concentrated blood from the purest source, no filler or by products." A.J. knew she sounded like an infomercial, but it was true. The blood was the best her company could get, legally. "How do you think I've stayed sane this long? I haven't fed on a human in ages. Now a vampire, that's different." A.J. smirked, remembering making love to Clarissa last night.

"Last night, huh?"

"I don't kiss and tell."

"You don't have to, it's written all over your face. Geez."

Pulling into the underground garage A.J. felt her nerves prick. Being a Sunday there were few cars in the cavernous space. A security guard waved at her as she passed the guard shack. Trying to shake off the nerves she let out a deep breath with a sigh. She hadn't felt this anxious in a long time, but it didn't matter. *What's done is done,* she told herself.

Both women were silent in the elevator. A.J. knew Selene would wait for her lead so she didn't say anything. Walking into the lab the only noise was the humming of the overhead fluorescent lights. A.J. picked up the phone and called Dr. Mayfield.

"Hi Doc. I'm at the lab. Where's Kevin?" A.J. looked around the room and focused on a locked door to her left. "Got it. Thanks."

Pulling a key off the wall, A.J. walked to the locked door. There wasn't a window on the wall or in the door so A.J. wouldn't know what she was walking into when she unlocked it. Looking back at Selene, who had already taken a knife from her holster she said, "Mayfield said he locked him in here yesterday. Seems he practically took the door off its hinges trying to get out. Then nothing."

"You think he knows what's up?" Selene stood near the opening waiting for A.J. to swing the latch.

"Yeah, you don't get locked in the freezer by accident." A.J. tossed the lock on the table and pressed her shoulder against the door. "Ready?"

"Ready when you are."

Swinging the door wide, both women raced inside, then stopped suddenly. Lying on the floor in a pool of blood was Kevin Armstrong. He had slit his own throat with a piece of broken glass. Bending down, A.J. turned him on his back. His neck was practically sliced in half.

"Fuck. Kevin, you fucking worm." A.J. stood and kicked the dead body, blood splattering on her black boot. Running her fingers through her hair, she stood over Kevin's body and cursed her luck. He had taken even that from her. Now she wouldn't have the satisfaction of telling him she knew who he was. How would she find out about De Marcus now? Looking at Selene she shook her head and walked out of the freezer.

"Well, look at the bright side."

"What bright side? He took his secrets with him, fucker." A.J. slammed her fist on the work table, rattling the specimen jars. "De Marcus must be some kind of asshole for these fuckers to find death a more welcome companion. Shit."

A.J. felt Selene grab her shoulder before she spoke. "Look, if it's any consolation, we have De Marcus."

"You don't understand. Kevin worked for me for eighteen years. I trusted him and he betrayed that trust. He owed me the satisfaction of dying by my hand."

"Did you really want that on your conscience? You have Clarissa now. Be happy about that. You don't want that kind of blood on your hands. Trust me, A.J." Selene's words rang hollow for A.J. She wanted revenge for Clarissa, for what he had done. Now, she would have to accept that she would never know why Kevin did it. Pulling her cell phone, she called Mayfield again.

"Hey, Doc. It's me again. We got a biohazard in the freezer. Yeah, Kevin Armstrong killed himself."

"I guess we better get back to the penthouse." A.J. slammed the door to the freeze and stalked out. "You better get De Marcus. I don't think he'll take the coward's way out. Do you?"

"Hardly." Selene said, following A.J. and shutting the lights off.

Chapter Forty

Clarissa walked around the huge penthouse admiring its simplicity. It definitely felt like Alexandra's home. The style, while modern, had her flair. From the big masculine leather sofa and chair to the simple black and white photography that graced the walls. Each item spoke of another time, of simple, yet elegant tastes. It was hard to pass by the huge windows and not look out at the great cityscape that unfolded before her. Turning the huge chair around to face the window, Clarissa settled into the soft leather. The morning was beautiful. Perhaps it was just her, but she felt like a new person, as though a veil had been lifted from her gaze and she could see a future for herself.

Opening her cell phone she dialed Carol's number. What would she say to her friend? What would her friend say to her?

"Clarissa? Oh my god, are you alright?" Fear oozed from the other end of the phone. Carol sounded beside herself.

"Carol, are you alright? Selene told me what happened." Clarissa felt her eyes start to tear as she listened to Carol sobbing on the other end. She explained what had happened and how Selene had probably saved her life from a killer. Why hadn't she suspected anything, Carol cried. Clarissa wished she could explain everything to Carol, but it was better this way. The less she knew the safer she was, reasoned Clarissa.

"Why don't you relax? I'll cover for you at the university. Besides, after what you've been through you deserve a break." Clarissa hoped Carol would listen to reason. Until they knew what was happening with De Marcus, Carol wouldn't be safe. "I'll call you when I hear from the police and let you know what's happening. I want you to be safe. Please?" Pleading, she finally got Carol to agree to a much needed vacation. After a few more minutes of chit chat, both agreed to call the other daily.

Clarissa's safe, neat little world was changing faster than she could imagine. Her mind was a jumble of images making it hard for her to concentrate. The past blending with the recent events of the last two weeks had Clarissa wondering what to do next. She had lived an easy, obscure life in education and now it was fractured. Shards of her life littered the floor of her mind as she tried to reconstruct the past century. What was a lie? What was the truth? She had been living a lie the past half century and De Marcus had let her. Had he been watching the whole time? Nothing made sense and the more questions she asked the more confuse and angry she became. Perhaps Alexandra would have some answers to her questions when she returned.

Thinking about what Alexandra was doing sent a shiver through her. Could she do it, take someone's life? She had purposely avoided Alexandra so she wouldn't be faced with that decision, but looking at the situation, if she was in Alexandra's position could she kill someone? She had fed to survive, but that was different. But revenge killing, was it in her spirit to protect someone she loved? Absolutely. In fact, she knew she would kill De Marcus if she had the opportunity. He had robbed her of her family and her own mortality. A man like that served no useful purpose, so his death wouldn't be a loss for anyone. What did her ability to rationalize his death say about her she wondered? Thinking more about it, she knew she wanted to be there when Alexandra confronted him. She had a right to face him, question him or at least watch him die. Revenge was a bitter sandwich to eat, but she had to take a bite or it would haunt her for the rest of her very, very long life.

###

Flipping the phone closed, Selene turned to A.J. "You're not going to like this, but the Coven wants De Marcus brought back. They want to take care of him." Selene braced herself for the onslaught she knew was coming.

"Are you fucking kidding me? They knew where he was the whole time and didn't do a fucking thing. Now, they want him brought back to face their justice. Oh that's ripe. Assholes." A.J. slammed her fist against the steering wheel. "I want to talk to him first, Selene."

"I can't, A.J. They're sending a plane for him tonight. I'm supposed to meet them at the airport in two hours." Looking at her watch she continued, "That barely gives me enough time to get home, pack a bag and meet Sgt. Gilmore at the airport. Sorry, A.J. Maybe it's better this way." Selene tried to look on the bright side, but A.J. wasn't having any of it.

"How? After what he did to Clarissa, how is this better?"

"No blood on your hands."

"He robbed me of my happiness for the past century and you think I'm worried about a little blood?" A.J. hated the rules of the Coven. She didn't owe them anything.

They were a useless bunch of geriatrics that only imposed rules when it suited their purposes. "Why now?"

"I think they want to save face. Maybe try and take back control over the 'congregation', so to speak. Selene made a set of air quotes around congregation, knowing there really wasn't a word that described the disorganized group of seekers, masters and slaves that existed in the world today. "Things have gotten way out of control. I think the Coven will use this to send a strong message that says they aren't above killing an old master. The younger vampires have walked away from the old ways and they're trying to bring back some law and order."

"Yeah? Well I'm not part of their law and order. So when you see them, you can tell them not to count me in on their 'congregation'. In fact, you can tell them I said to go fuck themselves. Clarissa and I won't be bound by their laws. I'm kind of surprised you're working with them. Last time I checked, they didn't do you any favors."

"It's hard to explain, A.J." Selene hoped A.J. didn't press her for an explanation. Selene still had attachments to the Coven and while she looked the other way on a lot of what happened in the human world, she couldn't ignore a direct order from the Coven. "Look, I'm not happy about this either, but I have to do this. Until things change there, I'm still bound by a few rules. This is one of them."

A.J. just grunted her disapproval. It wouldn't assuage her anger but one way or another De Marcus was a dead man, either by her hand or by the Covens.

"You just make me one promise, Selene?"

"What's that?"

"You stick around and make sure they kill that bastard."

"Deal"

Chapter Forty One

The last few days had been pure bliss. Waking before her lover afforded A.J. the pleasure of watching Clarissa sleep. It seemed to be her favorite pastime lately. The quiet solitude of her penthouse was in stark contrast to the last few weeks' events. They had spent time rediscovering each other and found little had changed between them. The easy banter they had enjoyed a century ago was back, along with talk of a true future together.

Clarissa had asked few questions about Kevin's death, relegating his suicide to a guilty conscience and nothing more. But A.J. knew differently. She hadn't the heart to tell her that both assassins and Kevin found death preferable to going back to De Marcus in defeat. The request of the Coven was another matter and A.J. didn't sugar coat her anger with them. But Clarissa had surprised A.J.

"It's probably for the best, Alexandra."

"How can you say that? You of all people know what kind of man he is. He doesn't deserve a humane death. He deserves to be punished, to be tortured like he's tortured others."

Clarissa wrapped her arms around A.J. and rested her head on a strong shoulder. "That may be true, but I don't want that blood on your hands. Does that make sense? I am happy to know that you didn't have to take a life on my account. I'm not sure I could live with that."

"I wish I had your compassion, my love. You're an angel that has brought light back into my life. Thank you," A.J. said, kissing Clarissa's hands.

Clarissa never ceased to amaze A.J. with her gentle, quiet reserve. She had lost her family and almost lost her life and yet she always looked on the brighter side of things. She had even tried to put a positive spin on things when Carol had finally come back. A.J. and Clarissa had told Carol that her boyfriend had been wanted for murder in another state, hence his sudden departure. A lie, but one told to keep her safe and asking as few questions as possible. Carol seemed to take everything that had happened in stride.

A.J. snuggled closer to Clarissa, enjoying the intimate time together. Soon she would have to get up and go to work. It was time to start to think about making a move. Changing jobs for Clarissa would take time and energy, but for A.J. it would be a matter of setting up a new company, staffing it and giving it time to get established. She had done this time and time again and it was nothing new to her. However, this time she was bringing someone along for the ride. Before she made any plans, she needed to talk to Clarissa first.

The phone on the night stand vibrated with the incoming call. Looking down at the number, A.J. smiled and whispered into the phone.

"Selene, it's been a while. I'm assuming you have good news." A.J. pulled her sleeping lover closer.

"I'm afraid not, A.J. De Marcus got away in Montreal."

A.J. felt her stomach drop as she bolted up, spilling Clarissa to the bed. "What do you mean he got away? When? How?"

A few minutes later, A.J. hung up the phone and

threw it against the wall. Leaning against the cold glass she cursed the Coven, De Marcus and the world. She had him right in her grasp and yet he still slithered away. Arms reached around A.J. and a head leaned against her back.

"Don't worry, it'll be alright, Honey."

"How do you feel about the Northwest?" A.J. grabbed the hands that held her and pulled them tighter around her. Time wasn't their friend. Circumstances had changed and they would have to speed up their timeline on things.

"Anywhere with you is home now." Clarissa rubbed her cheek against A.J.'s back then turned her around. "What happened?"

"It's what didn't happen," A.J. said, wrapping her arms around her lover. She explained everything Selene had told her. "The Coven promised Selene they would find De Marcus, but now he's out there somewhere, free. I know we'll never be free of him until I kill him so..." She saw the look on Clarissa's face and knew it would take her time to come to terms with what A.J. needed to do.

"I hear they get a lot of snow up there?"

Smiling, A.J. pulled Clarissa tighter. Life was finally worth living, even if she had to take care of some unfinished business.

Jett Abbott lives in California with her wife, and three sons. When she isn't writing, you can find her riding her motorcycle with her wife and friends. You can contact Jett at: jettabbott@sapphirebooks.com. Or check out her face book page to keep up to date on her current writing.

www.ingramcontent.com/pod-product-compliance
Lightning Source LLC
Chambersburg PA
CBHW061552100726

47898CB00002B/343